SEE
WHAT
I HAVE
DONE

SARAH
SCHMIDT

Atlantic Monthly Press
New York

Quote from "We outgrow love like other things" J 887/F 1094 by Emily Dickinson from *The Poems of Emily Dickinson*, edited by Thomas H. Johnson, Cambridge, Mass.: The Belknap Press of Harvard University Press, Copyright © 1951, 1955, 1979, 1983 by the President and Fellows of Harvard College.

First published in Australia and New Zealand in 2017 by Hachette Australia

Published simultaneously in Canada
Printed in the United States of America

First Grove Atlantic hardcover edition: August 2017

ISBN 978-0-8021-2659-7
eISBN 978-0-8021-8913-4

Atlantic Monthly Press
an imprint of Grove Atlantic
154 West 14th Street
New York, NY 10011

Distributed by Publishers Group West

groveatlantic.com

17 18 19 20   10 9 8 7 6 5 4 3 2

For Cody.

And for Alan and Rose who left before I could finish.

We outgrow love like other things
And put it in the drawer

Emily Dickinson

Knowlton: "You have been on pleasant terms with your
  step-mother since then?"
Lizzie: "Yes sir."
Knowlton: "Cordial?"
Lizzie: "It depends upon one's idea of cordiality, perhaps."

Lizzie Borden's inquest testimony

PART I

ONE

LIZZIE

August 4, 1892

HE WAS STILL bleeding. I yelled, "Someone's killed Father."
I breathed in kerosene air, licked the thickness from my teeth.
The clock on the mantel ticked ticked. I looked at Father, the way
hands clutched to thighs, the way the little gold ring on his pinkie
finger sat like a sun. I gave him that ring for his birthday when I
no longer wanted it. "Daddy," I had said, "I'm giving this to you
because I love you." He had smiled and kissed my forehead.

A long time ago now.

I looked at Father. I touched his bleeding hand, *how long does it
take for a body to become cold?* and leaned closer to his face, tried to
make eye contact, waited to see if he might blink, might recognize
me. I wiped my hand across my mouth, tasted blood. My heart
beat nightmares, *gallop, gallop*, as I looked at Father again, watched
blood river down his neck and disappear into suit cloth. The clock

on the mantel ticked ticked. I walked out of the room, closed the door behind me and made my way to the back stairs, shouted once more to Bridget, "Quickly. Someone's killed Father." I wiped my hand across my mouth, licked my teeth.

Bridget came down, brought with her the smell of decayed meaty-meat. "Miss Lizzie, what . . ."

"He's in the sitting room." I pointed through thick, wallpapered walls.

"Who is?" Bridget's face, prickly with confusion.

"I thought he looked hurt but I wasn't sure how badly until I got close," I said. Summer heat ran up my neck like a knife. My hands ached.

"Miss Lizzie, yer scarin' me."

"Father's in the sitting room." It was difficult to say anything else.

Bridget ran from the back stairs through the kitchen and I followed her. She ran to the sitting room door, put her hand on the door knob, *turn it, turn it.*

"His face has been cut." There was a part of me that wanted to push Bridget into the room, make her see what I had found.

She pulled her hand away from the knob and turned to me, owl eyes swooping over my face. A length of sweat trickled from her temple to collarbone. "What do ya mean?" she said.

Like a tiny looking glass inside my mind, I saw all of Father's blood, a meal, the leftovers from a wild dog's feast. The scraps of skin on his chest, his eye resting on his shoulder. His body the Book of Apocalypse. "Someone came in and cut him," I said.

Bridget was a-tremble. "What do ya mean, Miss Lizzie? How could someone cut his face?" Her voice soured, a tear. I didn't want her to cry, didn't want to have to comfort her.

"I'm not quite sure," I said. "They might have used an ax. Like taking down a tree."

Bridget began to cry and strange feelings popped across my bones. She faced the door and twisted her wrist, allowed the door to crack open an inch.

"Go get Dr. Bowen," I said. I looked past her, tried to see Father but couldn't.

Bridget turned to me, scratched her hand. "We should attend to yer father, Miss Lizzie . . ."

"Go bring Dr. Bowen." I grabbed her hand, all rough and sticky, and walked her to the side door. "You'd best hurry, Bridget."

"Ya shouldn't be alone, Miss Lizzie."

"What if Mrs. Borden was to come home? Shouldn't I be here to tell her?" My teeth were cold against my teeth.

She looked into the sun. "Alright," she said. "I'll try ta be quick as I can."

Bridget ran out the side of the house, let the door hit her on the backside, a paddle, and she bobbed as she ran onto Second Street, her white house-bonnet a sail in the breeze. Bridget looked over her shoulder towards me, her face dumb with worry, and I shooed her along, my wrist a flick and crunch. She kept going, hip and shouldered an old woman, made her drop her walking cane, made her cry out, "What's the hurry, missy?" Bridget didn't respond, *how naughty*, disappeared from sight, and the woman picked up her cane, made it chink against stone, made a tacky-tacky sound.

I watched people pass by, liked the way their voices filled the air, made everything feel whole, and I felt my lips turn a smile as birds jumped over and under tree branches. For a moment I thought of capturing them, placing them in my pigeon aviary in the barn. How lucky they'd be with me to look after them. I thought of Father, my stomach growled hunger and I went to the pail of water by the well, let my hands sink into the cool sip sip. I brought my hands to mouth and began drinking, lapping with my tongue. It was soft, delicate. Everything slowed down. I saw a dead pigeon lying gray and still in the yard and my stomach murmured. I looked into the sun. I thought of Father, tried to remember the last words I said to him. I took a pear from the arbor, walked back inside.

On the kitchen counter were johnnycakes. I wormed my fingers into their middles until they became small pieces of flour-rocks. I threw a handful of johnnycakes against the wall, listened to them crash in stale waves. Next I went to the stove, pulled the pot of mutton broth close to me and took a deep breath.

There was nothing but my thoughts and Father. I walked towards the sitting room, sank my teeth into the pear, stopped at the door. The clock on the mantel ticked ticked. My legs began to shake and drum into the floor and I took a bite of my pear to make them still. Behind the sitting room door was the smell of tobacco pipe.

"Father," I said. "Is that you?"

I opened the door wider then wider, sank my teeth into pear. Father was there on the sofa. He hadn't moved. Pear skin crisped in my mouth and I caught the smell again. "You ought to stop with the tobacco, Father. It makes your skin smell old."

On the floor next to the sofa was Father's pipe. I hooked the pipe under my teeth, my tongue pressed against the small mouthpiece. I breathed in. Outside I heard Bridget call like a banshee, "Miss Lizzie! Miss Lizzie!" I placed the pipe back on the floor, my fingers grazing circles of blood, and as I walked out of the room and half closed the door I took a peek at Father.

I opened the side door. Bridget looked a-fire, flame red, and she told me, "Dr. Bowen's not home."

Her response made me want to spit at her. "Go find him. Get someone. Get going," I said.

Her head jarred backwards. "Miss Lizzie, shouldn't we get Mrs. Borden?" Her voice an echo in a cave, *enough with questions.*

I cracked my heel into the floorboards, made the house moan then howl. "I told you, she's not here."

Bridget's forehead creased. "Where is she? We need ta get her right now." Annoying, insistent.

"Don't tell me what to do, Bridget." I heard my voice fold around doors and corners. The house; brittle bone under foot. Everything sounded louder than it should, hurt the ear.

"I'm sorry, Miss Lizzie." Bridget rubbed her hand.

"Go find someone else. Father really needs help."

Bridget let out a breath and I watched her run down the street, past a group of young children playing hopscotch. I took another bite of the pear and started to move away from the door.

From across the side fence I heard a woman call my name, felt the drilling of it, "Lizzie. Lizzie. Lizzie," bore into my ear. I squinted at a figure walking towards me. I pressed my face into the screen door, pieced together the shapes of familiarity. "Mrs. Churchill?" I said.

"Are you alright, dear? I heard Bridget hollering up and down the street and then I saw you standing at the door looking so lost." Mrs. Churchill came closer to the house, pulled at her red blouse.

On the back step she asked again, "Dear, are you alright?" and my heart beat fast, fast, fast and I told her, "Mrs. Churchill, do come in. Someone's killed Father."

Her eyes and nose scrunched, mouth hollowed into an O. A loud bang sounded from the basement; my neck twitched.

"This doesn't make sense," she said, a small voice. I opened the door, let her in. "Lizzie, what's happened?" she asked.

"I don't know. I came in and I saw him all cut up. He's in there." I pointed to the sitting room.

Mrs. Churchill slowed into the kitchen, rubbed her fat, clean fingers over her red-queen cheeks, rubbed them over her gold cameo necklace, covered her chest with her hands. There in all its shine, her gold and diamond wedding ring, *I'd like to keep that*. Her chest heaved, soft, child-suckled breasts, I waited for her heart to burst through ribcage onto the kitchen floor.

"Is he alone?" She was a mouse.

"Yes. Very."

Mrs. Churchill took steps towards the sitting room door then stopped, looked at me. "Should I go in?"

"He's very hurt, Mrs. Churchill. But you could go in. If you wanted to."

She receded, came back by my side. I counted the times I had seen Father's body since I found it. My stomach growled.

"Where's your mother?" she asked.

I wrenched my head towards the ceiling, *I hate that word*, then closed my eyes. "She's gone to visit a sick relative."

"We really must get her, Lizzie." Mrs. Churchill tugged at my hand, tried to make me move.

My skin itched. I pulled away from her grip, scratched my palm. "I don't want to bother her right now."

"Lizzie, don't be ridiculous. This is an emergency." She scolded me like I was a child.

"You can see him, if you want."

She shook her head, baffled. "I don't think I can . . ."

"I meant, if you saw him, you would see why it isn't a good idea to fetch Mrs. Borden."

Mrs. Churchill placed the back of her hand on my forehead. "You feel very hot, Lizzie. You're not thinking straight."

"I'm alright." My skin slid from underneath her hand.

Her eyes widened, threatened to outgrow the boundaries of bone, and I leaned towards Mrs. Churchill. She flinched. "Perhaps we should go outside, Lizzie . . ."

I shook my head, absolute. "No. Father shouldn't be left alone."

Mrs. Churchill and I stood side by side, faced the sitting room door. I could hear her breathe, could hear saliva swish thick over her gums, could smell Castile soap and clove in her hair. The roof cracked, made the sitting room door feather open an inch and my toes wiggled a step then a step until I was a little closer to Father. "Mrs. Churchill," I said, "who do you think will wash his body when it comes time?"

She looked at me as if I spoke foreign words. "I'm . . . not really sure."

"Perhaps my sister could do it." I turned to her, watched sadness tiptoe across her brow and gave her a smile, *cheer up now, cheer up.*

Her lips parted, a sea. "Let's not worry about that."

"Oh. Alright." I turned to face the sitting room door again.

We were quiet for a time. My palm itched. I thought of using my teeth to scratch, went to bring my hand to my mouth when Mrs. Churchill said, "When did it happen, Lizzie?"

I rushed my hand to my side. "I'm not sure. I was outside then I came in and he was hurt. Bridget was upstairs. Now he's dead." I tried to think but everything slowed. "Isn't that funny? I can't remember what I was doing. Does that ever happen to you, forgetting the simplest of things?"

"I suppose so, yes." Her words slurped out.

"He said he wasn't feeling well and wanted to be alone. So I kissed him, left him asleep on the sofa and went outside." The roof popped. "That's all I can remember."

Mrs. Churchill placed her hand on my shoulder, patted me, made me warm and tingle. "Don't push yourself, dear. This is all very . . . unnatural."

"You're right."

Mrs. Churchill wiped her eyes, made them red with tears and rubbing. She looked strange. "This can't be happening," she said. She looked strange and I tried not to think of Father alone on the sofa.

My skin itched. I scratched. "I'm really thirsty, Mrs. Churchill," I said.

She stared at me, ruby-eyed, and went to the kitchen counter. She poured water from a jug and handed me a cup. The water looked cloud warm. I sipped. I thought of Father. The water was tar down my throat. I should have poured it onto the floor and asked Mrs. Churchill to clean it up, get me something fresh. I sipped again. "Thank you," I said. I smiled.

Mrs. Churchill came close to me, wrapped her arm around my shoulder and held tight. She leaned into me and began whispering but there was the smell of sour yogurt snaking out from somewhere inside her and it made me dizzy. I pushed her away.

"We need to get your mother, Lizzie."

There was noise coming from outside, coming closer to the side of the house, and Mrs. Churchill ran to the side door and opened it. Standing in front of me were Mrs. Churchill, Bridget and Dr. Bowen. "I found him, miss," Bridget said. She tried to slow her breathing, *she sounds like an old dog.* "I went as fast as I could."

Dr. Bowen pushed his silver, round-rimmed glasses up his narrow nose and said, "Where is he?"

I pointed to the sitting room.

Dr. Bowen, his wrinkled forehead. "Are you alright, Lizzie? Did anybody try to hurt you?" His voice smooth, honey-milked.

"Hurt me?"

"The person who hurt your father. They didn't try to hurt you too?"

"I've seen no one. No one is hurt but Father," I said. The floorboards stretched beneath my feet and for a moment I thought I would sink.

Dr. Bowen stood in front of me and reached for my wrist, *big hands*, and he breathed out and in, his air swiping my lips. I licked them. His fingers pressed into skin until they felt blood. "Your pulse is too fast, Lizzie. I'll remedy that as soon as I check your father."

I nodded. "Would you like me to come in with you?"

Dr. Bowen. "That's . . . unnecessary."

"Oh," I said.

Dr. Bowen took off his jacket and handed it to Bridget. He headed for the sitting room, took his brown, weathered leather medical bag with him. I held my breath. He opened the door like a secret, pushed his body into the room. I heard him gasp, say, "Lord Jesus." The door was open just enough. Somewhere behind me Mrs. Churchill screamed and I snapped my head towards her. She screamed again, the way people do in nightmares, and her noise rattled through my body, made my muscles tighten and ache. "I didn't want to see him. I didn't want to see him," Mrs. Churchill screamed. Bridget howled, dropped Dr. Bowen's coat on the floor. The women held each other and sobbed.

I wanted them to stop. I didn't appreciate how they reacted to Father like that, *they are shaming him.* I went to Dr. Bowen, stood next to him at the edge of the sofa and tried to block sight of Father's body. Bridget called, "Miss Lizzie, don't go in there." The room was still and Dr. Bowen pushed me away. "Lizzie," he said, "you mustn't be in here."

"I just want . . ."

"You cannot be in here anymore. Stop looking at your father." He pushed me from the room and shut the door. Mrs. Churchill screamed again and I covered my ears. I listened to my heart beat until everything felt numb.

After a time, Dr. Bowen came out of the room, all pale and sweat, and yelled, "Summon the police." He bit his lip, his jaw a tiny thunder. On his fingertips were little drops of blood *confetti,* and I tried to imagine the ways he had touched Father.

"It's their annual picnic," Mrs. Churchill whispered. "No one will be at the station." She rubbed her eyes, made them raw.

I wanted her to stop crying and so I smiled and said, "It's alright. They'll come eventually. Everything will be alright, won't it, Dr. Bowen?"

Dr. Bowen eyed me and I looked at his hands. I thought of Father.

———

I was four when I first met Mrs. Borden. She let me eat spoonfuls of sugar when Father wasn't watching. How my tongue sang! "Can you keep secrets, Lizzie?" Mrs. Borden asked.

I nodded my head. "I can keep the best secrets." I hadn't even told Emma that I loved our new mother.

She spooned sugar into my mouth, my cheeks tight with the sweet surge. "Let's keep our sugar meal between you and me."

I nodded and nodded until everything was dizzy. Later, when I was running through the house yelling, "Karoo! Karoo!" and climbed over the sitting room sofa, Father yelled, "Emma, did you let Lizzie into the sugar?"

Emma came into the sitting room, head bowed. "No, Father. I swear it."

I ran by them and Father caught me by the arm, a pull at my socket. "Lizzie," he said while I giggled and hawed, "did you eat something you weren't meant to?"

"I ate fruit."

Father came right into my face, smelled like butter cake. "And nothing else?"

"And nothing else." I laughed.

Emma looked at me, tried to peer into my mouth.

"Are you lying?" Father asked.

"No, Daddy. I would never."

He had searched me over, searched dimpled cheeks for signs of disobedience. I smiled. He smiled. Off I went again, running and jumping and I passed Mrs. Borden in the kitchen and she winked at me.

———

When the police arrived a short time later they began taking photos of the dark-gray suit Father wore to work that morning, of his black leather boots still tied over ankles and feet. Flashbulbs broke every six seconds. The young police photographer said he would prefer not to photograph the old man's head. "Couldn't someone else do it? Please?" he said, wiped the back of his hand over his forehead, like oil was dripping from his head.

An older officer told him to go outside while they found a real man to finish the job. They didn't need a man. A daughter would suffice. I had lovingly looked after Father all morning and his face didn't scare me. I should have said, "How many photographs do you want? How close would you like me to get? Which angle will lead you to the murderer?"

Instead, Dr. Bowen gave me a shot of beautiful warm medicine underneath my skin that made me feel feathery and strange. They seated me in the dining room with Mrs. Churchill and Bridget and said, "You don't mind that we ask each of you some questions, do you?"

The little room was cloying and heavy with the odor of warm bodies and grass, of police mouths smelling of half-digested chicken and damp yeast. "Of course not," Mrs. Churchill said. "But I shall not discuss the state Mr. Borden was in." She started to cry, made a whirlwind sound. In my mind I drifted away to the upstairs of the house where everyone became an echo. I thought of Father.

An officer kneeled in front of me, placed a hand over my hand and whisper-spat into my face, "We will find who did this and come after him with our full force."

"Men do such horrid things," I said.

"Yes, I suppose they do," the officer said.

"I hope Father didn't feel any pain."

The officer stared at his hands and cleared his throat. "I'm sure he didn't feel too much." He gripped his notebook. "I wondered if you could tell me everything you remember about this morning?"

"I'm not sure . . ."

"There are no wrong answers, Miss Borden." A sing-song voice. His Adam's apple bobbed, made me think of Halloween games.

I looked the officer in the eye and grinned, *there are no wrong answers*, how kind he was to put me at ease. I knew for sure God would smile on him from now on. "I was outside in the barn and then I came in and found him."

"Do you remember why you were in the barn?"

"I had been trying to find lead sinkers for my fishing line."

"You were going to go fishing?" Scribble, scribble.

"My uncle is going to take me. You should see what I can catch."

"You're expecting him to visit?"

"Oh, he has already. He's here."

"Where is he?" the officer asked, a pony searching for feed.

"He's out conducting business. He arrived yesterday."

"We'll need to ask him questions."

"Why?" My fingers beat together, pulsed beat, beat, beat, beat, all the way into the center of my body. I followed the feeling, looked down at myself, noticed a soft, gray pigeon feather stuck on my skirt. I picked it off, rubbed it between my fingers, got all hot and boiled.

"Miss, I hate to be blunt, but a murder has occurred. We must ask your uncle if he saw anyone unusual outside."

I flashed up at him, "Yes. Yes, of course." I stuffed the pigeon feather into my palm, carried it like love.

The officer kept with questions. I glanced around the room, then up at the ceiling, tried to see through spiderweb cracked plaster and wood into the rooms above: a few hours before I had been up there, had seen Father and Mrs. Borden help each other ready themselves for the day. Mrs. Borden had plaited her light-gray, thick-mop hair and pinned it to the top of her head and Father had said, "Always charming, my dear." They did that from time to time, their being friendly and pleasant to one another. The officer kept with questions and a fog settled in my mind.

Next to me, I heard Bridget squeak to a second officer, "Her sister is visitin' a friend in Fairhaven. She's been gone for . . ."

"Two weeks," I interrupted. "She's been gone for two weeks and it's time she came home."

The second officer nodded, gruffed, "We'll send for her immediately."

"Good. This is too much for me to take alone."

Then Bridget said, "I lock the doors. House is shut tight all the time." The second officer took notes, wrote furious until sweat formed through his thick mustache. Sometimes Father's beard would wet with anger and when he spoke to you, came close to your face so you could hear his words, the wet would stroke your chin and sink in. A fog settled in my mind. I had the feeling of wanting to stroke Father's beard and face until he looked like the past. I glanced at the sitting room.

"And you know for sure the doors were locked this morning?" the second officer asked Bridget.

"Yes. I had ta unlock the front door this mornin' ta let poor Mr. Borden in when he came home early from work."

The way Bridget spoke about Father made me smile. I turned to face her and the officer. "Actually," I said, "sometimes the basement door isn't locked."

Bridget looked me over, her caterpillar eyebrows cracked like earth, and the second officer took notes, took notes. My feet traced circles across the carpet. I opened my eyes wide, felt the house move left then right as the heat ground into walls. Everyone pulled at their necks to unloose their tightly wound clothing. I sat still holding my hands together.

Outside, I could hear swarms of people lining themselves out the front of the house. Voices sounded cannon fire. I swayed with the heat, heard the nails in the floorboards give themselves up. The sounds of pigeon feet tacky-tacked across the roof and I thought of Father. The sun moved behind a shadow and the house popped. I jumped in my chair. Bridget jumped in her chair. Mrs. Churchill too. "Seems we all have fright," I said, wanted to laugh. Mrs. Churchill started crying again, made my skin shiver. Inside my head a butcher pounded all sense out of my ears and onto the dining table. My corset groped my ribs and small pools of sweat filled the spaces between arms and legs. Bridget stood from her chair, pulled her dirt-white skirt away from the backs of her thighs and went to Mrs. Churchill, comforted her. They spoke. Police took notes, entered and exited rooms, watched me.

I wiped my palm across my face, let the feather fall onto the carpet, noticed tiny droplets of blood sitting on my fingers. I put them to my nose then my mouth. I licked, tasted Father, tasted myself. I swallowed. I looked down at my skirt, discovered blood spots. I stared at the stains, watched them become rivers across my lap, *I know these rivers!* and I thought of the times I played in the

Quequechan River with Emma when we were younger, the way Father would yell out to us from the banks, "Don't go in too deep. You can't be sure how far down it goes."

My body craved a past with Emma and Father: I wanted to be small again. I wanted to swim then fish, have Emma and me dry ourselves under the sun until our skin cooked. "Let's be bears!" I'd tell her, and we'd grow brown and giant, our bear paws swiping each other's black noses. Emma would draw blood and I'd dig into her fur-covered ribs, touch her heart with my claws. Emma would want to swipe me again but Father would say, "Emma, be kind to Lizzie," and we'd embrace each other.

———

It was only two years ago that I was on my grand European tour. The freedom I had. Emma wasn't there to tell me how to behave or what to say and so I got myself a life. On Father's insistence I went with cousins, Bordens of blood and of marriage who I barely spoke to back at home, and we set sail, gulped ocean winds, learned how to stand against waves. The things we did.

Rome. My Boston-made shoes got stuck in mosaic-stone sidewalks, made me stumble, look a fool. I bought new, Italian calf-leather boots, walked straight lines, walked as a lady should without raising eyebrows. I'd walk, ears full of that fast Italian, made me want to jump into that sing-song, be spoken from one mouth to the other.

Everything reminded me of how small Fall River was, how big I was finally becoming. Over there the Spanish steps, covered in blooming lavender and carpet-red-colored azaleas, men and women climbing to the top, sun-kissed faces, kissed lips, two white and black goats pulling a small gray wooden cart of orange and green vegetables, my cousin and me standing at the base of a marble fountain, pointing to a deep, Roman-red building, whispering, "John Keats lived inside!" *aren't I the cultured one.*

Over there, men wearing rabbit-felt fedoras sat in circles drinking mud-heavy coffee. Over there, girls dressed in Virgin-laced communion. Over there, three people reading. Over there, pigeons shaking out wings, pecking seed. How I wanted one to take home. Over there, over there, over there. Eyes widened with all the things I saw. I knew more about the world than Emma did and that made me happy. I sent her postcard after postcard so she wouldn't feel like she was missing out, gave my love, gave her reason to miss me more.

I ate and drank what I wanted in Paris. Butter, duck fat, liver fat, triple-cream brie, deep cherry–red wines, pear, clementine and lavender jelly, crème cakes, caviar, escargot in sautéed pine nuts and garlic butter. I did what the French did, licked my fingers, didn't care if people saw, what they thought. Father would've hated it, would've told me I was uncouth. I ate everything up, ate his money, was delightful everywhere I went. I learned how to wrap my tongue around accented vowels, spoke to this stranger and that. Nobody knew me, didn't expect anything from me. I wanted to stay like that forever.

I the explorer. The strolling I did. One day I saw a woman throw herself into the Seine, swim like a swan under arched white-stone bridges, under Pont Saint-Michel. The noises she made, an opera. She smiled, floated along, disappeared. I clapped my hands, bravoed the way she had taken charge of herself. If only Emma had been able to see. How far a woman could travel if she really put her mind to it. And I put my mind to it.

————

My skirt stuck to my thighs, *Holy! Blood leeches*, and I began peeling the heavy fabric away, tried to cover the tiny bloodstains on it. From the sitting room, Dr. Bowen opened one of the doors that led into the dining room and said, "We need sheets for the body." The way he said body made my teeth grind. I shifted in my seat, tried to sneak a look into the sitting room to check if Father was alright.

Mrs. Churchill asked, "Bridget, where are the Bordens' sheets?"

"They're in the cupboard in the guest room. I'll come with ya."

"You'll need to take the back stairs," an officer told them. "Keep away from the sitting room, ladies."

They nodded, left the room and feet sounded out small percussion rhythms as they walked up the back stairs across the carpet. Someone handed me a glass of water. I sipped. The clock on the mantel ticked ticked. I sipped again. Dr. Bowen placed his hands on my forehead and asked me how I was feeling. I began an answer when two long screams sounded from the floor above. "What in God's name?" Dr. Bowen said.

Two long screams again. "Somebody! Somebody help us!" Bridget yelled. The screams, the screams.

TWO

EMMA

August 4, 1892

I PRESSED AGAINST Helen's windowpane, felt the morning sun; warm like Mother's touch. How it prickled my skin. How it made me think of her, all these years without. She would come into my bedroom and raise the curtain. I wanted her to stay, wanted to be her, just so I could have her forever. But baby Alice would cry from another room and mother would leave me. Alone. Then years later baby Lizzie would cry and I began to understand that there was no such thing as forever.

The morning sun. A bird flew by the window and I put Mother thoughts away.

Everything in Helen's house was quiet: not a clock, not a foot on floorboards, not a raised voice, not a slammed door, not a father, not Abby, not a sister. My cheeks rounded to the size of a hot-air balloon. I had not had a sister for two weeks, had not had to think about someone else's needs, feelings, heart. In this house my mind had been all for myself.

I pressed harder into the windowpane, thought about how, after I finished here in Fairhaven, I would run away, travel distances of foreign blue-stoned streets, sketch them in my workbook, color my fingers with pastel wax crayon. Afterwards I would cleanse my hands in deep seas and on the off chance that I might think of my family, send a postcard that would simply read: Adventure continues. I would make a point to send a postcard from the places Lizzie had never reached on her own European tour, remind Father that I had sacrificed a lot to keep Lizzie well behaved and that I was deserving.

And when I did eventually return to American soil, I would move away from Second Street and live hermitically, quietly. Live like Maria a'Becket, paint my own *Northern Lights*. There would be no more Lizzie, no more Father, no more Abby. Finally, at forty-two, there would be no more pretending.

The sun shifted and my shoulders widened. My body growing. Downstairs in the kitchen, Helen thumped a cast-iron kettle on the stove, made me jump.

Helen called out, "Emma, tea?" She almost sang it.

I smiled. "Yes. Always yes."

The difference between houses.

Before I travelled those sixteen giant miles to Helen's house in Fairhaven, Lizzie had begged me to stay at Second Street, not to leave her.

"No," I had said. Everything I dreamed of was wrapped in that small word: I was going to be taking a private art class, my clandestine rebellion against Father.

She had looked at me, glass eyes. "You're making a terrible mistake going away." Lizzie, a locomotive, tried to push me into guilt. I raised my hand, had thought of slapping her, but instead I left my sister in her room calling out. I ignored her, let her cry.

Two days after I arrived in Fairhaven, Lizzie began sending letters:

> Well, I'm not having a good time of it, I'll tell you that much, Emma. You wouldn't believe the things I've had to listen to at the dining table. Father is an absolute bore. Have you ever noticed how his lips tighten when he says "today"?

I had not. At first Lizzie's letters amused me. I read them out loud to Helen over dinner, and we roared laughter. Then Lizzie started writing about Abby:

> I overheard Mrs. Borden telling her ridiculous sister about how "secure" she felt now that she was going to own all of Father's properties when he dies and that he wasn't going to leave us anything. Emma! What a scampy liar. Imagine the nerve. What are we going to do about it?

I could hear their voices in my head, old headache, heard them yelling across the parlor to each other, across the kitchen, the front stairs, through the walls of bedrooms. Sixteen miles away and I was still at home. I folded Lizzie into small pieces.

But the letters did not stop.

> I'm having those strange dreams again, Emma. I thought they had really happened. You must come home.

Going home. I thought of Lizzie in her sheet-white bedroom, lying on her bed twisting ostrich feathers between her fork-long fingers, the feathers hanging from the headboard like overripe fruit. She would be clicking her tongue and sucking her cheeks, the way she did, and I clenched my fist, thought of beating my thighs, that old frustration, my patchwork of bruised skin. Instead, I kept burning letters.

I was slow to adjust to living away from the family. In those first days, I looked over my shoulder, prepared for confrontation anytime Helen and I happened to knock elbows or spoke at the same time. Staying at Helen's house had been a release. I forgot the awkwardness of Abby lumbering through our house, Father's curled arthritic fingers on his left hand, the constant thud of the fall and rise of foot traffic out the front of the house, the putrid smell of trapped breath each morning before the house was aired, Lizzie's night-time sighing.

To ease the way into accepting a life without my family, I went into town and sketched scruffy cats, floral arrangements on restaurant tables, mothers and their children, those pleasant things. The way fingers knitted around fingers. I buried myself in strangers. On the way back to Helen's I would stop to pick purple and yellow wildflowers. The smell of them: afternoon sun on petals, tall grass that had rubbed against stems, dried dirt. The things that came to me:

1. Raspberry jelly only needs a hint of sugar if you use apple juice.
2. Leaning over Mother in bed. "I promise to always look after Lizzie." A kiss on her cracked lips.

3. Mother handing me baby Alice to hold for the first time. "She smells like icky icky poo." Then when Mother gave me baby Alice to hold for the last time after she had convulsed herself to death, Alice didn't smell like anything at all.

4. The time I was meant to be watching Lizzie and locked myself in my room instead, drew geometric shapes until my wrist ached. Lizzie broke her arm sliding down the front stairs banister. Father broke my pencils.

5. One day I will see Jacob's coat of many colors at the Ashmolean Museum.

6. I wish Father had died instead of Mother.

7. Lizzie clinging to Abby's legs. How could she love her so easily?

8. How quickly does the body forget its history?

The sun settled on my fingers. I was reminded of the last time I saw Father cry. Mother had died. He covered all the forgotten places of her body, the inside of an ankle, the underside of an eyebrow, the spaces in between fingers, with kisses. It had frightened me to watch.

———

One afternoon when I came back from town, I opened Helen's front door, went to the sitting room, filled a vase with the flowers. Helen came behind me, said, "Were you expecting a visitor?"

"No." Please do not say that Lizzie had visited.

"A man came looking for you. He claimed he was your uncle."

My jaw tightened. "Did he have slightly enlarged front teeth?"

Helen nodded. "That's him. Your favorite is he?" She smiled.

"No. That's John. He's my mother's brother. Why in the world would he be coming here to see me?" I pulled at my throat. How had he known I was here? Lizzie? Surely she would not send him to make me come home? She knew I wouldn't listen to him, that I had come to hate his visits: hated the way John spoke to Father, like he wanted things; the way Lizzie fawned then asked for pocket money and got it; the way he seemed to always be up to something; how he kept telling me I looked like Mother, made me miss her all the more.

"Did he say whether he was coming back?"

"I didn't get a chance to ask. He looked angry, almost slammed my own front door on me. He really wanted to talk to you."

I shook my head. "I'm sorry he did that." Always apologizing for family.

"You know you can stay for as long as you like." Helen came close, took my hand. The warmth. Helen, the good friend. I held tight. The possibility of not going home. I would take that. What a new life would mean.

"Would that be a burden for you?" I said.

Helen shooed her free hand towards me. "Don't be ridiculous. You could live here a hundred years as long as Lizzie doesn't move in."

A century of me. Finally doing what I wanted. I could not wait to tell Lizzie I was staying longer.

I wrote my own letter to Lizzie. Then I took a long route to the post office, walked until paved streets became dirt roads, houses turned into fields. I held wildflowers and leaves to my lips before pulling them apart and studying the structure of nature. Rebirth. Trees welcomed me with birdsong, encouraged me to keep walking, not to turn back. My ankles loosened. The sun hit grass, warmed the dirt underneath and I sat, ran my fingers over blades of green and yellow.

———

I pushed away from the windowpane, slowly began to dress, rubbed my hand over my body to loosen muscle. It was as if I was home alone at Second Street, as if I were reliving a morning from over twenty years ago, as if Father was out on business, as if Abby had taken a chattering Lizzie out for ice cream sodas. Abby had asked me if I would like to join them.

"No." I was blunt, had already made plans for myself.

"You're being rude! You shouldn't talk to Mother like that," Lizzie said, waggled her ink-stained finger.

"Again, no, thank you." Then I was left alone in the house. I waited a few moments before shrieking, before filling the house with my voice and body until the glass tumblers chinked inside the dining room cabinet. Father would have severely disapproved of this childish outburst. But there was no one to tell me to act my age and so I did what felt best. I stood in the sitting room and listened to the house, to the way it swayed ever so slightly with the wind, made cooing noises in the walls. The house made me feel as if I were standing inside a giant, inside a pyramid, inside an ocean-deep well: like I would be swallowed up. I smiled. What a thing to want.

I walked around the house as if I owned it. I went to my bedroom, stood in the little doorway that led to Lizzie's nun-sized room. If things were fair in life, I would make Lizzie move to the guest room, make the tiny space my studio. I would not have to worry about Lizzie running off to Father and telling him everything

I said or did. Father could never understand the problem with sisters living on top of each other.

"It's a room within a room. Doesn't it make you feel like you've always got her near?" Father and his salt-and-pepper chin-length hair, the way it moved when he was trying to be helpful.

"That room is supposed to be a closet!"

"Rooms are rooms."

"And she talks in her sleep. It's distracting."

He had clicked his fingers, made my eardrum itch. "There's a door. Shut it and you've got a separate space."

At twenty-one, I knew my room was still decorated in fantasy. On a dark-wood desk: a world globe, a photograph of me sitting on Mother's knee, a postcard of the Paris opera house (found in my aunt's travel case), a set of charcoals. On a shelf: encyclopedias, a collection of sheet music, a small leather-bound Bible given to me by John. After Mother died, he had hoped I would use it to find a way to God, to find peace and acceptance. I did not want to accept. For a time, I had blamed Lizzie. If she had been more of a loving child, Mother would have had more reason to stay by our sides. The dust that Bible has collected.

Right there in the silent house, all alone, I lifted my skirt above my ankles and removed my stockings, was shocked at how pale I was. Then I took my skirt off. How I could move. I went down to the sitting room, sat on Father's sofa, rested my head on the backboard and widened my legs, a mimic of manhood. I had invaded my father's space. I had thoughts of how I would run the household if I were in charge. If this could be a future, I had much to look forward to. I smiled.

A small pigeon flew into the closed window, its breast bone slamming hard before its beak tapped on the glass. I pulled my legs together, sat up straight, calmed my heart. I looked down at my half-nakedness. Should I be ashamed? The day for being myself was over.

———

Helen called out again. "Emma, tea is ready."

I made my way to the kitchen. Helen had made banana pancakes, had set a pot of apple marmalade on the table. "How did you sleep?" she asked.

"I am afraid to say that I was a bit too excited about the class to sleep properly."

"Are you sure you're not ten?" Helen poured tea, poured milk, dolloped cream, blew brown hair out of her eyes.

"Not cute, Helen." Laughter.

We buttered pancakes. Helen looked at me, said, "Are you alright? You look like you've got a plague of hives."

"I'm fine." But I knew this feeling. It was happening again. Years before I had heard Abby complain to Dr. Bowen of rising temperatures, of volcanic anger. He had said nothing and Abby continued to live with her moods and weeping eyes. Then I started to feel it too, like a strange hereditary gift, this thing that was traded from woman to woman, whether it was wanted or not. It was the same when I first menstruated. For a long time, I thought I was defective, broken inside. I was late to it all; seventeen. The last of my friendship circle to be seen as a woman. My friends made fun of me but Abby had been kind about it. "I was late too. Once we get this, it's there for years." The way she insisted on "we," like she and I were from the same seed.

"Look on the bright side," she said, stroked my shoulder. "You'll be able to be a mother now." I considered what growing a baby might be like, the expectation of children. Once, after baby Alice died, I foolishly prayed to God that she would be returned to me, come live in my body. I would do what mothers did and push out screaming skin, and together we would pick up our sisterhood where it had left off and live happily ever after. Then Lizzie came along. Would I be disappointed if my daughter was not like Alice, turned out like Lizzie instead: one part love, one part brilliance, one part mystery?

"If it's so good, why don't you have children?" I did not mean it the way it came out; unkind.

Abby shrugged. "Sadly, that's how life goes sometimes. We don't get everything we want when we want. You'll learn that eventually." Something about what she said felt instantly true, made me hate her.

———

We heard carts roll down the street, heavy wood grinding into stone at the mill. Helen yawned, made me do it too. Funny how doing so little makes you tired. "I guess I should start my day properly," Helen said.

"Or not. You should relax." I caught myself in my ear. I almost sounded like Lizzie.

"If I don't get this baking done, there won't be anything for the Woman's Temperance Union to sell on Saturday."

"That's why you need a maid. Lizzie usually gets Bridget to bake for her chapter."

"I wouldn't expect anything less," Helen said.

"Still. Bridget's soda bread raises a lot of money."

We sipped our tea. Then Helen said, "You should probably get yourself ready for your big afternoon."

I looked at the little gold watch hanging from my chest. Ten o'clock. The day was slipping. I let it go, and it swung a pendulum. "I think I'll go outside, let the day inspire me."

Helen clapped. "Marvellous."

I dug out a notebook and pencil and headed for the empty lot behind Helen's house. I sat in direct sunlight. Everything around me glowed and for a moment I understood how it was possible for Lizzie to believe in God as strongly as she did. The leaves on trees; slow movements of branches; the way the wind blew wheat grass; patterns that were made then erased: this was what I sketched. When I was still at school, I used to draw pictures for Father. I gave my best drawing—"Landscape with horse"—to him as a gift. I went to Father while he was in his bedroom, took a gamble that I would be allowed in. I had wanted a private moment between us, and I anticipated his compliments. "Emma, so beautiful."

And he would kiss me on the forehead.

But when I gave it to him he said nothing more than, "Oh." He cleared his throat. He put the drawing on the ground. "Go find out what your sister is up to."

Out I went, shut the door. My fingers curled into small deflated balls.

———

I found myself drawing a small child who was playing in the nearby creek. I made it plump, like Lizzie had been. I drew the baby's head large, gave it a mass of curls, a butterfly wing mouth, soft blubber cheeks. This cherub of a being.

There have been times when Lizzie was away from home that I nursed absence. Always two ways of feeling: relief and loneliness. The longest absence between us was when Lizzie took her grand European tour. Only thirty and seeing the world. I cried foul: as the eldest, I had been denied my chance, more than once, was told that I had far greater responsibility at home, that the family, one of Fall River's richest, couldn't afford it. I suspected that the real reason Father didn't want me to go to Europe was because he knew I would never come back, would encourage Lizzie to move out of the house too. And if I wasn't housebound, I wasn't Borden-bound. And he would be right.

When Lizzie had asked Father over dinner if she could travel with our cousins, he said, "Yes, of course." He sounded almost joyous.

Lizzie had not mentioned any plans to me. That sneak.

Abby wiped a napkin over her mouth and smiled, showed her graying teeth. "We know how much this means to you, Lizzie. You're going to have a wonderful time."

Lizzie grinned triumph. "Emma, isn't this so marvellous and unexpected?"

I was furious, lost my appetite. "Very."

Father pointed a finger at me. "You be happy for your sister."

I loosened my necktie. "May I be excused?" I pushed away from the dining table, left them behind, took off to the backyard, and tried to calm myself. How long had Lizzie been cooking up this plan? I wanted to scream but thought better of it. I did nothing, let crickets surround me. Later, Father came outside, kept his reason for letting Lizzie go simple: "For once you need to put Lizzie's needs before your own. You're the mature one. Let her see the world and become a woman."

It took all I had to say nothing.

In the months leading up to the trip, Lizzie held court in her little nun room, packed and unpacked her travelling trunk for days on end. "I just can't decide what to bring." Lizzie knew nothing about practicality. I knew what I would take: a few dresses, notebooks and pencils, a book, Mother's fur coat. I thought about all the time I would have away from Abby, away from Lizzie. Things unlikely. There would be an upside to her leaving.

As the departure drew near, Lizzie buried herself at Father's side, spoke softly and followed him to church. Father's little girl returned. I often overheard Lizzie tell Abby, "I'm already beginning to miss you." All that love she pretended they shared.

Afterwards Lizzie would tell me, "I hate her, Emma. Father's just as bad."

And then Lizzie was gone. The morning she left, a white coach pulled up at the house, the white draught horse's bridle decorated with vermilion rosettes and ribbons. "Do you like it?" Lizzie asked me before stepping out the front door. "I made them dress her up. It adds a certain touch, doesn't it?"

Half the street had come to see Lizzie off and she waved to them. "Don't go changing Fall River on me while I'm away." Some laughed, others glared. Mrs. Churchill gave Lizzie a piece of cherry pie to take with her for the journey. "Don't you forget what home tastes like." Lizzie kissed her on the cheeks, sniffed the pie, licked it, placed it on the coach seat. I wanted the street to open up, swallow them all.

The driver lumbered Lizzie's trunk onto the coach and Lizzie came to me, a bear hug, whispered, "I'll miss you, Em Em."

Childhood names. I wasn't that cold-hearted. "You too, Swizzy."

Lizzie kissed me dead on the lips. We were warm. The driver said, "It's time to go." We separated. Lizzie said last goodbyes to Father and Abby and before we knew it the horse was clopping down Second Street, and the crowd went back to their own lives.

The house was quiet. Sometimes I would open the bedroom door that separated us and stand in the middle. I raised my arms above my head, a lack of knowing what to do with myself. I had that feeling: happiness and loss hitched together. It felt like I was missing a limb.

I became more attuned to Father's and Abby's presence, their winter-years bodies, the way they slurped their food, the way Father held his breath when he snored, Abby's too-round face that made the dimple in her cheek look like a crescent moon. They were always there.

Occasionally Lizzie would send me a postcard: "Small walks taken through Rome," "Endless Spanish steps," "The food, Emma! The glorious food." I swallowed Lizzie's words. Some of that should have been mine. I took countless walks through Fall River, tried to take my mind off things. But it was hard to take the summer heat on my back without her.

I walked. The cotton mill's industrial calls thumped over stone. In the mornings factory steam covered Fall River in a summer fog, thick with a chemical smell that made me cough on my way downtown. Every so often I would pretend Fall River was the French Riviera, an impossible feat without the prospect of an ocean. Downtown was always the same: birds in cages, cawing and singing, hung from house verandas and shopfronts; horses and carts carried human movement; children jumped over curbsides, boiled sweets pushed hard into swollen cheeks; Mr. Potter, the Western Union Telegraph officer, waved to businessmen, trying to hide the extra pinkie finger on his right hand. On the hottest days, the police station would open the outer doors of cell rooms, exposing the screaming and cursing drunkards behind iron bars to the street. Once I watched a prisoner pull down his pants and take his penis in his hand, wave it around before letting warm urine stream down his legs. "Hey, love," he called to me, "Oh, love. How sweet it is."

At the end of my walks, I would stand outside the confectioner's store and stare at the yellow cheesecloth curtains, remember all the times Lizzie and I had spent there. I waited for the doors to open and inhaled sugar. Then I would walk away.

When Lizzie finally returned home, I welcomed her with kisses. She demanded we swap rooms.

"I think it's time you let me have it." Lizzie chewed each word as it came out, a dragon spitting out carcasses. She'd barely asked me how I was, how I had spent my time.

"I don't think so," I told her.

Lizzie closed in, squeezed my cheeks. "I'll tell Father your big secret," she whispered. Samuel. I pulled her hands away, squeezed them in my own, made Lizzie's blue eyes widen like sky. I wanted to break a bone. Instead, Lizzie got the room and I shamed myself for missing my sister as much as I had.

———

"Oh, God, Emma!" Helen shouted, filled the paddock.

I snapped to attention. Behind me, feet sounded small thunders across hard land. My name again. I twisted around, pulled towards the voice.

"What is it?"

"It's terrible news." Helen stood back. There was the loss of gravity as images presented themselves: a burning home, Mother's grave desecrated, Father striking Lizzie, Bridget abandoning her station. Thoughts of being alone with Abby.

"There's been a terrible accident." Helen, a quake.

A small fist settled at the bottom of my abdomen. Lizzie. What had happened to baby Lizzie? I wanted our mother.

Helen handed me a telegram. My legs pulled me towards the house even though I wanted to stand still. Somehow bags were packed. Then I was in a horse and carriage on the way to the train station, the way home. Down the road. Further down the road. My lips dried, throat tight. Further down the road my hands shook. Horses' hooves: cymbals. Down the road. Down the road. I arrived at the train station.

I was uncomfortable on the train's leather seat. My body stammered, muscle memory: "Your mother is not well," Father had told me when I was only ten. "She'll need you to help her around the house." For weeks Father had avoided looking me in the eye. I took his impending grief for disappointment and resentment towards me. I had tried to be the best I could by staying out of his way, by making sure that little Lizzie was bathed, was read to at night. Every now and then I would sit on Mother's bed and recite the day's news: marriages, births, important business, district policy. Obituaries were never mentioned. "Doesn't anyone die anymore, Emma?" Mother laughed. But they did, they had. She would. Lizzie had simply wanted to hold Mother's hands and stick them in her mouth. I did not understand how her world kept spinning. "Lots of wet kisses," Lizzie told me, and then she would yell, "Mama, wake up! I eat you."

On the train back to Fall River I watched a coughing child and fussing mother. Further down the track. Further down the track. A terrible accident. I remembered two months before, the way Lizzie had crawled into my bed at dawn and whispered, "I just want to make him suffer . . ." The way she had laughed. "Imagine if he fell down the stairs! What sound do you think he would make?"

I had thought nothing of it. The train went further down the track. Further still. Further still. The telegram in my lap the entire time:

Father hurt. Mrs. Borden missing. A terrible accident. Come home.

THREE

BRIDGET

August 3, 1892

THE FIRST TIME I tried to leave the house, Mrs. Borden miracled herself an almighty flu, got her arms and legs shaking, got herself all hot, all sweat, all types of pain. Dr. Bowen had to be summoned over and he told her, "Bed rest, love and attention is what you need." Mr. Borden told me to take care of his wife. I'd take food to her, chicken broth and scone dumplings, have it splashing down the bowl, down my fingers, and she'd be propped up on white cotton-covered pillows, her royal blue bonnet tied tight around her sagging jowls, and she'd say, "What would I do without you? You're looking after me just like you would a mother." She'd slurp her broth, dribble a little. I'd mop her up. Oh, she wasn't anywhere close to my mammy, but I felt for her. I'd be there, cloth in hand, dabbing her forehead, telling her stories from home, rubbing cramps out of her feet, her lips curling like a cat, pushing her cheeks into plump. I felt for her. And that's how she made me stay the first time, made me give her the love and care until I had no choice but to stay.

The second time I tried to leave, after Emma and Lizzie temporarily split the house in two by locking all the adjoining doors, Mrs. Borden raised my wages to three dollars a week and gave me Sundays to myself. "Don't let them put you off," she'd said quietly. "It happens from time to time. We'll get over it."

I weighed my options. I was the luck of the Irish. I took the money, took everything that came along with it. Mrs. Borden said I'd made the right decision. I had no other choice. I could send money home and one day money could take me back home, to moss-green fields and craggy rock, to the place where smells of fresh salmon and bottom-mud water swam through the air, the place where I laughed most, to where Nanna's ghost was waiting for me, to where my childhood lived in streets and trees and my cramped, thatch-roofed house, to the place where people talked about love like it was part of breathing.

I listened to the house, heard nothing but a crack in the roof and I stretched my legs out long in my bed, cotton sheets stuck to my skin. How long could I keep serving the Bordens? I thought of my family, all those faces, those suffocating hugs, those voices saying, "God love us," when things went wrong, and "Bridget this, Bridget that," those people around me all day and night, loving and bickering, my nanna and granddaddy, mammy and daddy, my brothers and sisters, all in that house, all together. Sometimes it could be too much and not enough.

I rolled over and lit the kerosene lamp, shined it at my wall. Seven years gone from them. The lonely time. On my wall, the photo taken at my American wake, my nineteen-year-old skinny-fed body, towards Nanna's little old lady face, her body bones in her chair. We couldn't afford the photographer but Mammy insisted, said, "We'll pay the price later." Two copies were made: one for me and my journey, one for them and Ireland.

"I'll see ya again," I told them. "I want ta see ya again."

I left the next day.

Now I was twenty-six. Now I was with the Bordens. It was getting hard to go back. Oh, but I had tried.

I didn't want to face another day with Lizzie, not another day with any of them, not another day of God knows what. It was hot in the attic. The walls popped around me, the old wood, and looking at Nanna, at my family, I told them, "I've a plan to tell Mrs. Borden that I'll be leavin' soon. I'm gonna come home." I smiled. It felt good. I sat up in bed, stretched. Then I was on hands and knees on the floor, my arm under the bed. I pulled out a heavy, round metal spice tin, green paint flaking, and coins rattled inside. I lifted the lid, lifted my St. Matthew card, kissed him on the lips, counted my savings. One hundred and four dollars. Almost two years of saving in secret. It was enough for the ship home, to tide me over till I found another job.

When I had first arrived in Fall River from Pennsylvania, Mrs. McKenney, the work agent, told me, "I'll place you with the best families." The best families would bring higher wages, four dollars at least. The best families would bring me closer to my own. Mrs. McKenney had checked me over, had read my references.

"They don't always like us Irish in their homes but we're the most loyal."

I nodded.

"You look like a wonderful domestic. I know a family who could use you well." So she sent me along with my bag down Second Street to see Mr. Borden. The street was lined with beech and poplar trees, the green blocking the sun, making my skin pimple up. I passed St. Mary's Cathedral, heard a choir hymn the Lord and I quickly Father, Son, Holy-Spirited myself, kept walking, was pushed to the edge of the sidewalk by a bald-headed child, his paw-hands chubbed against my legs. I knew women back home who'd've clipped him across the ears. Oh, I thought of it, and laughed at him. Second Street was full of manure, little green wildflowers in the middle of the street. I crossed the road, weaved through the manure field and knocked on a green door. A tower of a man, Mr. Borden, his gray hair all neat, a pipe in his hand, answered the door, then let me in. "I pay two dollars a week," he'd said. It wasn't what I'd hoped for.

I ran my fingers over the coins, sniffed old grease nickel and the tinge of nutmeg on my skin. It stung my nose and I sneezed. I put the lid back on, pushed the tin under my bed. My heart beat loud under my nightie. It was time to meet the day.

I went down the back stairs, held the lamp high, smelled kerosene like a miner. When I reached Mr. and Mrs. Borden's door I put my ear against it, waited for their bed to squeak, waited for Mr. Borden to pass gas, for Mrs. Borden to roll over in bed. I didn't have to wait long. Oh, how I knew them.

Down the stairs, in the kitchen, the clock struck double time to mark the half-hour. Five thirty.

Outside, the faint wind-chime sound of glass bottles, the milkman dropping off fresh fattened milk. It would be our turn soon. I stood by the side door and waited until he arrived.

"You beat me to it, Bridget." He placed his wooden crate on the step, stretched a bit.

"It was too hot, couldn't sleep."

He handed me a bottle, cool to the touch. "Old Borden say anything more about going off to the Swansea farm so you can have some peace and quiet?"

"They'll go nowhere now. Last night I heard Mr. Borden sayin' he's got some property sales he wants finalisin'. That got Miss Lizzie all boiled up."

"Nothing new there." His mouth had the habit of opening too wide when he spoke, always showing his chipped teeth.

"It's just 'cause she misses Miss Emma. I don't reckon she'll be comin' home anytime soon."

"I'd stay away too."

"It's not always bad," I said. Oh, but it gets bad.

"You girls all say that." He bent down to pick up our empty bottles, hips cracked from the strain. Not even Mr. Borden's body did that. He lifted his crate. "Well, I'll be seeing you tomorrow."

"Sure, sure."

He left. I took the fresh milk inside, unscrewed the lid and took a sneak sip from the bottle. The thick cream, a taste of grass. I set the milk in the icebox in the scullery, went about stacking a fire for the stove. On the kitchen counter was the large pot of mutton broth we'd been eating at luncheon for days. The thought of having to eat it one more time made my stomach flip. I went outside, got some fresh air. I heard a pigeon coo in the barn and I got to thinking that Lizzie would be up soon to check on her beloved birds, gently nursing them against her chest, stroking a wing, a head, letting them feed off seed from her hand. She should've long been out of the house and into her own family. Birds are no substitute. Once, she asked me to come into the barn and help keep the pigeons still while she checked for lice. I held the birds against my chest, used my left hand to stop necks from moving. I was afraid I'd strangle them. Their little claws at my wrists, not a thing I was used to, nor what I liked. Lizzie parted feathers, leaned in close, said, "Pretty, pretty bird," and whistled. The pigeons cooed. I'd never seen her face soften so quick.

"Ever think of gettin' a dog, Miss Lizzie? It'd be nice ta have one runnin' about."

She preened her pigeon, nipped her fingers together like tweezers, pulled a little critter from its body. "And risk them being hit by horse and cart around here? I wouldn't have it." She squished the critter between her fingers, wiped her hand on her skirt. Lizzie spread the pigeon's wings, all delicate, and said, "Look how far you can go!"

———

I began preparing breakfast. From the icebox out came the thick-cut pork steak I got from Whitehead's market two days before. Oh, the meal I was going to make. Spoons of butter, salt and pepper, bread to scoop the juices. A little something nice to start the day. I did things and I did things.

There was hard, loud walking down the back stairs, like bricks falling on bricks. There was a cough. Mr. Borden. He was on the bottom step when he said, "Bridget, where is the castor oil?"

"Sir, we don't have any left."

His arms crossed his stomach and he leaned against the doorjamb.

"Would ya like a chair, Mr. Borden?"

He waved me away. "I'll be fine. I'm queasy is all." He took a moment before heading out the side door. I rushed after him, heard him heaving in the backyard, long and deep, a cow laboring. I hoped he'd not messed himself. I did not care to clean his suit.

When he came inside, he eyed the steak. "You've cut the meat too thick." He poked the pork with his finger. Mr. Whitehead's butcher boy had cut it. I thought it a fine cut.

"They said it was a large pig, Mr. Borden."

He grunted, let me alone, went to the sitting room and I heard him pull a book from the bookshelf, pass wind, old trumpet. The frypan reached its heat and I lumped butter into it, watched the creamy yellow melt and bubble, begin to brown. On went the pork. The sizzle. I set about making johnnycakes and the morning continued like always.

Later, Mrs. Borden came down, just as pale. "You right, marm?"

She shook her head. "My stomach is feeling violent."

"Again? Mr. Borden is the same."

She rubbed her balloon stomach. "I'm beginning to think we're being poisoned." The drama of her, how she sweated, pulled her face tight.

"I'd never, marm."

She came close, touched my elbow. "I didn't even think it."

"Is Miss Lizzie sick too?"

She shrugged. "You'd know as much as me."

I flipped the pork steak. Her stomach made all kinds of noise. It wasn't long before she took herself out the side door like Mr. Borden had, and was sick. When she came back, she wiped her arm across her mouth, said, "Do we have any castor oil?"

"None, marm."

"Oh dear." She scratched at her temples and left the kitchen.

I went back to cooking and soon breakfast was ready. I set everything on the dining table and cut the pork steak into portions. Mr. Borden came in to see, said, "Go get Lizzie. I want her eating with us."

I nodded. I didn't like the chances. I went into the scullery, over to the sugar sack. Inside was a little thimble and I filled it with sugar, put it in my apron pocket, went up the front stairs, made them holler under my feet. As I got closer to Lizzie's bedroom, I heard, "As the Lord liveth, there shall no punishment happen to thee for this thing." She'd been saying the prayer for weeks. There was no love in what she said, no rhythm or heart. I'd a mind to tell her sometimes: He is deaf, it doesn't matter how much you pray, things go unanswered.

I knocked on the door.

"What?"

"Miss Lizzie, yer father says ta come down for breakfast."

Her feet across the carpet. She opened the door. Half her hair was plaited and rolled on top of her head, the other half in auburn semi-curls dragging below her shoulders, a horse's mane. "What are we having?"

"Pork steak."

She chewed the insides of her cheeks, puckered her mouth. "Is there anything extra special for me?"

I shoved my hand into my apron pocket, pulled out the thimble. Lizzie snatched it, licked her pinkie and stuck it in, sucked sugar. "Are they waiting?"

I nodded, she sighed. "Fine. I'll be . . ."

"They've been sick this mornin'."

"Really? How bad?"

"Stomachs are a-talkin'. They've already been out the backyard."

She smiled at this, stuck her tongue in the thimble. "I'll fix my hair and come." She gave the thimble back and closed the door. I was sick of this routine.

———

I was standing against the dining room wall, waiting to be of service, when Lizzie came down, sat at the end of the table. "Good morning," Mrs. Borden said. I wondered why she bothered. Lizzie broke a johnnycake in half, stuffed it into her mouth.

"What are your plans today, Father?"

"Work, of course."

"Of course, Father."

"And what will you do today?" Mrs. Borden asked her.

"I've Sunday school planning." Lizzie sweet as the thimble.

Mrs. Borden sipped tea. "What will you teach the children this time?"

Lizzie cocked her head. "What would you teach them?" Her voice was a tart raspberry pulling on cheeks.

Mrs. Borden blushed. "I wouldn't know. I'd probably stick to hymns."

Mr. Borden chewed slowly, said nothing.

Lizzie rolled her eyes. "You can't teach children the moral life by singing, Mrs. Borden."

Mr. Borden placed his knife and fork on the clean tablecloth, made pork butter stains. One more thing I'd have to clean. He cupped his hand over his mouth and belched. "And sometimes you can't teach children the moral life no matter what method you use."

Lizzie reddened. "Father?"

"I'm surprised the Reverend lets you teach as often as you do."

Lizzie's jaw angled. "I'm a good teacher, Father. The children like me."

"Children like children, I suppose."

"Andrew . . ." Mrs. Borden choked her words.

I pushed myself into the wall, wanted to disappear inside of it, did not want to see a grown woman squirm in front of her father. The wall was hot against my hands and Lizzie shot me a look, made my face burn. I did not care to see, did not care to listen to the conversation.

Lizzie said, "What's wrong, Father?"

"Your mother and I have been ill."

Lizzie straightened her back, got stiff. "Bridget mentioned."

"There's no reason we should be."

"I'm not sure . . ."

"Unless, of course, there's disease in the house."

"There's not, Father."

He arrowed a finger towards her. "You've not got rid of your pigeons, Lizzie."

"That's because I shouldn't have to. They're kept safe in the barn."

"Nonsense. You let them out and they come inside through the roof and leave their filth around." He pointed to the ceiling, the sky, to God.

Lizzie tightened her fists under the table. I did not care to be in the room.

"I've not done that, Father."

"I want you to get rid of them."

"No."

Mr. Borden pushed himself upright, a giant. "Don't defy me, Lizzie."

"But they're mine. You should fix the roof if you're so worried about disease." Her eyes wide. I sunk against the wall, hard in my back. Lizzie should've known better.

"What's that you teach the children? Obey and honor?" Mr. Borden leaned into his chair, made it creak, made me think he'd fall back and Jack and Jill his head.

Lizzie slammed her hands on the dining room table, made her piece of pork jump off the plate and onto the floor. "That's different."

Mr. Borden stood then, adjusted his trousers and came towards Lizzie. I'd seen this before. I prepared myself. I could see little yellow string-saliva in his beard. He went in close to Lizzie, slapped her across the face. Oh, the sound filled the room, that noise of skin, a cleaver working meat, and Lizzie's head snapped to the side, her shoulders metered wide, wings, and my heart raced, my knees weakened, brought sweat to my brow. Lizzie stared at her father.

"Andrew, please." Mrs. Borden held her napkin tight.

"You better start listening to me, Lizzie."

Lizzie shook her head. "You're a nasty."

Mr. Borden struck her again. I did not know where to look. Lizzie ran out of the dining room, went up the stairs and slammed the door. Mr. and Mrs. Borden didn't say anything and I collected the dishes, careful not to make too much noise. I left the room, my face ran hot, the feel of wanting to cry. How I wanted to leave the house right there and then.

———

I sympathized with Lizzie in that moment, the suffering. There'd been that moment back in Cork at the estate where I worked. I'd been touched one too many times by the master of the house. He was a giant hand, reached for my breasts as I poured him coffee, the way he did, and this time I looked at him, his dirty-red wine-colored, mushroom-bulbed nose, his English matchstick teeth, and I slapped his hands off me, slapped his chest, slapped his face. Hot coffee went everywhere, made him leap from his chair.

"Look at what you've done!" he yelled.

"Ya keep yer bloody hands to yerself. Ya shouldn't've touched me."

He came close to me, smelled of damp wool, of coffee grounds. "I'm the one who gives orders around here. Who do you think you are?"

I was beginning to find out. I was sent packing, was sent without a recommendation. It had been my third posting. I was running out of options.

"Ya didn't need to go do that," my brother said. We were all standing in our warmed kitchen when I told them what had happened.

"Ya know nothin' about what it's like."

He ran his stubby fingers through his hair. "If yer so smart, whatcha gonna do now?"

Like women and men before me I counted out money, counted out how far it would take me. Away from here, away from grubby landowners. America. Mammy and Daddy didn't want me to go, said they'd miss their baby girl, said to at least try Dublin.

"I'm hearin' girls are makin' more money there. Let me have an adventure," I told them.

"It'll kill us," Nanna said, "but it would kill ya more to stay," and she stroked my cheeks with her half-sized finger, the one she lost when she fell under a horse, and it was smooth and knobbly like a newborn bird head.

Just like that I got my ticket for the SS *Republic* down in Queenstown. A grown woman full of decisions. I knocked on doors in streets around our house, said, "I'm havin' my American wake. Come see me off."

Come they did. They filled me up with food and drink, cabbage and bacon, mutton with soda bread. Mammy made loaves of brack, made sure there were chunks of plum, my favorite, and for hours I was toasted with mulled wine, toasted with all their home-grown drops.

They filled my ears with fiddle and drum, flute and cruit, got my heart beating in time with "The Devil and the Bailiff," and I was danced from one neighbor to another, danced from a brother to a sister to a brother. Everyone laughing, screaming out song. I took that in, tried not to think about it ending.

Daddy had organized the photographer and so we stood there, arms around shoulders, all of us sweating against each other, staying still, trying not to blink, and Nanna said, "I'll die before this bloody photograph is taken." Oh, that sent us breaking, made the photographer stomp his foot, tell us we were useless. "Now I'll have ta take it again."

I didn't mind.

We'd been celebrating for hours when the keening began. I laid myself out on the sofa, looked up at them, all the people from my girlhood, who knew me too well. They had come over to me, one by one, to kiss me on the forehead and lips, tell me that I'd be missed, that they hoped to see me again, that I was already a little bit dead for having to leave them behind.

My face was covered in their wet salt, how we cried, and when it was Mammy's turn to love me and say goodbye, she let out the banshee wail, lay her hands on my body and howled in my ear. She sounded like a killing wind, moaned low and deep, and then my sisters joined her, then Nanna, then the women, a circle of grief thundering towards me. I was frightened. On they went, like cats, like foxes, heating in the night.

Then Daddy sang "Blow the Candles Out," got his voice singing beer-sweet, and just like harbor waves, everyone joined in, was accompanied by Uilleann pipes, that sorrow sound washing over me, made me cry, made me realise I had no idea what to expect in America.

I went to my nanna, who sat small in her chair, and I got on my knees, wrapped myself around her, touched her empty, old cheeks, and cuddled her onto her feet. The butter smell of her hair. She was yellow, skin tight to bone. Yellow her face, yellow her arms, yellow her half-finger. Her eyes were wrinkled half-moons, still deep brown like mine, still watching me with love, and I held right on to her for our last hold. I was able to reach my arms all the way around her, could feel her ribs struggle against me. Hold tighter, I thought. Bridget, hold tighter. But I was afraid I'd break her. Nanna breathed in my ear, short and tired and her heart beat into mine. What a sound.

"I love ya, Nanna," I said.

"I love ya too."

I lost it then, started keening over her, let nineteen years of love wail at her. I'd never heard myself like that before. It made Nanna's body shake and I held tighter to her and she said, "Will I ever see ya again?" I didn't answer.

The next day I was on the ship, was with dozens of others leaving. The ship's horn bellowed and I threw up over the railing. Thought America better be worth it.

———

As things calmed, Mr. Borden left the house for work and I went about my morning, found it hard to shake off the slap. Hard to shake off that Borden fever.

Mrs. Borden came looking for me. "Are you alright?" she asked. She held her stomach, looked in pain.

"Just continuin' along, marm."

"I have something to cheer us up," she said. In her hand was a telegram. "Look what I got yesterday. Did I tell you? I'll be having guests this Saturday."

She had not. "Who's it, marm?"

"Some old friends." The way her face became bright. It made me smile. "I knew them from school. Fancy that. After all this time."

"It'll be nice for ya."

"Yes." She read the telegram to herself again, said, "You and I have a lot to do in two days. You'll need to begin cleaning and thinking about what you'll cook for meals. I don't want to disappoint them."

I didn't see how cleaning for visitors would cheer me up. She told me to start with the parlor rug. "Take it out and beat it clean." That old heavy wool thing with its ragged yellow and white iris and violet flower pattern, green stem arches that went round and round. She'd be better off buying a new one. But I went and got the wicker slapper from the basement and threw it in the middle of the rug, rolled the whole thing into a long tube.

I dragged the rug through the parlor to the sitting room, worried that I would knock over the small tables with Mrs. Borden's porcelain ornaments on top, those ugly glazed cats and shy dogs, tails between their legs, paws begging for food. The rug rubbed against the floor like a saw, cutting up weeks of foot traffic. My underthings stuck to my lower back. I dragged it some more and there was a thwack and a drop. I put down the rug. "Pshaw," I said.

It was enough to bring Lizzie downstairs. "You're disturbing me." There was a little red Father mark on her cheek from breakfast time. Oh, I'd seen that all before.

"Sorry about it, miss."

She scrunched her nose. "What are you doing?"

"Mrs. Borden wants this cleaned. She's havin' guests Saturday."

"Who exactly?"

"Don't know."

"Father didn't tell me." Her hands went to her hips. "What's going on?"

"I've knocked the table." I pointed.

She glanced, a smile across her face. "Look at what you did." She held a porcelain dog, his ears pricked and tail raised. In her other hand, the dog's leg. Lizzie laughed, forced the pieces together, forced them apart, teased me like that, and I wiped my mouth with the back of my hand, felt it against my lips like an earth tremor.

"It's the second one I've broke." My voice came out of me, a mewing.

"She needn't know." She closed her hand over the pieces, held tight.

"She will. She loves that one."

Lizzie stuck the leg against the dog. "Stop being so dramatic. If I were you I'd throw it out." She handed it to me.

The pieces stabbed the inside of my hand, cut a little. How had she been able to hold it without hurting herself? "Maybe it can be fixed?"

She smiled, all crooked. "Or you could say someone took it."

"She'd not believe me."

Lizzie shrugged. I put the dog in my apron pocket. I'd think about what to do with it later. "I gotta get this rug done."

"As long as you don't destroy anything else."

I'd not thought her funny, wanted her to make it up to me. I pointed to the rug. "I shouldn't ask ya, but could ya help me drag it outside?"

"No. I don't do that."

"Sorry, miss."

"I'm heading out now anyway. Don't ever ask me to do your work again."

"Yes, miss."

She came near me, right up close so that I could feel her breath. "Aren't you going to ask what I'll be doing?"

"If ya like."

She stared at me. "Never mind. I don't want to tell you anyway."

"I'm sorry, miss."

Lizzie kicked the rug, went to the entrance cupboard and took her summer coat. "You're all rotten," she said, walked out, slamming the front door. I couldn't wait to leave the house, this family. I took the rug in my hands. The stupid, heavy old thing.

———

My hands and wrists were aching to snap by the time I got outside. I dragged the rug through long grass and I thought of the early days coming to Second Street, how Mr. Borden didn't believe I was worth his money. I'd been polishing the front stairs banister, Mr. and Mrs. Borden were in the parlor. She'd said, "The girl is very efficient." So I polished some more, shined it up so good I could see my teeth reflected, a prize at a show.

"She's not strong enough. Why keep her on when we have you and the girls?" he said.

"I can't do it all on my own," Mrs. Borden told him. "My back isn't what it used to be. She can do the heavy tasks."

Then he set tests. Mr. Borden had me lift wooden boxes above my head, had me pull objects like an Irish bullock. He didn't care that I could keep to myself or that I could cook a meal. He wanted a backbone for his wife. She wanted someone to give an order to, someone to keep her company. After he'd made me dig holes in the backyard, blister my hands so he could plant an extra pear tree along the fence, Mr. Borden looked me over, squinted those gray-blue eyes into sockets and said, "Fine. We'll keep you on. Just stick to what you're told."

I'd've jumped and clicked my heels if I wasn't that rundown. When Mrs. Borden found out she said, "I believe you're the girl we've been looking for. Our last one, Maggie, didn't seem to fit in."

"I can fit in."

"Wonderful. It's important I have someone here I can trust with everything."

"Yes, marm."

It was a few months later that she made me start running messages to her adult children.

"Bridget, tell them their father and I are going to Swansea."

"Bridget, can you ask them not to leave their teacups laying around."

"Bridget, tell me if they mention me in any way."

And I'd go to them, knock on their doors like I was banging a drum in a field.

"Yer mother says . . ."

"Yer mother is . . ."

And Lizzie would get all in a flap and say, "Tell Mrs. Borden that we'll come down when we're ready."

It had been funny at first, this fairy-tale way of speaking about each other. But when I saw Emma in the sitting room turning Mrs. Borden's photos face down on the mantelpiece, I wondered what exactly did fitting in mean?

———

I unrolled the rug, tried to throw it up high over the clothesline. The rug landed hard on the ground. I didn't have it in me. I went to the weather-stained pine fence we shared with Dr. Kelly, climbed onto a wooden crate, upped my head over the fence.

"Ya there, Mary?" I called out. I waited a moment, tried not to look at the Kellys' basement—the place, Lizzie had told me, where the bad thing happened.

"Father's sister used to live in that house. She did it when no one was looking," Lizzie had said.

"Did what?" I had been with the Bordens six months at the time, had complained to Lizzie that it was much too tiring to be walking water up and down the basement stairs.

"You want to know what tiring is? Picking up a kicking child." The story came out of her like she'd been wanting to tell me since we met.

She spoke fast. "She drowned her children, Holder and Eliza, in the cistern in their basement."

"Holy Father."

"Guess what she did next?" Lizzie pushed her dried lips together. I didn't care to know.

"She went inside the house and slit her throat." Lizzie said it plain face, like it was nothing, like it was a daily occurrence.

"What came over yer aunt?"

"No one knows. Father says that she was always melancholy and then she was out of her head one day."

The first of many secrets I learned. For a while, the only thing I could think about was the cistern. What sound was made when the children's heads went under water, whether their mother struggled to keep their kicking legs from hitting her in the face, whether she said anything to them.

It was Emma who noticed me staring at the steps to the basement a few weeks later.

"Who told you?" she asked.

"Miss Lizzie."

Emma rubbed her hands over her face, muffled a breath. "She shouldn't have."

"Did she really throw 'em in?"

She was pale in the cheeks, shallow in the eyes. "Yes. The only child she didn't drown was Maria."

I couldn't stop myself. "And she hurt herself?"

"She did."

"When did it happen?"

"Before I was born. We don't think about it much anymore. There's no use."

"Oh."

We both looked at the basement steps and then Emma closed her eyes, mumbled to herself and walked back to the house.

I'd heard other domestics say it was the maid who found the mother after bringing in a pail of water from the well, found her with her eyes and mouth wide open, razor in hand like she couldn't let go. It's always us who do the finding. The bad days at work.

I called loud for Mary again and she came, a sore waddle through the yard. "What's wrong with ya?" I asked.

"Dropped the iron on me foot." She pointed down her lank leg, down at a bandage, a little stain of blood.

"How many times do I have to tell ya, ya can't iron out cracked heels?"

"One more time, maybe, Bridget." She smiled wide, grimaced when she felt pain.

I mimicked a queen, plummed my voice. "You Irish may not be bright but you do bleed well."

She two-finger saluted me and we laughed. Mary limped over to the fence, lifted herself onto a stoop and our eyes met. She had those deep brown eyes, like my sister did, bright, still enjoying the idea of making a living away from her mammy and daddy. A few months ago, Mrs. Kelly brought Mary over to introduce herself to me. "The Bordens seem happy with you. Teach our girl how to keep house properly." Mary didn't need any help. All she had to do was keep quiet, get on by.

"Why'd ya call me anyway?" Mary asked.

"Can ya help me swing the rug up?"

"Why she havin' you do that?"

"Surprise of the year, Mary! We're havin' guests Saturday."

Mary mocked a shock. "Someone's willin' to visit the house long enough? Alright, hold on." Mary disappeared, walked along the fence line then joined me in the Bordens' backyard. We each took an end and swung the rug, had to swing it again when we missed the line. Crumbs of dirt, of food, rained on our foreheads and eyes.

"Enjoy beatin' this one." Mary handed me the wicker slapper and I took a swing, the thud of wicker like beating an old cow. My mouth filled with dust, all that Borden living. I spat it out.

"Well that's not very ladylike." Mary waggled a finger.

"Good. I've been practisin'." I hit the rug. There was sun on my back, on my neck. I hit the rug. Then, all serious, Mary said, "Bridget, I've been seein' Mrs. Borden in the backyard."

I stopped hitting, spat it out. "What'd ya say?"

"She's been comin' out in the mornin's, sometimes at dusk."

"What she do? She see ya?"

"I'm not thinkin' so. I saw her this mornin' too. She punches herself in the stomach," Mary said, quiet. Somewhere in the distance I heard a door open then close.

Mrs. Borden had done this before. I'd heard Lizzie reading out Mrs. Borden's diary to Emma. How they laughed. Mrs. Borden talked about how she was getting her women's blood again even though she hadn't bled for years, said her insides felt bruised, like it might fall out of her. "Listen to this!" Lizzie had said, put on her best slow-pug voice. "I wake up sweating. Andrew won't come near me." Emma and Lizzie laughed. I felt for her.

Mrs. Borden went on and on about these horrible thoughts and feelings she had, that sometimes she wanted Mr. Borden to die, that the more she had the thoughts, the more she bled, like she was being punished. So she started punching herself in the stomach, tried to stop her terrible thoughts. The girls just laughed.

But now Mrs. Borden was being violent to herself again. I knew the things that followed. How she'd wake at night with red between her legs, an ache battering inside her. She'd quietly get out of bed, hold her nightie tight as a tourniquet and hobble down the back stairs to the basement and wash. She would never leave her nightie and sheets for me to deal with. Not like Lizzie has, not like Emma has. Mrs. Borden wouldn't want me to know her like that.

"What do ya think she's doin' the punchin' for?" Mary asked.

"I wouldn't know anymore." A horse and cart went by, tripping hooves on stone, a bridle jingle-jangle. "Maybe it's good I'm leavin' when I am."

"Since when? Ya said that last time and had nothin' to leave with."

"I've been savin' all me money ta go. I'll tell Mrs. Borden soon."

"She won't let ya."

"I don't care. All their fightin' and nonsense. Somethin's gonna happen. It'll drive me crazy."

"She'll never let ya go."

"I'll make her let me go." A pigeon cooed in the barn. "Well, I best be beatin' this, earn me keep."

Mary touched me on the shoulder and rubbed circles. "God love ya, Bridget."

I beat the rug, took mouthfuls of dust.

———

When I went inside, Mrs. Borden was in the sitting room, her eyes stony. "You took your time cleaning that rug."

"Mrs. Borden?"

"You've a lot of chores to get through."

I couldn't read her and so I went to the basement and got my cleaning things. She had me dusting photos, dusting shelves, dusting frames, piano, porcelain. The way she sat on the sofa, in Mr. Borden's space, her hands resting over her knees, like she was the master of the estate whistling commands. Mrs. Borden was hardening up. Oh, but she could when it was only her and me in the house. Lizzie must've upset her.

"I heard you out there with the Kelly girl." She spat it out all dirty.

I felt red, like I would burn and disappear. What had she heard me say? She pulled herself from the sofa, held on to the mahogany side table for support. Then she was right up close to me, her breath my breath.

"I drive you crazy, do I? What would dear old Nanna and Mammy think of you now, hmmm? You're making a habit of abandoning people, aren't you?" Mrs. Borden licked her lips. I hated her then, hated that she spoke of poor Nanna as if she knew about her dear heart. Hated that I'd told her anything about me back home. Her breath my breath, a stinking piece of pork caught between teeth. I pulled away from her. Mrs. Borden caught me by the wrist, held me, pinched my skin.

"Please, Mrs. Borden. Yer hurtin' me."

She gripped tighter, her dry paper-thin hands.

"Why were you telling her you're leaving the house?" Her eyes watered. Now she knew.

"I was goin' ta tell ya."

Her face came closer to me and I felt my breath bounce off her skin, warm. "It's time I moved on, marm."

"How many others have you told?"

"Just Mary."

"You've embarrassed me."

"I didn't mean ta."

Closer still she came, closer until our noses almost touched. Old woman freckles, blue-purple bruising under her eyes, river red lines on cheeks. "I paid you more, kept paying you more. Do you hate me that much? Am I that despicable?"

"No, marm. This place is no good." I didn't recognize my own voice.

Mrs. Borden slapped me hard across the face, the meat cleaver sound, my head snapping to the side, my body going with it, and the room echoed like that banshee's cave. I tasted blood in my mouth.

"You shouldn't be allowed to just leave!" she bellowed, she wailed.

Outside was the sound of a horse and buggy, the ringing bell of the iceman's cart, a man and woman walking by, her shoes tripping on bluestone trying to keep up with him. I could hear all those things from inside and I wondered if they could hear her out there. I raised my hand. I wanted to hit her back.

Mrs. Borden scratched her temples, scratched hard. I tucked my hand under my arm. "Go upstairs and do your job," she said, her voice then a calm creek.

"Marm, let me explain . . ."

"Go upstairs."

I got my cleaning rags, got my bucket. Mrs. Borden watched me. I walked past her, made my way to the front of the house and my skin brushed against hers, a whoomp sound, like sheets drying. When I reached the stairs, Mrs. Borden said, "When you finish up there I want you to explain this." She paused and I heard a rattle. I stopped. There was my money tin, all my hours and years of living Borden in her hand. Rattle, rattle.

———

In Lizzie's room, I dusted and dusted. I hated Mrs. Borden then. I was ready to cry in anger but held myself back, thought to play safe so I could get my money back. I dusted over Lizzie's trinkets, those ridiculous little things she didn't even touch. If I had half as much as she did. Over at the bookshelf, I dusted and let myself cry, let myself want Mammy and Daddy, want them to say, "We told ya America was no place for a girl like ya," want something, someone, to come into the house and make everything end, let me go walking out the front door and never return. My rags went over spines, over *A Connecticut Yankee in King Arthur's Court*, over *The Woodlanders*. When was the last time she even read these? Rags over *Frankenstein*, over *Wuthering Heights*, over *The Castle of Otranto*, and I got to thinking of home, of the times we'd sit around the kitchen table hogging stove warmth as we told stories to one another, hours of ghosts, hours of tales about cold hands crawling out of the darkness onto your face, stories of drowned immigrants sinking to the bottom of the sea before swimming back to shore, coming back to family.

There would be Daddy and Granddaddy pouring glasses of their homemade whiskey, waiting to be told they had a fine drop.

"Burn yer throat this lot would," Mammy's brother Frank would say, but he'd keep on drinking it down, drinking till it no longer burned.

I dusted spines, I dusted shelves, dusted over Lizzie's bedhead, right over to her dressing table. Lizzie fancied herself, her little collection of flower-painted porcelain vases, her bottles of jasmine and civet perfume smelled like unwashed bodies. I noticed her jewelry box was unlocked. I shouldn't have. Inside it, her crosses, wooden and silver, different sizes of her love of the Lord. There was a sapphire ring, the large stone encased by tiny gold claws, a tiger with prey. I'd never seen her wear it. It must've been new. I picked it up. Underneath the stone was a small price tag. Forty dollars. A ring Mr. Borden would never let her buy. I put the ring back in the box, shut the lid. Lizzie had been bad again. Just like she had been the year before when she told Mr. Borden, "Oh, Father! Someone came into the house and raided your belongings."

"How do you know?"

"I heard him. I think I scared him away before he had a chance to take anything else."

We were in the sitting room when Mr. Borden asked me what I knew, as if I had done the deed myself. "Nothin', sir. I was down the basement washin' laundry." Emma knew nothing either.

His finger back and forth between me and Emma, like choosing teams. "How is it no one heard a man break in except Lizzie? Are you all lost to the world?"

"Father, the house was locked. I didn't suspect a thing out of order," Emma told him, out of breath, out of depth.

Mr. Borden made the three of us walk through the house with him like naughty children. He'd point to windows, ask me to rattle them, see if any came loose. None did.

"Father," Lizzie said, "is it really necessary we do this?"

Mr. Borden didn't answer.

After an hour of searching the house, we were in Mr. and Mrs. Borden's bedroom. We stood by the window as Mr. Borden looked through drawers. Emma scratched her elbow. Lizzie watched her father.

"He took tram tickets." Lizzie stepped towards him, rested her hand on his arm. Emma breathed deep, her throat making accordion sounds. The air in the room got thick.

Mr. Borden pulled his arm away. "Seems an odd thing to take."

"Maybe he thought they could be cashed in." Lizzie shrugged.

Mr. Borden looked at his daughter. They looked at each other. Lizzie's face flushed pink, eyes widened. He made a fist, unmade a fist.

"Father." Emma was loud. He turned to her. "Lizzie needs rest. It must've been frightening to hear that commotion and not be able to call out. Let's stop searching."

Mr. Borden took a good look at the open drawers around him. "Looks like a few dimes and a necklace have been taken too."

"Father, if I can think of anything else I might've heard I'll tell you and you can tell the police." Lizzie sweetened up.

Emma stretched her hand to Lizzie. It was taken. The sisters left the room, went down the back stairs, clumped along like toddlers. I went to leave.

"Stop," Mr. Borden said. He stood by his bed, rocked back and forth then got himself still. "Have you ever given your key to anyone?" His voice was small.

"No, sir. I keep it on me always."

Mr. Borden grunted. "You can go now."

I nodded and left.

A few days later I was doing laundry in the basement when I found a tram card stuck to the inside of Lizzie's skirt. I checked the other pocket. Another card. Lizzie had a lot to learn about hiding secrets. I tore the cards, clumped them together in the tub of warm soapy water, watched them turn gray.

FOUR

BENJAMIN

August 3, 1892

I MET JOHN in Fairhaven after a night of blood-letting fighting, of losing my last dollar, of ripping my leg on barbed wire. I met John the way I do most—by chance, by accident, the crossing of paths. It was dawn and I was water-full. I was with my gristle and chops in hand, urinating up an alleyway wall when an older, tree-height man quickly turned into the alleyway, came trudging towards me, vomited gravy-thick onto my boots. He held himself together then gave a gentleman's laugh. "That was rather unexpected."

"Damn sure was."

He wiped his mouth, looked me over, said, "I too quite like urinating in open spaces from time to time. It's freeing, don't you agree?"

I didn't care to be interrupted. "I just do what I need to do."

He nodded his head, said, "I like a man who doesn't overthink things. There's value in that."

Something my papa might've said. "Sounds like you're calling me stupid, old man."

He waved his hand. "On the contrary." He shifted eyes down to cobblestone, grimaced and said, "My apologies about your boots. Drank some milk that was too far gone, I'm afraid." He rubbed his hand over his dark suit, reminded me of a banker.

"Didn't your mama ever teach you to sniff before you drink?" I was about to pull my trousers up when a voice boomed, "Hey, you! Stop what you're doing."

I quick-turned, saw a pimple-faced, slightly hunched officer at the alleyway entrance. I ignored him.

The officer came closer, scraped his boots. I ground my teeth, felt one loosen. I was tucking myself in when the officer started up like a master, said, "You dirty cur."

I faced him. "Tsk-tsk. Name-calling isn't a way to get someone to cooperate."

The officer closed in on me, dug his finger into my chest. "I speak however I want." Then he took a look at the older man, raised his eyebrows. "Got ourselves a father-son act, do we?" The officer chuckled, pointed to the man's groin. "Get your codge out, did you?" The man reddened.

This officer was one for humiliation. I didn't care for his tone.

"It's not like that," the older man said. "It's hardly what you think."

"Public urination is an offence, did you know that? Give me your name," the officer said.

"John."

"You don't strike me as the filthy kind, John. Not like this one here." The officer came in close, sniffed us up like a dog.

"Get away from me," I said. All low.

"You don't have a say in the matter. I make the rules around here." The officer pulled his baton from his belt, tapped it against the brick wall, then tapped it against John's leg. John buckled like old kindling.

"Get away from me," I warned.

The officer, closer again. "You dirty, dirty cur."

I'd had enough. I slapped the officer across the face, my iron palm, and the officer's head twisted. A warm-up. I knuckled up, punched the officer until I heard a crack, made him fountain blood, made him double over, drop his baton. John grabbed it, thunked it into his palm, and for a moment I thought he would use it against me.

"I wouldn't," I told John.

"Neither would I." He handed me the baton. The officer was hands and knees between us, a tabletop of blue cotton and wool. I lifted the baton, struck it hard against his body. The officer cried out. I lifted him, got his blood all over my hands and said, "That's for hitting an elderly man."

The officer lay there, spat out a tooth. He would not be getting up. Then John said to me, "That was rather unexpected."

I looked at him, saw the beginnings of a grin, saw a little gap between his front teeth. He stuck out his hand and I grabbed it, gave a handshake. His skin was elderly-soft, someone who never had to use their hands for work. There was blood on my thumb, on my wrist, and when we finished shaking hands, there was blood on his too. He took out a white cotton handkerchief from his breast pocket, wiped himself clean.

"Benjamin," I told him.

"I'm so glad to have met you, Benjamin. Who knows what might have happened if you hadn't been around?" John eyed me, pointed to my barbed-ripped thigh. "You seem to have gotten yourself into a spot of bother."

I looked down at my frayed trouser leg, at the gash underneath. "Nothing I can't handle."

"I'm beginning to see. But you'll need to take care of that."

"In good time."

John wiped his hand again, inspected his fingernails. His stomach gurgled and he belched. "Pardon me," he said, rubbing his stomach. "Seems I've still got some issues here."

My leg began to ache, remembered the fire-tear of steel as I jumped over a fence, remembered a man's bloody tooth jammed into my palm after I had smashed him. I must have winced because John asked, "You need a rest?"

"I'll be okay."

"Why don't we go somewhere, get ourselves a rest? Get a drink? I feel I owe you for sticking up for me." John, overfriendly, overinsistent.

I looked down at the officer, still passed out from knocking. Would John rat me out if I didn't go with him? Some men scare easy, some men are the scare. I knew what I was. I'd gamble about John. "Alright," I told him. "Let's rest."

John smiled. "I know a quiet place but we'll need to walk. Can you manage?"

"I've had plenty worse injuries."

We left the alleyway, walked deeper into Fairhaven, past the scaffolding around the roofless city hall, past all things gentlemanly, walked to a quiet, dusty corner storefront. "No one to bother us here," John said. I nodded.

We went in, smelled the dirt-whiskey fumes, saw men there. Men holding on to half-empty glasses, men holding on to their bollocks, men playing their last chance at card games. Men there like my papa. They paid us no attention. We sat at the bar. I could smell John, could smell that he didn't belong in places like this. I breathed him in—clean-smelling, just a hint of sweat.

The barman came over, dragged his weasel legs behind him. "Get you anything?"

I fingered my pocket, had nothing inside, looked at John, who reached into his jacket pocket, pulled out a fold of notes. "Two whiskeys to warm us up."

The barman poured, handed them over, left us.

We sipped, my throat liquid-warm, and I nodded my head. John smiled. "What were you doing out this morning anyway, Benjamin?"

"This and that."

"A man of secrets. I respect that."

"What were you doing?" I asked.

"I'd been up and down through the night vomiting, I thought a walk might do the trick, but alas . . ."

"Alas indeed."

"Besides, I think we all should be up in the early hours. Early birds catch the worm." John winked, sipped whiskey, made a gurgling sound as he swallowed. A peculiar man.

The bar was noise and drink. Men challenged men then quickly gave up the fight. After a time, John asked where I had come from.

"It's a story," I said.

"But you're not from around here?"

"No." I didn't care to be friendly like this with him but we were under unusual circumstances. "You from here?"

"No, not me. I'm here to visit before moving on to Fall River."

"What's there?"

John rubbed his nose. "Family. Of sorts."

"Of sorts?"

"My sister's daughters live there."

"But not your sister?"

He smoothed palms over his hair. "She died many years ago."

"I've sisters." I said it like we were becoming buddies.

"You get along with them?"

"I used to. I haven't seen them in a while."

This made him smile. "So you like to keep your distance from people."

"Sometimes."

John looked at me like I was a calculation. "What is it you want?" I asked.

He palmed his hair again. "I'm just trying to get to know the person who helped me."

"I see situations and I fix them," I told him. A half-truth. If only he knew.

John grinned. "I bet you do."

We stared at each other. John bit his fingernails, like he was thinking things over, and after a time he said, "I hope this doesn't push our newfound acquaintance, but I wondered if you would consider helping me one more time." A waver in his voice.

"In what way?"

"I need someone to take care of a problem."

"What kind?"

"Familial."

I nodded. "I know about those."

He smiled. "I had a feeling you might." John looked me over again, looked down at my leg. "That needs to be seen to."

Blood was resting on the surface of my pants, my leg giving off all types of smells. "I've had worse injuries."

"Still, you wouldn't want a cut like that to get in your way."

"Guess I don't."

The men in the bar kept up their drinking, kept up their card-playing, kept up. Outside the sun brightened, cast long shadows into the bar. I thought about the officer, whether he'd been found yet, whether he had sent anyone to come for me. Sitting still was a danger. I said to John, "This problem you have, is it in Fall River?"

"Yes."

"And you want the problem to be taken care of soon?"

"The sooner the better."

"What exactly do I have to do?"

"I'm having trouble deciding. I don't want it to get out of control."

"I'm very controlled."

John nodded. "Yes, you are, but can you disappear? Can you keep secrets?"

I got the rush feeling of danger, felt it push along my body. I'd been asked this type of thing before. There would be gold times ahead. "It's what I'm good at."

John nodded and nodded, his head bobbing for a tipping point. "Good. Because we're very private people. We simply need help.

We need someone to be a kind of mediator, someone who doesn't know us and won't play favorites." His gap-toothed smile.

"Who exactly needs help?"

"My wonderful nieces." He paused. "Unfortunately, they don't see eye to eye with their father. He's a stubborn man, doesn't take too kindly to anyone who questions him."

I knew about fathers. Origins are important. There was a time when I wouldn't have been able to take care of such business.

John studied his fingernails then slid them one by one over his teeth.

"Do you want me to talk some sense into him?" I asked.

"I want you to be forceful with the man. He needs to listen to reason."

"What message do you want me to send him?" I thought of the ways I could do that. The fun it would be.

"I want him to know that I've been paying close attention to how he's been treating his daughters lately." He paused again, thought some. "And I want him to reconsider where he's spending his money."

Rich people. This I was interested in. "I understand. How far do you want me to go?"

"I just want the girls to feel that I've taken care of them, the way I promised their mother."

———

I used to be butter—the way I'd disappear at the sign of heat. There had been all those schoolboy days of knuckle busting skin, taunts about my chicken coop smell. My papa was a tall, hulking fist. He had ways of shaping children into adults. I used to wake at night, sweated lumberjack fever, to find my papa kneeling above me.

"You're not going to school today."

"Why?"

"I'll be teaching you how to be a man."

Being men, we would head out, guns in hands, and stalk through trees fighting off cold-spine shivers each time Papa slapped my head for missing a target.

At home, Mama was a dust keeper. Hours then hours of menial tasks to keep herself from thinking, "If I stop, I'll leave and I'm not sure I'd take the children." But there she stayed, haloed us with love.

My sisters and I would watch the way Papa kissed Mama, always with a danger tongue, demanding knuckles under skin. "Let me love you my way," Papa would say.

"No, not now. The children."

"What good are you?" Papa would slap her. "You're ugly, anyway."

I wanted to get him off her but never could work up the nerve. What was wrong with me? How was it possible I could look an animal in the eye, dagger a throat, but be too scared to pull Papa away?

Then one night Papa came home and said, "This family's gone to shit." He spat on the floor before sitting down at the table. We watched him eat the cold mutton soup that had been lovingly prepared for him that afternoon. He slurped.

"What's gotten into you?" Mama was a mouse. She moved to him.

"Shut up, woman." He slapped her across the face.

I cleared my throat, tried to be the man Papa wanted. "Don't you hurt her."

He stood from the table, inched and inched towards me until nose touched nose. For the first time I noticed wild-boar–like hairs covering the sides of his nostrils. "You questioning me?"

"God will punish you. That's our mama," I said. I got knotted up, heart pounded, thought I'd vomit.

Papa pushed his index finger into my throat. "You're wrong. I can't be punished."

The index finger pushed, pushed harder, and I could feel my breath trap underneath the weight of Papa.

He packed his bags and lofted his hat onto his head, he gripped my shoulder and said, "You're it." My sisters waited for him to say he loved us, that he might come back for us one day. I tried not to get my hopes up—I loved and hated. But all Papa did was leave and that was it.

That night Mama sat on her knees and crossed her chest. I walked through the house nursing a hurt so big it made me feel like I would break. He had to come home. I thought of tracking him, wondered if I might need to take a gun. I wasn't sure I had it in me. Instead, I walked to the Mackenzie River, sat on the bank, thought about the time Papa had let me hold his fishing rod. Light wood against the current. "Am I doing it right, Papa?"

"Yes, sir, son. Yes, sir." He even young-pupped me on my back.

Papa had said that nice thing once.

I needed to cool off and so I walked into the water until it filled my boots. I looked up at the moon. "Why's he get to do this to us?" I said, I cried. Once when I had killed a deer and sobbed, couldn't stop my shaking, Papa had said, "The first time doing this is always hardest, but it gets easy. Trust me." Hitting, fighting, blooding, yelling, strangling. A lot of things were meant to get easy.

Mama once told me, "You ask God for the right thing to do and he'll tell you the answer is always in you. You just gotta trust it."

I looked up to where the Lord might have been and said, "God, I want to make things better. What's the right thing to do?"

I waited for an answer. I thought of Papa, all the hurt that he had made, thought about what he might do in my position, thought of him back home with us, what that could mean. I thought about holding a rock above Papa's face, teeth smattering over lips, blood on cheek and chin. From a very dark place, I told myself, "It's right to protect and it's right to take care of problems." In my mind I smashed the rock into Papa's face, felt a whole lot better. I didn't hear God tell me what I was thinking was wrong and so I willed myself into being Papa's son. I would make him pay, make him come home and everything would be right. I walked out of the river, water rushing from my clothes. A baptism.

Several weeks later, my uncle stood on our steps, his hat tilted low over his eyes, and with a clotted mouth told us, "Just saw him. Your papa's been living just over in Rising Sun. I saw him at a wedding."

My sisters breathed in shallow rhythms, burst into crying. They held each other's hands and pulled at finger webbing as they called Uncle a liar. It made me want to hold them, tell them everything would be okay, that I would take care of everything.

"He a guest?" I asked.

"It was his wedding. I saw him's bride hold a new baby child. Looked a lot like him. Like you, even."

I said, "Do you know where he lives?"

"Don't go looking for him, Benjamin," Mama said. "You stay right here with me."

Uncle smoothed his fingers through his beard. "Yup. I followed him home. 'Bout a quarter mile from Baptist church you . . ."

I spat onto the ground. My tongue curled from a rancid metallic taste and I sucked it away.

I pushed past my uncle, began the hunt for Papa. I walked. As I entered Rising Sun, the smell of burnt hay and mud welcomed me after twenty long miles. I walked around town for hours, looked through windows and under fences for signs of new family life. Some houses were a ransack, others bare and ghost-like. I walked on.

And then, just like that, I happened across Papa and his bride. They were tucked behind a red fence. The wife, red hair and too-long dress, sat on the front porch reading a woman's palm. Papa cut grass by the side of the house, wiped his mouth on his shirt sleeve. He looked happy. I had thoughts of rock, teeth, blood.

When the wife had finished with the woman, Papa walked over, kissed her on the forehead. "Gotta get these cutters fixed," he said. I imagined Papa's lips on foreheads—Mama's, sisters', mine. I lifted my hand to my mouth.

"I love you," the wife told him.

"I love you too."

What a thing it was to hear Papa say those words, like he had said them all his life. He took off down the street and the afternoon breeze picked up.

Papa's wife saw me, came out from behind the fence. She smelled sickly sweet, her hair, around fingertips, threads of her blouse, stupid lips and full cheeks. Papa's wife's brow shadowed. "You alright? You seem lost."

Sweat cracked along my back. "Not entirely."

She grinned then. "Aha, well, I can make you see the light, all God's good things. Get His spirit into you."

I grunted at her. I did not care for magic.

She reached a hand towards hand. "I'm Angela."

"Benjamin." We shook. I sucked my tongue. Angela, her face peach-calm, pretty like a faun, and I smiled back, got an idea. I got the idea that Angela would be punishment for Papa.

Angela.

"Come inside." Chirped like a bird.

I followed. I clenched my teeth and bit my lip.

"Please take a seat. Be comfortable." And she sat beside me. "You've such an angelic face. Look at your dimples." She leaned in, looked right through me. "Your eyes remind me . . ." Her voice wet, made my spine convulse.

Angela giggled. "You met the devil somewhere?"

"Maybe."

Their house was filled with books and furniture, more than what we ever had, and in the sitting room there was a small statue with a bulging belly. "What's that?"

She waved her arm towards it, like shooing a fly. "That's Buddha. Gotta make sure you cater for everyone."

For a moment I wondered what it would be like to see inside of her, all the red. "You're young to be out on your own," she said, scooping hair from her neck.

I tried to think of what she would want to hear. "I don't really have a family." The sitting room windows were half open, the light breeze waltzed into the house carrying with it the smell of sycamores and chicory.

"It must be difficult for you."

I nodded.

"Well, once you let God's light in, you'll never be alone."

I laughed, a little boy. "Sounds strange."

"My husband thought so too when I met him."

"Was that him cutting grass?" I leaned towards her.

Angela sat back, pressed a finger to her lips. "Yes, it was."

"Is he a good man?"

She nodded. "One of the best."

I would not let her off the hook. "How did you meet him?"

"Out walking one day." She rubbed her eyebrows, as if I was giving her pain.

"What were his first words to you?"

Angela shook her head, whispered, "This moment isn't about me. I'm more interested in healing you."

"Did you heal him?"

"Yes."

I thought of her bones. "How did you fix him?"

"With love." Angela's cheeks rosed round.

"Does he stick it to you?"

Angela shifted back on the sofa, got pale. "That's very rude. I'm not sure I can help you today."

"But I was looking forward to it."

"I'm sorry, you have to leave." Angela went to the front door.

I didn't care to be told what to do. I reached for her. She locked eyes with mine, mouthed a silent God rhythm, red lips sugar dancing. I took a deep breath. Her eyes pulsed. I gripped her hard. I wanted to drag all that blood and life out of her.

I ground my teeth. Somewhere in the house a baby cried. Angela tried to push against me, looked towards the back of the house.

There would be no escaping me. Outside two women walked past the house, their heels diving into rock and soil. I breathed deeply, held Angela's bony wrists tight, and pulled her into me, her cheek on my cheek.

"You need to let go of me," she said.

A surge of electricity carried through my veins then skin, hands trembled. Her breath became shallow, saliva dripped onto my chest. She was so warm.

The baby cried. Angela pushed against me again, said, "Please, let me go."

"I have something to tell you, Angela."

"What?" she whispered.

I choked her into my body, felt her tense. "Your husband's already got a family."

The baby cried. "Please, let me go to her," Angela said.

"Before he stuck himself inside you and gave you a baby, did he tell you about his other children?" I was the sound of a boulder rolling.

The baby cried. Angela sobbed. "What are you saying?"

Together in embrace we made a shadow across the wall. Then I threw Angela into the sofa.

"Who are you?"

"I've come to have words with your husband. You should be thankful, really. He'll eventually get tired of you, especially when you get ugly."

"Let me go."

"Let's play a game now, Angela . . ."

Angela had tried to curl herself into a ball when my first punch landed. I stepped back and watched her face burn and I thought of

Papa, the time I told him, "I love you," and was ignored. I lifted my fist in the air and brought it down hard into Angela's cheek. A bone cracked.

"It's your fault Mama isn't smiling."

Another punch. Angela slumped deeper in the sofa as each fist came for her. I closed my eyes, my face wet. The baby cried. Everything was becoming right and the air smelled of blood, honey-sweet.

It wasn't until Angela hoarsed, "Please, no more," and the front door opened that I stopped. The smell of leather, a sourness, hit me. I snapped my head towards the man standing in the doorframe. Papa. He dropped his keys at the sight of Angela. My knuckles sang.

He almost sobbed, "What've you done, Benjamin?" All that caring in his face. Where was his anger?

The baby cried. Angela howled a call of pain. I pushed past Papa, gave a jaw snarl, went out the front door and down the road. I ran, I ran.

When I finally reached home, Mama was waiting on the porch. "Police came here looking for you. Christ, where you been?"

I reached for her. "I've been out fixing. I love you, Mama."

She wrenched her head, hit my hands away. "You've got blood all on you."

I looked at my hands; the small cuts and lion-bulge knuckles, the dried blood and ripped fingernails. "It's okay, it's not mine."

"Police said you were in your papa's house."

I didn't answer her.

She lifted a kerosene lamp to my face. "Did you hurt that woman?"

"I didn't hurt her. I hurt Papa. I was doing the right thing for you."

Mama shook her head like she would cry. "I don't know you. I'm sending for the police."

"Mama, please . . ."

She slammed the front door. I stood on the bottom step. This wasn't meant to happen. I thought she loved me.

I banged on the front door, yelled, "Who's gonna look after me?"

She whimpered back, "I can't have someone like you in the house. It's too much."

I banged again.

"If you don't leave, I'll get the police."

I didn't want any of that. I just wanted to explain how I was making things right. But instead I had to run. I took in the house a last time, hoped that one day when she realized what I had done for her, she would love me like before. I ran then, into the woods, ran, thinking of how one day I'd return to Mama, ran, until I was deep into trees.

———

John was searching for safety at home. I knew this want. I could give it to him. I moved my tongue over my teeth. "Do your nieces know you're helping them?"

John shrugged, smiled. "Who could say? I like the idea that I'm simply helping them out before they realize themselves that they need it."

"What are their names?"

He waggled his finger at me, said it wasn't important, and I huffed from my nose, gave him a hard stare. John said, "Have it your way. Emma is the eldest, Lizzie the youngest. But only Lizzie will be home. You're not to go near her."

I nodded. The less people involved the better. "What does she look like?"

"Why do you need to know?"

"If I'm not to go near her . . ."

He was tight-jawed. "Lizzie is the young woman in the house, a little shorter than average height. Then there's Bridget. There's nothing much to say about her other than she looks like a maid, will have a uniform on." He smiled, bared his teeth.

I nodded.

He told me that all he needed from me was one night, that he would get me out of Fall River, that things would be easy. Fine things, but I wanted more. I had my own problems to take care of. So I asked John about payment.

He looked me over. "You'll get your leg fixed."

I laughed. "My leg isn't payment. I want money."

John rubbed his beard. "How about a thousand dollars, if it goes well?"

More than I expected. He really did have a big problem to solve. The things I could do. I thought of Papa, how I could finish his punishment. What a gold visit that would be. I nodded my head and nodded my head.

"And their father. What's his name?"

"Andrew Borden. His wife is Abby. She's rather heavyset, if you know what I mean. I doubt you'll have to talk to her."

I churned everything through my mind, started thinking of the talk I'd have with Andrew. "Let's go to Fall River."

We made our way from the public bar into the light. The town clock chimed ten o'clock. We wound in and out of people all the way to the train station without saying a word. After John bought tickets he said, "Don't forget it's Fall River."

"I know where we're going. You and I are going to have an interesting train ride together."

He patted me on the back like I was his young pup. "I didn't mean to confuse you." He gave me my ticket and pointed to the end of the train. "You'll be down there."

I didn't like the way he said it. He left me then, went to the front carriages. There's always someone thinking they're better than me. I had second thoughts about helping him. I started walking to the end of the train. My leg ached, started to bleed like a little creek. I thought about payment. The train whistle blew. I thought about fathers, the problems caused. I would have to keep my eye on John. I hopped on the train. And the train slowly rolled forwards.

PART II

FIVE

LIZZIE

August 4, 1892

I WAS ALMOST five when Father and Mrs. Borden got married. Emma and I watched them like tiny gods from the doorway, watched Mrs. Borden plait then pin her hair into fibrous loops by her temples. Father had looked on, his teeth sucking in air, a tin whistle. "Do you need help? I can ask Emma . . ."

"No," Mrs. Borden said. "A bride needs to do these things on her own."

The church was full of flowers, white and crimson, and bells filled the air then my ears; tiny angel wings. As Emma and I walked down the aisle, dropping rose petals at our feet, I could smell the dresses of the women, violet-honey and camphor. I sneezed and there was laughter. Emma squeezed my hand tight, tugged my wrist to her belly, and we walked towards Father, organ music pumping blood. We stood and waited for Mrs. Borden to walk the aisle.

I swayed to the music, my feet jumping, small click beetles, and tried to make Emma dance with me. She was still, marble-limbed, looked like she might cry, so I huddled into her side, wrapped my arms around her legs, watched Father and Mrs. Borden give each other silver-moon rings then kiss.

After, I heard people say, "He'll completely dominate that woman." Others said it would mend his broken heart after Mother had died, *what about our hearts?* "Abby will have the children she has always wanted." These things people said.

These memories that came to me as I thought about Mrs. Borden's body on the floor, the way red and purple carpet flowers would be pressed against her teeth and eyes, *let's make flower presses, Emma,* and it made me feel like there were small pebbles tumbling through my stomach, a skippy-skippy-do-da rhythm.

Two officers ran from the dining room, ran up the stairs, ran until their feet stopped above my head, sank into the floor. A pause. "Good Lord. Get the doctor right now," a voice bellowed. The house popped, sent cracks along windows and doorframes. Dr. Bowen turned to me, his mouth a tinge of purple, said, "Lizzie, you must stay here." I nodded. A fog settled in my mind and everything slowed.

When Bridget and Mrs. Churchill came back into the dining room, they came to me, sat at my feet, looked half dead. I sat straight, tall.

"Miss Lizzie, it's awful. It's all bloody up there." Bridget's eyes glassed, were wet.

"What?" I asked.

"We found her, Lizzie. Abby is up there." Mrs. Churchill seesawed her head to the ceiling, made all kinds of cracking sounds.

The back stairs were a thunder of boots. Another police officer came into the dining room, blue cap in hand. "Miss Lizzie," he said, "I'm afraid to say there's been another death. Mrs. Borden . . ."

"Oh, did she finally come home?" I asked. I'd been waiting to hear.

The officer stared blank. "No. She's killed."

I thought of Father. Then I thought of Mrs. Borden. "Did someone cut her too?" I said.

The officer stared blank, then looked towards the ceiling where Mrs. Borden was lying face down in a swelling pool of dark red, her arms by her side, her feet crumpled in her soft leather boots. Her hair, plaited then rolled tightly around the crown of her head, hacked off and tossed aside onto the bed. What a horrid thing.

Mrs. Borden's hair used to taste like lavender. When I was seven, she would swoosh it around my face, all those thick strands tickling my cheeks. But then her hair grew gray and began falling out into bowls of food. She never noticed how she ate a piece of herself each night.

More police officers came into the dining room, formed a semicircle around me, *let's find out how many more people we can fit.*

It made me hotter, feel like I needed to vomit. "What's going on?" I asked.

"Miss Borden, under no circumstances are you to leave this room," an officer said.

"Should I be very frightened?" My hand moved across my stomach.

Bridget cried. Mrs. Churchill cried. Those high-pitched wails.

"We have reason to believe that the killer is still in the house."

"Good heavens," I said. My stomach tightened. "I need my sister. I really need my sister."

———

An officer sat across from me, said, "What's the matter, Miss Borden?"

"Pardon me?" I said.

"You keep rubbing your head." He leaned closer, made the wooden dining chair creak, sinking wood logs in a river.

Fingers caught at the top of my forehead, *a widow's peak, a widow's peak*, and I pulled them away, placed them in my lap. "My head is feeling rather strange, Officer."

"It must be the commotion."

"Yes. That would be it," I said.

The pebbles tumbled. In the corners of my eyes, Mrs. Borden lay like a giant stone crypt, waiting for me to come in. My body jumped, surprised me.

"What is it?" the officer said.

"I've had the most hideous thought. Mrs. Borden is up there all alone, all hurt like Father."

"We'll make sure she's taken care of," the officer said.

I imagined Dr. Bowen by her side, checking her pulse, rubbing her shoulders as comfort. The kitchen walls popped, echoed, pushed a wave of nausea over my head. She was being cared for. *But what about me?*

The house filled with talk, one voice after another on top of each other until voices sounded like a wasp swarm. The way it hurt the ear. On one side of the room, Mrs. Churchill and Bridget, *these banshees*, as they told officers:

"I didn't notice anything else in the room."

"No, there was linen on the bed . . ."

"I only noticed her body . . . do I call her a body? . . . on the floor when I closed the cupboard in the guest room and I turned around."

"I touched her back ta see if she might move."

"We were inside and didn't hear anythin'."

"I feel sick. I feel sick."

Everything they said made my head numb, a drum full of echoes, coming back to me slow and vinegared. Through the other side of the wall, someone, a man, said, "And this here is where I suspect the last blow landed. My guess is this was the blow that cut the eye out." I thought of Father. A few weeks before, he'd complained to Emma that the world wasn't looking the way it ought. She'd patted him on the back, *she's trying to be the favorite*, said, "You should see someone about that."

Father shrugged. "They'll charge me an arm and a leg to fix my eyes."

"Some things are worth the money, Father." Emma shouldn't have spoken to Father that way. I should've been good and told her to watch her caustic tongue, remind her what he could be like.

But Father shook his head, laughed like a good time. "I suppose you might be right."

"Mrs. Borden would agree with me, I'm sure," Emma said, seemed pleased with herself.

"Yes, well. I'll have Abby take me one of these days."

"Very well, Father." Emma patted Father on the back again. I thought of her touching my shoulders now, the way I would want her to make me feel comforted. She'd warm my blood, erase numb feelings. She'd never leave me alone in a house again, *Emma makes everything better.*

The men continued to speak. I hoped one of them was massaging Father's shoulders the way Emma would, the way I might have done.

There were voices in the sitting room, voices in the kitchen, voices above me a muffle-muffle and dragging feet. Everything louder than it should.

A hand grabbed my wrist. The officer stared. "Miss, are you alright? You were talking to yourself. Should I summon the doctor again?"

I looked around the dining room: a face, then a face, then a face, all in my direction. One of the officers had a crooked mouth, the kind that ran through Mrs. Borden's family. The officer blank-smiled at me, a grim tooth shooting over his lip. Mrs. Borden had smiled at me like this before. My head ached. I rubbed my forehead.

The tip of my tongue shivered, *I want Emma.* "Yes," I said. "Yes, you had better fetch him," and the officer went to Dr. Bowen.

I thought about Mrs. Borden upstairs. The clock on the mantel ticked ticked. Everyone around me slowed, limbs saltwater taffy. From the top of the stairs I heard her voice, "Lizzie, dear Lizzie. Come and help me." My heart rumpled, my toes electric. "Quickly, Lizzie." I stood from my chair, said, "Mrs. Borden?" and two long lines of sweat worked my spine. "Lizzie, I've fallen," Mrs. Borden said.

I walked towards the sitting room. Then someone took my hand.

"Miss Borden, where are you going?" An officer stood in front of me.

"I'm going upstairs."

"You can't." He showed his teeth, a dog, sounded almost furious.

"Why not?" My stomach tightened, *pigeons walking through me.* I was going to help Mrs. Borden. I was going to be helpful.

Mrs. Churchill stood by my side. "Dear," she said, her voice salty-sweet. "Your mother is up there . . ." *Not my mother but Mrs. Borden!*

"It's best you stay downstairs with us, miss," the officer said, gobble, gobble, gobble.

I was led back to my chair and told to wait. The clock on the mantel ticked ticked. Dr. Bowen slumped into the room. "The officer tells me you're in pain, Lizzie."

I nodded. "The very worst kind."

He looked at me, tired eyes hazed, and I could feel him walk into my body, survey my insides and see all the things I was made of, *jolly good things.* I smiled. Dr. Bowen burrowed into his medical bag like a scavenger and took out the syringe, filled it with my favor. Into my arm it went. "There now, Lizzie. This will make it better for you."

I started thinking all manner of ways. I wondered if Mrs. Borden was hurt like Father, would we still be able to have an open-coffin funeral? *These are bad things to think.* I knew Father would need some healing, but I wanted everyone who would come to the funeral to be able to see them one last time, get their lasting memories. I would have to ask Emma what she thought was the best way to present Father and Mrs. Borden in the coffin. We would both agree that Father deserved the very best.

"We will place them in the parlor," Emma would say.

"With the sunlight behind them like they're glowing," I'd tell her.

"There will be wreaths."

"And I will have one of the children from church play a hymn on the piano," I'd say.

"Uncle should give the eulogy for Father so that he can talk about his life with Mother."

But I'd tell Emma it should be me that gives the eulogy. I'm used to writing little sermons for my Sunday school pupils. I know how to deliver the word of God in bite-sized pieces.

"Just think, Father and Mrs. Borden will be there the whole time, so peaceful and resting," I'd say.

"Yes."

"Emma, what do you think will happen once they are in the ground?"

"To us?"

"Yes, to us."

A heavy hand hooked onto my shoulder, meaty fingers digging into my skin. "Miss Borden," an officer said.

"What is it you want?"

"If you're able, we would like to ask you some more questions." Sweat poured down the side of his face into his thick mustache.

"Hmmm-hmmm." My tongue fat in my mouth.

"Officer, perhaps it's best we leave Lizzie to rest," Dr. Bowen said. "She's experiencing trauma."

"We understand, but there have been two deaths in the house."

Dr. Bowen paced the room, his face pale sick. "Poor Andrew would be outraged," he whispered. The way he said Father's name made it seem he was still alive. It made me want to curl into a small ball on the ground.

"You know the family well, Doctor?" The question sounded like an accusation.

"I've been treating them for years." Dr. Bowen dug his fingers into hips, claws.

You get a boiled sweet if you've been good.

"Dr. Bowen last came to the house when everyone was feeling unwell," I said.

"When was this?" A notebook was flipped open to a new page.

"A few weeks ago. Mrs. Borden said she was so ill she felt like dying," I told him, hoped he captured my words perfectly.

"It seemed a simple case of food poisoning," Dr. Bowen said. "It was lucky Lizzie and Emma didn't fall ill to it."

Yes, it was lucky.

The officer took notes. The clock on the mantel ticked ticked. I thought about that morning, how I had told Emma, "Don't eat breakfast today."

"Why not?"

"I just heard Mrs. Borden and Bridget vomiting."

"Oh." Emma stroked her throat. "I've already eaten some porridge with Father."

Later in the room, I heard Emma moan, her body shifting, shifting in the bed. But she didn't call for help and so I didn't tell Dr. Bowen when he came to the house for the rest of them. It took them days to fully recover. I allowed myself to eat pears in the sitting room when I wasn't supposed to, *I got those sticky fingers.*

"How has everyone's health been recently?" The officer was a stickybeak.

"I think they were all sick again, Officer," I said.

"When?"

"This morning. That's why Father came home early from work."

"What did he tell you, miss?"

I tried to conjure Father's words in my mind but there was nothing but blood and his open head. My forehead throbbed and I rubbed. "I don't know."

"I'm sure you will remember in good time." Dr. Bowen was calming, soothed me.

"I hope so. I want to remember as much as I can to help the police."

"Rest assured you're doing a good job, Miss Borden." The officer smiled crooked, tooth over lip.

My stomach hardened, rock intestine, and the more I saw the tooth the more I wanted to reach up and rip it out, watch the gum bleed, *but what to do with a tooth?* I snaked my tongue over my teeth, *years ago now,* felt the little hole at the back of my mouth. It was Emma who had decided that my tooth should be pulled when I was seven. "If you do it, you'll get money," she said. I liked the sound of that. We sat on her bed, our legs dangling over the side like we were riverside.

I pinched my molar between fingers and wriggled. "It's like a little trapdoor!"

"Maybe you could put Abby in there," Emma said. We laughed, filled the house with cracking.

I reached for my tooth again, made it wiggle. "I'm too scared to do it, Emma."

"Don't worry. I've had lots of experience." She stood in front of me and squinted. "Open wide." I opened wide and her fingers rushed in. The taste of salt, of honey. She pinched my tooth and pulled. Inside I was the sound of weeds uprooted from a garden.

"Karoo! I got it," Emma said as if she'd found gold.

I screamed. Blood danced on my tongue. I spat onto my skirt. Emma studied the tooth. "It's huge, Lizzie."

"I don't feel so good." Blood continued.

There was the sound of feet on the front stairs then the bedroom door opened. Mrs. Borden stepped inside, was cross. "Girls, what on earth are you doing up here?"

Emma held the tooth high. "I got it!"

Mrs. Borden came for me, a tender face. "Lizzie, are you alright?"

"She's perfectly fine," Emma said, arms folded across chest.

I shook my head.

"Open up. Let's see how bad it is."

I opened and blood dribbled onto her hands. "Oh dear," she said. I cried. She pulled me into her body, warm with the smell of kitchen fat, warm with love, and said, "You've certainly had quite the adventure today." *The absolute worst kind.* She pulled away. My blood sat on her shoulder, trickled down towards her heart. She smiled at me. Teeth popped over lip.

———

I overheard an officer tell another, "We found a green tin full of money upstairs in Mr. and Mrs. Borden's bedroom. Do you think whoever did this knew there was money hidden in the house?"

"Who could say? Take it as evidence."

What secret is Mrs. Borden hiding now?

Somewhere along the floor I thought I could hear my name, the house whispering, *There's something down here you should see.* I lowered my head just enough to see under the dining room table. There on the carpet, condensed meat and bile, the leftovers of rotting. "Where has that come from?"

An officer cleared his throat. "I'm sorry, what did you say Miss Borden?"

I tried to size up the mess, compare it to all the vile vomit of Bridget and Mrs. Borden I had seen in the morning.

"Nothing. It's nothing," I said. Where had it come from? *Is that Father's?* I was in the house this morning and then I was out of it. Bridget made noise, Mrs. Borden made noise. I walked through the house and then Father came home. How did I miss the rotting?

"I heard you say something," the officer said.

I better be good. "There's something strange under the table." I pointed, watched the officer tilt forwards like a cuckoo.

"What in the world . . ." He crawled the floor and for a moment I considered straddling his back, riding him like a prized pony, *I just want to be taken away from here.* I'd command my little pony around the room, kick heels into his stomach.

"I told you they were sick," I said, was right.

"Did you see it happen?"

"Of course not. I would've had Bridget clean up if I did." Where had it come from?

Everything hurt. A throbbing behind my eyes began every time the officer asked a question. "Where was your mother?"

"I don't know," I said. "I think I was upstairs."

"What were you doing?"

Memory coiled like a snake. "I don't remember." The clock on the mantel ticked ticked. I'd had enough of speaking. I wanted Emma to come home.

"It's very hot in here," I said. "Can we open a window?" The house let out a sigh as windows opened. People spoke about me as if I didn't exist.

———

They sent for Alice Russell to keep me company until Emma came home. When she arrived she said, "Lizzie, what on earth happened?" She stroked my hand, *like she should*, and I told her, "They are dead. Just as I feared."

"How?" Alice was hysterical, was too much.

I played with her hand, pinched her skin like dough. Her skin was softer than mine. I didn't like that. I pinched harder and she eyed me. I smiled. "Someone came and cut them," I told her.

"Oh my Lord!" Her mouth dropped open like everyone else's. I was tired of the look, the way it made me feel like hiding.

"I don't think I believe it myself," I said.

Someone had opened the window in the dining room and the house filled with more noise. I heard a pigeon coo-coo in a tree. I felt empty inside.

The officer asked, "Did you see anyone unusual loitering around your house this morning?"

"No, not this morning."

He paused. "You mean, there has been someone before?"

My heart skipped its beat. *What's the answer?* "We were robbed last year."

"Who was the culprit?"

Footsteps above us became louder and louder, echoed in my head. "What are they doing with Mrs. Borden?"

"There are procedures to follow," he told me, offhand.

"Oh." I wanted to be there, to make sure things were being carried through properly, *isn't that the right thought?*

"Miss, did they catch who robbed you?"

"No."

"Can you tell me anything more about this morning?"

Everything was lost inside my mind, all the jitter-jitter of the morning cutting away the things that made sense. I wanted Emma.

Everything became too bright. Voices were pinpricks in the ear. My hands ached from resting under my knees. I pulled them out from underneath me, saw a small cut on one of my fingertips, blood dried around the openings. I put it in my mouth and I shifted in my seat.

The officer looked at me with little eyes. "Now, did your mother . . ."

"Stepmother," I told him.

The officer held his pen in the air. "I thought . . ."

"Mrs. Borden is Father's second wife." Facts need to be stated. I smiled.

"I see." He flung his pen back into the inkwell and pounded his fist against the yellow-white paper. I tried to look past his fingers to the notebook. He guarded his thoughts well.

"After breakfast, your stepmother, Bridget and yourself were home alone, correct?"

"Yes."

"Can you remember details relating to the time after you found your father?"

I shook my head. *No, no, not I.*

The officer said, "Let's try. Where was Mrs. Borden at the time, Lizzie?"

I thought ever so hard. "She had been sent out to a sick relative." The walls knocked together around me, made all the red and blue and green of the wallpaper swirl. I felt nauseous. I threw my hands across my eyes and waited for the rush to leave me. There was too much to remember. I blocked everyone out.

All I could see was a moment from a few days before, when Father, Mrs. Borden and I had sat around the dining room table and sipped mutton broth. Mrs. Borden slurped from her spoon, *carnivorous pig*, and I watched her tongue flick her lips, gray and thick. I imagined her tongue inside Father's mouth. What they must taste like.

"You must be missing Emma." Mrs. Borden, jolly.

"Must I?"

Father sat at the head of the table, peeled skin from an ink-spotted banana. "Answer properly, Lizzie."

"Very well. I miss my sister. I'd do anything to make her come back." I traced my fingers over the lace tablecloth, got snagged.

"I miss my sister too. I wish I could see her every day." Mrs. Borden's voice hammered my head, just like her voice hammered my head this morning, keeps hammering.

I opened my eyes and stared at the officer. The sound of pigeon claws on the roof. Tack-tack. "Officer, I remember something from this morning. I came downstairs a few minutes before nine . . . I should say about a quarter before nine. My uncle had already left for his business outing."

"And your father?"

"He was with Mrs. Borden. They were speaking about things."

"What kind of things?" His tongue lapped at his lips, sloppy.

My head ached. "Just common things. I asked them how they were."

"And how were they?" The way he was trying to find meaning made me angry.

"They seemed happy," I said. "We were looking forward to having dinner with Uncle tonight."

The officer dipped his pen and lightly ran his fingertip over the nib. Above our heads the floorboards stretched as far as they could. The clock on the mantel ticked ticked.

"Mrs. Borden asked me what I wanted for dinner. I told her not anything. Then she said she had been up to the guest room and made the spare bed, but would I mind taking some linen pillowcases for the small pillows because she'd just received a note from somebody sick and she had to go out. Then I think she said something about the weather. I don't know."

All the spaces between an hour, between life and death, came towards me. I could see everything clearer and I could tell the officer because it was right there in my head waiting to be told. I could tell him that I then went outside and stood under the pear arbor for a short time, took a pear off the tree and then went to the barn and ate it. I could tell him that I took another pear and ate it in the middle of the yard, and how hot the sun felt for early morning and how I could see small beads of sweat on the attic windows. I could tell him that I went back into the barn to look for a lead sinker, that Uncle and I had decided to take a fishing trip the next day like we used to. I ate pears again. They were delicious and dripped down my wrists, sticky and sweet-smelling. Birds perched in trees. Neighbors were outside talking. Then I went inside the house, to iron handkerchiefs in the dining room. *I almost forgot*, I could tell the officer, "I read a magazine in the barn. I was there for maybe half an hour reading." Everything was right there. I could even see myself speaking with Mrs. Borden, how we talked about the time we found a frog in the basement and couldn't catch it, how that was such a fond memory for both of us, though it is hard to remember everything I told her. Perhaps I would have asked her about the time she met Father and did they love each other immediately and, if they did, what did that love feel like and did she think it would ever happen to me? I could tell the officer all of this because it was the truth. All of this happened in the house at some stage.

Should it matter when it happened?

I leaned forwards and said to the officer in a whisper, "The more I think about it, I did speak with my father when he came home! I told him that Mrs. Borden had gone to visit a sick friend. He smiled and said, 'She's always looking after others.' That's when I left him to rest on the sofa and I went outside and then I found him . . ."

The officer reached out his hand and placed it on mine. He said, "It must have been such a shock," and I told him, "At first I did not think what had happened was real. I noticed he'd been cut, but I did not see his face properly because he was covered in blood. I was so afraid. Officer, I didn't know that he was dead at the time."

There was a cracking sound on the back stairs and I could hear men talking.

The low voice said, "It's hard to say without confirming through an autopsy, but the blood has congealed and dried significantly. I would suggest Mrs. Borden died earlier in the morning."

I looked out the dining room window. The clock on the mantel ticked ticked. I wanted all things at once: for the questions to end, to keep talking, to be left alone, to be surrounded, to continue with the day as normal, to check Father, to make sure Mrs. Borden really was gone, to have Emma come home and tell me everything would be alright.

SIX
BRIDGET
August 3, 1892

I DUSTED, I DUSTED, thought of old Mrs. Borden, of her in my room looking for ways to keep me with her. It must've been hard for her to be on hands and knees, look under my bed. The effort it must've taken to get back to standing, holding my tin, all her sweat on my sheets. I dusted. Mrs. Borden and her sad eyes. Mrs. Borden and her tyrant talk. Mrs. Borden outside overhearing me. How that must have hurt her. I stopped dusting. Lizzie had a neat pile of whites on her velvet swooning sofa. I picked up the pile. Three long-sleeved white aprons and a bonnet. Perhaps they were meant for me. I tried on an apron, saw myself in the full-length mirror next to Lizzie's dressing table. I looked a ghost, looked like one of Whitehead's butcher boys, looked like I was drowning in fabric.

I took it off, refolded the aprons, put them back on the sofa. If chance arrived, I'd ask Mrs. Borden about the aprons, see if she knew why Lizzie had them. I looked out Lizzie's window. The view I had. So much of Fall River in front of me, a patchwork of street, people, house. There was nothing out there for me. I saw the rooftop of Mrs. McKenney's service office down Second Street. What could've been had she sent me to another family.

The sun came over the pane and I heard Mrs. Borden walk through the house, rattling my tin box as she went. There was a pain in my chest, like someone had punched me there, stopped me breathing. Rattle, rattle, rattle.

I was bent over, trying to breathe the pain away, when someone knocked on the front door. Three big thunder raps, the big bad wolf looking for his piggies. I waited for Mrs. Borden to answer the door. The knocks came again. I called out, "Mrs. Borden? Ya expectin' company?"

She didn't answer.

I downed the front stairs, pulled the house key out of my pocket and unlocked the door. I pushed it open, sun hit my face, made my lips part. A man stood there.

"Hello, Bridget."

I looked at the man, stood back a little and took him in. Uncle John.

"Mr. Morse."

He smiled, lips crooked, wrinkled face, worn leather. He wore a black woolen suit, hard to clean, made him smell like paddocked sheep.

"You going to invite me in?" A cigared voice.

I thought about swinging the door closed in his face. "Of course."

In he walked, stooped a little as he went through the door. I went to get his bag but there was none.

"Mr. Morse, where're yer things?"

"I didn't bring any. I'm only here to visit a short time."

"Mrs. Borden is the only one in at the moment." I came back inside, locked the door. John stood close to me, the way he does. He took a deep breath, smelled me, the way he does. "Care for me ta hang yer jacket, Mr. Morse?" I held my arms out, expected him to lay the jacket across. I did not care for the way he stared at me. Like he was seeing something else.

"Give me a hand?" he asked and so I had to. He lowered himself for me and I unhooked his jacket from his bone-thin shoulders, saw clumps of skin knotted in his hair where he'd been scratching the back of his head. A piece fell onto my hand. I shook it off good.

"Alright, Mr. Morse," I said. "I'll pop this in the cupboard."

He straightened. We stood for a moment and I stared at him. I hung his jacket, felt his eyes on my back. I hoped it would be a quick afternoon visit. From the kitchen, the pound of feet walking tired into the sitting room. I pulled myself to attention, saw Mrs. Borden wipe her mouth with the back of her hand. She looked at John, held her palm across her heart.

"Goodness. John."

"Have I startled you, Abby?" He said it like a game.

John left me behind in the entrance, went to Mrs. Borden, his arm stretched towards her, his fingers little hooks. He shook her hand, as if she was a rag doll.

"Pleasure to see you, Abby."

"And you as well. What brings you here today?" She could barely speak.

"Didn't Lizzie tell you?"

Mrs. Borden inched her eyes together, creased her brow. "About what?"

"I wrote a few weeks ago letting her know I'd be in town for business and that I'd come visit." His long, bony jaw moved like a grip broiler and toaster as he spoke. Mrs. Borden smoothed her hair.

Lizzie didn't always tell us things. The only letter to arrive of late had been for Emma, inviting her to Fairhaven. The trouble it caused. Lizzie had slammed her bedroom door, had screamed, "You're not leaving me here alone with them."

"Don't be silly," Emma said.

On and on it went. Then Lizzie cut the arm off one of Emma's dresses. "You can't leave if you have nothing to wear."

"What is wrong with you?" Emma asked.

"You know very well I can't be here alone." Lizzie, scissors in hand.

"You're reacting like a spoiled monster."

"Well, don't force my hand." She snipped, just a little, made cotton threads rain onto the carpet.

It went on for days. I'd go into the basement to get away from their hacking voices, their slamming doors. I found Mr. Borden down there once. He leaned against the brick wall, let it hold him up.

"Hello, Mr. Borden."

"Bridget." He nodded his head, sharp.

"Hope I'm not disturbin' ya."

"Not at present." He closed his eyes, looked like sleep.

The basement was cool, half lit like a cave. I could hear both of us breathing, slow and breathy. We stood that way, then he said, "I'm sure you have some work that needs to be done."

"Yes, sir." I left.

Back upstairs there was peace now. I'd thought the sisters had left but I found them in the parlor, Lizzie resting her head on Emma's lap, Emma stroking Lizzie's forehead. The heat that came from their bodies. I wanted to open the windows.

"Bridget," Emma said, "could you make us a pot of tea?"

I could see their chests grow big then small together. Lizzie kept quiet, her eyes bay-blue and soft. Someone had won.

———

Mrs. Borden cocked her head, said to John, "Lizzie hadn't mentioned anything."

John sucked saliva through his teeth, made the hair on the back of my neck bristle. "Well, here I am." He laughed.

I didn't care for that.

Mrs. Borden gave a half-smile, scratched her temples. "How long do you intend to stay?"

"Overnight. Possibly a day or two."

She tried to look behind John. "But you didn't bring your luggage?"

"It's the funniest thing. I didn't think to bring any."

I wished he'd go away.

"I'm sure you can borrow something from Andrew."

"How very hospitable, Abby." John sucked saliva through his teeth again and Mrs. Borden called my name, like I wasn't even there.

"Prepare Mr. Morse some tea and give him dinner."

"Yes, marm."

"Don't go to any trouble on my behalf," John said.

"Nonsense, we've plenty of food, haven't we, Bridget?"

"Yes, marm." I went by them in the sitting room, went to the kitchen and put the mutton broth on the heat. I heard Mrs. Borden tell John to sit, to be comfortable, and then they said nothing else to each other. Oh, it was quiet. It was so quiet that I could hear Mrs. Borden's tongue click each time she opened her mouth.

The mutton warmed, filled the kitchen, and then I ladled the broth, felt the meat plop as it landed in the bowl, splash up on my cheek. How I itched, how my underthings stuck to my stomach, to my underarms, the insides of my legs. It was like being wrapped in wool, made to sit in front of an alcohol fire. I blew breath onto my palms, tried to cool myself, pretend I was on the way to Cobh, to the sea. Blow, blow, blow.

I heard John say, "What have my nieces been up to?"

I put his bowl on a serving tray, I put the teapot on the serving tray.

"Lizzie is downtown. Emma is in Fairhaven."

"Well, I'll be. I was in Fairhaven yesterday!"

"On business?"

"I'm always on business." He laughed. "I had things to take care of. Had I known Emma was there, I would've popped in to say hello."

"She's been away for two weeks."

"Must be lackluster around here with her gone."

"It's unusual."

"Yes, I suppose it would be, used to having both of them around you all day."

"Not many days go by without seeing one or the other." Mrs. Borden's tongue clicked.

"You're lucky in many ways."

"How so?"

"To have them at home. To have people to talk to."

"Yes."

"It can become rather lonely for men like me, I'm afraid. Living alone."

I picked up the serving tray, took it into the dining room.

"Sounds like your meal," Mrs. Borden said.

"Splendid."

I stood back from the table as they walked in, and Mrs. Borden pulled a chair for John, was red-faced, hands a little shaky.

"I'll be in later ta collect dishes," I said.

John sat at the table, bent forwards over the bowl and breathed in deep. "This will hit the spot."

Mrs. Borden took a quick look at me, like she didn't want me to leave. "Perhaps, Bridget, you may like to wait around, pour Mr. Morse some tea?" Mrs. Borden used her sweet voice, the one that pulled me in.

John slurped his broth. We watched him.

"As ya like, Mrs. Borden." I stood with my back against the wall, waited to be useful, waited for it to be over.

"Tell me, Abby: how's Andrew's business going? He serving on any more boards? Acquiring any more property?"

Mrs. Borden shook her head. "That may be a question you ask him."

John slurped. "Quite right, Abby. You'll have to excuse me."

"That's alright." A polite smile.

"But he is doing well? He's in health?" He rammed the spoon in his mouth, hit his teeth.

"You know Andrew, he shan't be slowing down anytime soon."

John gave the table two quick knocks with the spoon. "Good old man!"

Mrs. Borden smiled. "Care for tea, John?"

John raised his eyes towards me, looked me up, looked me down. "Splendid." Him looking at me like I wasn't a real person, Mrs. Borden saying nothing about it. I'd the mind to take his spoon, poke his eyes.

I went to the table, poured tea, my arm right close to his arm. "Sugar, Mr. Morse?"

"Two scoops."

I spooned them in. His breath on my hand, on my arm through sleeves. I caught Mrs. Borden watching me. "Thank you, Bridget," she said. I went back to the wall.

They sat in silence.

———

In the scullery, I washed their dishes, my fingers wrinkled as I got to thinking about getting my money tin from Mrs. Borden. There was no polite way of getting it. Depending on where Mrs. Borden hid the thing, I'd have to break locks throughout the house, break open her secret places until I found it.

Since the daylight robbery last year, she'd taken to hiding valuables in the basement in a safe, in little wooden boxes in the scullery, in locked dressing table drawers. I once found a bottle of Calcarea carbonica in an old soap box under a sack of flour. For her, everything out of sight, out of mind.

A hot breath on my neck. My neck shuddered like someone was pulling on my skin.

I spun around. John stood, arms by his side, leaned toward me, eyes big.

"You left my napkin behind." His voice the sound of a stone road, he held up the dirty cloth, jiggled it in front of me.

"Thank ya, Mr. Morse." I went to reach for it and John pulled it away. I didn't want to have to go after it.

We stood for the longest time. Just us. The creases around his mouth, a piece of mutton resting in his beard. Wrinkles pinched around his eyes. Slowly his hand, the napkin, came at me, winter-twig fingers ready to snap. I kept at the dishes, swirled the cloth in the water as quiet as I could. John jiggled the napkin and dropped it at my feet.

"There somethin' else ya needed, Mr. Morse?"

"Not at all." John smiled at me, walked from the scullery, through the kitchen and into the rest of the house. My legs were stiff, started to shake a little. I looked at the napkin, the stewy outline of his mouth.

I went to the stove, put the napkin inside, and watched the flames blacken linen, raise smoke.

———

Mrs. Borden sent John with me when I went upstairs to prepare the guest room. His boots clomped, hand sliding over the polished-wood banister.

"Thank you, Bridget," he said coming into the room.

"That's alright, Mr. Morse."

John put his hands on his hips. He went to the dressing table, wiped his finger across it. "No dust."

"Yes."

"You certainly do your job well, don't you?" John admired himself in the vanity mirror, picked up the wooden-handled horsehair brush on the dresser, ran it through his hair. I didn't care to answer him. He put the brush down, came towards me by the window, stared out onto the street.

"Look at them down there. Everyone so busy."

I glanced down, saw men storm the footpath, their summer coats flocking behind them. John wheezed beside me. It was enough for me to forget my mind, want to jump out the window and get outside. I saw Dr. Bowen across the road in the front of his house, talking to a woman. She opened her mouth lion-wide and Dr. Bowen put his fingers inside, took a look.

"I wonder if anyone can see us?" John asked.

"They could if they stopped ta look up." Oh, how I wished they would, see what was going on in the house.

He was quiet for a time. Then he said, "Tell me, Bridget: are there any spare keys to the house?"

I turned to him. "No, Mr. Morse. I've my set, the Bordens theirs."

He rubbed his short beard, tapped his chin. "I see. I wonder if perhaps you might let me borrow yours while I'm here." He cupped his hand like a beggar. The corners of his mouth turned up.

I placed my hand in my apron pocket, felt my key. "I'm not able ta do that, Mr. Morse."

He stood closer to me, wheezed, "Not even for a few hours?"

"Mr. Borden likes everythin' locked, even when we're home. I need me key." He was so close, made everything hotter.

"What Andrew doesn't know won't hurt him." His teeth rested on top of his bottom lip.

My ears burned. "Mr. Morse, yer standin' too close ta me." I said it before I could think about the trouble I might get.

John pulled away. "I see. My mistake."

"There's always someone here ta let ya in."

"That's handy to know." His body pulled tight and he swallowed, Adam's apple bobbing.

"I'll be goin' now."

John stood aside, off I went, and he followed, told Mrs. Borden, "I'll be back this evening."

Mrs. Borden's shoulders relaxed. "Very well, John. I'm sure Andrew will be pleased to see you."

I gave John his jacket from the cupboard, pushed the front door open nice and wide. There was fresh horse manure on the street, sweet hay mixed with boggy dirt and rotting fruit; a waft of the Quequechan River stretching across the city. I hated summer in Fall River, the death smells it brought. John said, "What a glorious afternoon," and headed along Second Street, right out of sight. I shut the door, locked it good. Then it was just me and Mrs. Borden.

She had sat back down on the sofa, her hands on knees. "Bridget." She said the T sharp, a needle point.

I steadied myself, went to her. "Yes, marm?"

"I haven't forgotten our little problem."

"No, marm."

"You've made me quite unhappy." She looped her tongue around her lips.

"Yes, marm."

A few strands of hair fell onto her shoulder. "And you've been keeping things from me."

"Not really, Mrs. Borden." I made her red-faced, she rubbed her knees.

"Get out of my sight!" It came out rough, like it had ripped her throat. I dared not look at her.

———

Oh, but it was hot up in the attic, like anger had fired itself all the way up to the ceiling and hung like a curtain. I lay on my bed, rolled over and looked at my family, heard their voices in my ear, the sweet singing of "Blow the Candles Out," their sweet goodbyes before I took to the ship. I hummed along. I hummed along, my throat tight and homesick, my cheeks wet. I hummed along, kept my family close. I thought of Mammy's baking, smell of yeast rising from my mind out into my room, sending me close to a warm sleep.

I would've kept it up had it not been for the chocking sound outside. Chock, a flurry wind. Chock, an ax in wood. Chock, a grunting. Chock, chock. A man's voice: "Stay still." Chock. Mr. Borden. My stomach knotted.

I got out of bed, went to the window and looked down. In the backyard by the barn stood Mr. Borden, his jacket on the grass, white shirtsleeves rolled to elbow. He held an ax in one hand, an upside-down pigeon in the other, its wings wide, stiff from the blood rushing to its head, the shock of what was awaiting. My knees got to trembling and my bladder gave way a little, wet me between my legs.

Mr. Borden put the pigeon on the chopping block and swung the ax quick. Chock, the head fell to the grass and Mr. Borden threw the body into a metal drum. He wiped his arm across his forehead before reaching into the aviary and pulling out another.

Lizzie's pigeons. He'd finally followed through. Mr. Borden cricked his neck and my wrist itched, remembered a tiny claw. I hoped he wouldn't make me be the one to tell Lizzie about this. But I couldn't look away. He held a pigeon and the little thing beat its wings against Mr. Borden's left arm, made him drop the bird. The pigeon landed on the grass, was still a moment before flying into the tree above. Mr. Borden shielded the sun out of his eyes, shrugged his shoulders. He leaned the ax against the inside of the barn door, threw pigeon heads one by one on top of the bodies in the metal drum. He carried the barrel deep into the barn. I was surprised to see that there weren't many feathers on the ground; a little here, a little there, enough to make you think that a cat got lucky, was quick to pounce and tore into flesh.

I fixed my bonnet back onto my head and went downstairs, my heart a-jump as I waited by the side door, waited to find out what Mr. Borden would do next. I heard him walk up the path, the soles of his black boots sandpaper on stone. I quick-skipped over to the kitchen counter, made myself busy with a pot of tea, the tea-leaves like small trees falling as they hit the sides of the pot. The clock struck two. The side door opened and he came in.

"Bridget, I need soap." Mr. Borden's hands were stained, smears of jam-red blood along his fingers. There was blood on his collar, blood above his eyebrow, blood in the corner of his mouth. It made me lick my lips, my silent way of making him do the same, make him notice that he was covered in animal. He did nothing, as if he couldn't feel it.

"Yes, Mr. Borden." I ran down to the basement, got soap, ran back. He leaned against the counter looking at his hands, rubbed his fingers together. There was a strange musk smell. I started shaking. I didn't want to go near him. I held out the soap. "Here ya are, Mr. Borden." It was like I was holding a brick, the way my wrist wanted to snap. A step forwards, he took the soap from me and I could see sweat bead above his top lip.

"Mr. Borden, ya right?"

He turned the soap over and over in his hands, washed them in the basin, squelch and squish. "I'm fine."

"Did ya hurt yerself?" I was a terrible liar.

"No. I was just cleaning the yard." So was he.

"Oh."

He washed his arms next, soap-blood bubbles dripping.

"Have you seen Mrs. Borden?" he asked.

"Not since earlier, after Mr. Morse left."

He turned, scrunched his face. "Morse?"

"Yes. He's come ta visit."

"Where is he?"

"Out on business. He'll be back later."

Mr. Borden chewed the inside of his mouth, made his cheek-bones appear like wolf teeth. "When did he arrive?"

"'Round midday, sir."

"How long is that man staying?"

"I'm not sure, sir. Definitely overnight."

That man. Not a way to describe your beloved dead wife's sibling.

"Did you know he was coming?"

"I don't think anybody knew 'cept Lizzie."

"Where is she now?"

"She's out, sir."

Mr. Borden slammed his fist on the counter. "Why is no one around when I need them to be?" He wiped his face with a tea towel. He wiped his hands along his pants, cricked his neck from side to side. Off he went through the house.

SEVEN

EMMA

August 4, 1892

SECOND STREET WAS thick with skin. I slowed out of the horse and carriage, glanced at the swarm of onlookers at the front of the house, their strange-looking faces. My shoulder ached and I combed fingertips over knotted muscle. I was home. A few people in the crowd placed hands across their chests as I walked by and I recognized faces: Mr. Porter, the young carriage driver whose son always had a runny nose; Mrs. Whittaker, her cabbage cheeks ballooned in talk; little Frances Gilbert, Lizzie's least-favorite Sunday school pupil, scratching up her wild hair, her squirrel eyes gazing at the house. I tried to make eye contact. Somewhere a voice: "I wonder if she knows?" News traveled fast: what kind of accident exactly?

I looked at the sky, cloud shadows over my face, noticed a bird center itself on top of the roof. I blinked and everything became quiet. The house looked so ordinary and I kept thinking over and over "Abby missing." How was it possible a woman Abby's age could disappear? Had she slipped out at night? Had she forgotten to leave a note, forgotten to tell Father that she would be back and not to worry? Or had she decided to give in to one of her moods and leave for good, walked down to the river, stepped onto a boat and floated downstream until she reached the sea, where she jumped overboard, drank salt water and sank like an anchor?

The crowd parted as I walked towards them and ten women cried, their cheeks red with gossip. I heard, "Lizzie," slip from my mouth and step by step my thighs tightened, shoulders cringed, body scared.

A police officer emerged from the side of the house and said, "Miss Borden, please come this way."

It was true. There had been an accident. I was taken through the side entrance, hadn't wanted to think about what was inside the house, but then there I was. I stepped inside, noticed the heat immediately, the drying of my tongue. The door to the sitting room was closed. I heard the words, "Time of death," strange male voices that beat against my ear. My hands petrified.

"Your sister is in here." Fingers pointed to the dining room.

There: Dr. Bowen, Mrs. Churchill, Alice Russell. Strange men surrounded Lizzie, had reduced her to the size of a child.

"What has happened?" My hands, sweat.

Alice Russell came forwards, "Oh, Emma," and wiped her brow and temple.

My sister worked her fingers along her skirt, fidgeted in that way that always annoyed me. There were small indentations along Lizzie's jawline and I could tell she had been picking at her skin as if using her nails as tweezers. I knew this: she had tried to stop herself from worry. On Lizzie's skirt I caught a stain, small and rust-colored. My skin pulled tight around my ribs, hands sweated. "What has happened?"

In the corner of the room a police officer stuck out his chest, the shape of a wooded birdcage, smoothed a hand over his mustache and watched Lizzie. I coughed and the officer straightened and lengthened his fingers across his stomach. The air, salty thick.

"If you would like to sit down, Miss Borden." The officer's tone was high-pitched, too rehearsed.

"What has happened?"

Heads hung low.

"Your parents," someone said.

"Father," Lizzie said, her voice quiet.

"Your father and mother have died."

My head began to throb. "Why are there so many people here?"

"Emma, it's a tragedy." Dr. Bowen was solemn, almost too hard to hear.

I locked eyes with Lizzie, her face was stone. How strange she looked. Words were unsaid. Lizzie swallowed hard, made the sides of her throat move in and out, a frog's mouth, said, "I'm so glad you've come back, Emma," and she put her hand out in front of her, fingers stretched, and waited for me to take hold.

"What happened?"

Breaths were held. I sat next to Lizzie and tied my arms around her shoulders, breathed her in. An odd smell. Side by side our bodies stitched together and I felt like I was drowning in salt and sweat. The heavy drum kick of Lizzie's heart thumped along fingers and bone. She was too much for me to take. I closed my eyes, wished Lizzie would disappear each time I squeezed her.

"Emma."

I opened my eyes. Lizzie stared back, tried to pull away.

"Emma, let me go. You're making me feel faint." She pushed against me.

I let go of her. "What happened?"

Lizzie whispered, "Uncle is here."

That man. I scanned the room. "Why?"

"He came for a visit last night." Lizzie, almost sing-song.

"Where is he?"

"He's out running errands. He has to come back soon," Lizzie said. She chewed the inside of her cheek.

A pause, then, "Something very bad happened today, Emma," Mrs. Churchill said and sat beside me, took hold of my hand, stroked skin until it became numb. The facts were kept brief, tumbled out of Mrs. Churchill and the police officers as if they were one person:

"Someone killed your father and mother."

"Happened this morning."

"We had believed that Mrs. Borden was out visiting a relative, but . . ."

"Your sister is in shock."

"Lizzie found him in the sitting room this morning."

"Your maid and Mrs. Churchill discovered your mother in the guest room."

"Lizzie had sent Bridget to get help."

"No sign of forced entry."

I wanted something to make sense. How long had I been away?

"Emma, hold me close again." Lizzie like a cat.

The noise of voices continued. Mrs. Churchill spoke softly into my ear, " . . . I couldn't believe it was happening . . . oh . . . I saw Lizzie by the door . . . there . . . I asked her . . . we made sure . . ." I tried to shrug away sensations of pins and needles, forced voices out of my head. I caught Lizzie's tongue peeking through, swirling over her teeth. The noise it made. I smiled at my sister, stroked her temples, tried to get her to calm. Lizzie's heart beat through the sides of her head; rapid, mountainous, and cascaded into my fingers. I wanted the world to stop.

Dr. Bowen handed me a cold, wet washcloth. "For her." His voice a slow train. I placed it on Lizzie's forehead, applied pressure. Lizzie looked small. In that moment I wanted to carry her inside me, keep her safe and loved, the way I had promised Mother. Everyone stared at Lizzie with pathological sympathy, a curiosity. She kept her eyes on me, the way she used to after Mother died. I kissed her. Somewhere behind heated skin, the birth of tears.

I was surrounded by faces, identical horrors, and everything seemed smaller. Somewhere in the house there was a strange wailing sound, the way blood might sound as it rushed out of the body. I winced, glanced towards the sitting room, to Father and, beyond that, Abby, and prayed that nobody was going to make me walk through those rooms. I stared at my wrists; sun lines danced over veins, and for a moment I was back in the field at Fairhaven, pencil in hand, back on my own. I could hear Lizzie's tongue swirl inside her mouth and I pulled my sleeve over my wrist and wiped my sister's forehead.

"We understand it's a lot to take in," an officer said.

"Yes." But there were so many questions I wanted to ask.

"Emma, I feel faint."

"Perhaps you should take Lizzie upstairs to rest." The officer again.

Alice Russell bent over me and said, "Her room is out of sorts. Would you like me to fix it?"

"No. I'll do it." I was used to taking charge. I stood, I nodded. I would make Lizzie comfortable and prepare her room. "I'll be back for you soon," I told her and kissed her forehead. I would save my questions for later.

———

I headed towards Lizzie's room via the back stairs, knew I would have to go through Father and Abby's room. As I rounded the stairs someone said, "Likely she was the first to go. Found a piece of skull by the radiator across the room." That made me pause, muscles tighten, and then it happened: my stomach pushed bile from my body, again, again. I wiped my mouth, continued up the stairs and entered Father and Abby's bedroom. The room was quiet. A small clock on the dressing table had stopped ticking. There was the bed: fresh linen, careful tucking, ornate wooden bedhead; the dual spaces of marriage. I carefully touched the edges of the blanket, felt the thickness of loss. The smell of lavender and sage mixed with leather and dampened wool, soft against my hands. Abby had not long before been in here. I lifted hands to my face and gently wiped them over my skin. I knew from experience scent never lasts long.

There were traces of Father around the room: a small handful of nickels and dimes, copies of tax receipts, a crumpled piece of paper with instructions to purchase supplies for Swansea farm and Bridget to mend socks. On Father's side of the dressing table I found a small photograph of Mother. Her wedding day, her young skin. I kissed the photograph. Did Abby have to look at Mother every day?

I sat on the side of the bed and closed my eyes, conjured images of Father. It was hard to think of him as being anything but an old man. Two weeks ago he was an old man on the sofa, tobacco pipe in hand; one year ago he was an old man struggling to lift farm equipment out of the barn; a decade ago, two decades, three: Father old all the way back to when he met Mother, told her he loved her and planted me inside her.

My stomach lurched, the air inside the room was honeyed. I stroked my head, arms, passed through nothingness like a dream. I shouldn't have been in the room. Below, men crawled around the first floor, heaviness sang, and I stroked the bed: everything would be different. Mother, Father, Abby. All three of them had slept there, all three dead.

I crossed the room and rested at the far window, looked towards the barn. A place I hadn't been for some time. Its doors were shut tight. A police officer appeared in the yard, fumbled with his notepad and pencil. He stood at the front of the barn, examined the small building before touching the doors. Fingers caressed knotted timber. He took notes then opened the barn doors, stepped inside and disappeared.

The barn had stored our discarded possessions for years: plates and teacups lay broken, hoping for second life. There were lengths of rope, a container full of lead fishing sinkers, old hammers and nails, a wrecked splitting ax, stockpiles of wood. Father threw nothing out. Now everything would remain there.

Through the window, I saw the officer step towards the barn's upper level. He wiped his forehead with a flat hand before swiping a finger across the bottom of a windowpane. He studied the skin of his index finger, took notes. I pressed my forehead against the glass, made it rattle. I walked to the end of the room and opened the door to Lizzie's bedroom, unlocking the boundary separating Borden and Borden. Inside: aggressive movement, a trace of strangers. Photo frames had been tilted, books removed from shelves and thrown on the floor. Did Lizzie know of this destruction?

I caught my reflection in the mirror: rounded chin; slow, weary eyes; slumped shoulders. I couldn't bear to look anymore. I pulled Lizzie's bedclothes back, made a small linen cocoon. There had been years of making nests for Lizzie. I had grown tired of it but there I was. Underneath Lizzie's pillow was a small piece of damp white cloth. I lifted the cloth: a hint of metallic dressed in florals, those strange sister smells. I returned it to under the pillow.

A jug of light-brown water sat on the bedside table. I poured a glass for Lizzie, hands shook, heart leaped. I willed my body to be still, thought of the tone of the officer's voice when he had said, "No sign of forced entry," the way the tongue seemed to click, the slight whistle echoing from his chipped front tooth. I invented possibilities: a stranger knocking at the door spruiking the wonders of indoor plumbing, lost his temper when Father told him, "A waste of money, you scoundrel," and ordered him to leave. But it was hard to believe that "no" would carry such a harsh penalty.

There might have been a disgruntled tenant, furious that Father had raised rent without warning.

"There's another hole in the roof," he would have said. "Insects are coming through at night."

"The problem will be fixed when there's an actual need." Father's reply.

The tenant would shake his head, spit on the front steps next to Father's feet.

"Leave my property now!"

"Not today, Mr. Borden." And the tenant would push Father's chest, push him back through the front door.

But none of this could be. It all required a witness and nobody saw a thing.

With each movement I took a deep breath, inhaled a heavy, hot stench. What was that smell? A tree branch tapped on the window, made a screech sound, made me open the window, feel the sun bruise my face. A pair of boots marched up the front staircase towards the guest room. The boots became louder and then I remembered: beyond the doors lay Abby's body; Father's dead flesh twin. I tried to get on with things.

I noticed torn pieces of paper under her bed. Lizzie could be so filthy. I got down on hands and knees, picked up the useless words, saw a used knife and fork caked with dried food, slivers of saliva becoming mold. There was a used handkerchief and dirty blouse. I gritted teeth, felt a nerve twinge along my gum.

It used to be my room, uncluttered, dust-free, worthy. I had kept my books alphabetically, covered the most precious in dust jackets. I had chosen white for decoration—coverings, paint, furniture—but the room had since become covered with reds and yellows, large parasols and gaudy artwork. Lizzie had grown gigantic. Every day I was surrounded by my sister: clumps of auburn hair found on the carpet and in the sink; fingerprints on mirrors and doors; the smell of musk hiding in drapes. I would wake with my sister in my mouth, hair strands, a taste of sour milk, like she was possessing me.

The year before, Lizzie had insisted that my bedroom door, the only partition to separate us, remain open. "To know that we are always there for each other."

"I doubt it's good for adults to share space as much as we do. It makes me uncomfortable."

"It's what I want, Emma." She tilted her head, widened those eyes.

Quarrelling continued for weeks. Lizzie won; it was easier to give in. I was forced to listen to her daydreams, boorish and pedantic.

"One day I'm going to reinvent all of this," Lizzie had said pointing to herself.

"What on earth are you talking about?"

"I'm going to be a Grand Dame woman, the way I ought to be." She had gotten this idea from being in Europe.

"Grand Dames don't go around declaring childish wishes. Why can't you just be yourself?"

Lizzie wistful. "I'm waiting for the best moment to be my true self. Everything will be different then, you'll see." She stood from the bed and studied herself in the mirror. "Emma, what do you think we look like on the inside?"

The morbidity of curiosity. I watched her, followed the trace of her fingers as they smoothed over her chest above the heart. Lizzie touched her skin like it was night.

"We could reinvent each other, Emma."

"Stop it! I'm sick of this ridiculous talk. Go daydream to yourself."

Lizzie looked at me in the mirror, became serious. "You should consider the possibilities."

And I had thought about it: an artist in Europe, speaker of ten languages, a monk on a vow of silence, a scientist aboard the *Beagle*. These things I would never become. These things Lizzie had more chance of being, simply because Father let her do anything she wanted. I knew deep down that I ought to abandon the fanciful and take what was real, that I lived with my father and stepmother, lived with a sibling who would never give me up. My time to be anything, anyone, had slipped. I had to live with that disappointment and I wished Lizzie would do the same.

———

I continued to clean, made my way to a second set of windows, pulled the curtains apart. There, small cracks in the windowpane, a dead fly on its back. I scooped the fly in my palm and put it in my skirt pocket. I got tired, sat on Lizzie's bed and wiped my hands along the linen, thought about the speed of sound, how fast a call for help would take to be heard. How loud is death? Had Lizzie heard any of it, that sickening shock? I looked towards the guest room, thought of Abby, the way her heavy body must have slumped to the floor. There were questions I wanted to ask her:

1. Were you here when Father was killed?
2. How far was escape?
3. Was Lizzie in any danger?
4. Did you see this coming?
5. What happened? Who did you anger?
6. How much pain did you feel?

I stood and rested my hands in my skirt pocket, felt the fly.

Everything was ready. I made my way through Father and Abby's room, walked down the stairs and noticed for the first time just how steep they were, how angular and aged they had become, the way they made the body thick and dull. I looked out the window, noticed neighbors form parallel lines along the fence, their hands pawing at wood. What would they possibly want to see inside this house? My face soured and I hoped they saw me.

I was at the dining room door. "I'll take you away now," I said.

Lizzie stared at the sitting room door, her eyes like weighted lead, her tongue flicking along lips. She might have even smiled.

I walked closer to my sister, tried to settle my heartbeat, feet whispers along floorboards, and held out my hand.

"What do you think he looks like, Emma?" Lizzie, matter-of-fact.

"Lizzie . . ."

"He's all cut and red." She touched the side of her face, frightened me.

"She's in tremendous shock," Dr. Bowen told me.

"Come now, Lizzie. Don't talk like that," I said.

"But it's true. That's what I found."

"I've given her more sedative. She'll sleep soon." Dr. Bowen suddenly seemed old too.

"Thank you." I wrapped my arm around Lizzie's shoulders and pulled her onto her feet. She was heat and electricity.

"I've made your bed," I told her. "Come with me."

Lizzie sighed. Noise came from the sitting room: the sounds of men shifting dead weight. "Careful, the head."

We lumbered up the back stairs to Lizzie's room. In my right ear she hummed "The Song of Birds," a song we composed years ago. The melody popped with each step, danced over Lizzie's teeth.

"Lizzie, enough," I whispered and she smiled. What was wrong with her? I thought of Helen, her offer to let me stay longer. How would I tell Lizzie that I was moving on without her?

In bed Lizzie asked, "Did you miss me while you were gone?"

"Try to relax." I didn't want to play games with her.

"You never replied to my letters." Lizzie pouted.

"I was busy."

Lizzie poked my chest. "You should apologize."

Spikes grew along the back of my ribcage, made me cough, and I took her hand. It was soft like mine. There we were, me and my sister, our bodies inseparable. There is nothing that escapes blood.

I looked into Lizzie's rounded eyes: a pupil dilated, the corner of her right eye twitched.

"What happened today, Lizzie?" I needed to hear it all, did not want to hear it all.

"Nobody would understand." Lizzie looked past my shoulder towards the guest room.

I leaned closer. "What happened?"

"I can't be too sure." Lizzie's breath was fire in my ear.

"What did you see today?"

"They asked me that too. Why are you treating me like this?" Her voice on the edge of a song and scream. I did not want to be the one to push her over.

"I'm sorry. The police haven't told me anything. I just wanted to hear it from you."

"I found him on the sofa. Resting." She said it like she was solving a jigsaw.

"And?"

"I wasn't really sure then."

Lizzie's hand grew heavier in mine. The room was silent. Outside, a bird warbled sunny times. I let go of Lizzie and thought about what was left unsaid. I wished to be inside her mind, see everything from underneath her bones, eyes, skin.

When Lizzie was younger, I prayed to be carried into her mind. I would whisper memories of Mother and life before all the changes, before Abby came. I wanted to explain how lonely it had been before Lizzie's arrival, about the small ache that never seemed to disappear after baby Alice went to sleep with God. Nobody wanted to know how much a seven-year-old could cry. I learned to keep so many things to myself. Inside our house, the constant beat of adult rhythm, ageing breath, talk of melancholy and business, of Mother and Father not touching each other like they used to, Mother telling Grandmother that the pain of baby Alice was too much to bear. Sometimes Father and Mother forgot that I was in the room, forgot that I was still alive. I started wishing myself a twin, wanted to be able to stand in front of myself and hold hands, to communicate telepathically, to no longer be lonely.

Then, one day, Mother touched Father's hand, then touched his arms. I took to listening to my parents make love. I held my breath every night. For months I prayed, please, please, a new baby from Mama. Please, please, and I became the family anatomist, taking stock of any possible changes in Mother's body:

1. Some weeks her stomach and hips looked wider.
2. Her hair seemed thicker.
3. She used the word "ravenous."
4. She began to smell of musk and salt, an animal.
5. Her cheeks became flushed.

Eventually Mother said, "There will be a baby." Her body stretched and she complained about how she ached, how she could not wait for this part to be over. I helped her put shoes on when she could no longer bend over, rubbed her feet with lanolin and lavender so she could sleep better.

"You're a good girl, Emma," she said. "You're going to be a wonderful big sister."

I grinned at her but I knew all of this. I had heard it before, had been a big sister before. How could she have forgotten?

Time passed, Lizzie arrived, and I knew I had made it happen. I tried to find myself in this new sister. I would stand over Lizzie as she slept, watch her face for familiar expressions. I dressed Lizzie in my old clothes like a doll, carried her everywhere until my back gave way, told Lizzie my childhood memories in the hope that she would think of them as her own. Lizzie and I had the same shaped eyes, had the same way of opening a hungry mouth. I spent hours teaching baby Lizzie to talk like me, to say, "Emma, Emma," but the only word that came was "Dada," over and over.

There were brief triumphs: baby Lizzie liking the same foods as me, loving the same pieces of music, of thinking a horse's neigh and a rooster's crow were worthy of applause. Lizzie climbed over my body each morning, her saliva-wet baby hands warm and sticky on my back and legs. I was so excited to see myself reflected in another's face that I began to refer to me and Lizzie as I.

"I is looking upset."

"I is hungry."

"I love I."

Sometimes I would hear Father talk. "It's as if she's reverted back to primacy," he told mother.

"Perhaps she has still not coped with Alice leaving us?"

"Still. Surely she realizes they are not the same being."

———

There was silence between us. Lizzie pulled at my fingers and I knew she wanted me to come undone, give in to her.

"How are you feeling? Do you want to talk?" I wiped a hair from Lizzie's forehead.

"When do you think everyone will leave?" She was annoyed.

"I'm not sure what happens from here."

"Oh." Lizzie watched the door.

"They said Abby died first." I wanted to understand the day, how it could have started so differently from mine only a few hours earlier.

"Yes." Lizzie nodded.

There was something bitter on my tongue. "They told you?"

"I figured it out."

"How . . ."

"Quiet. Emma, I don't want to discuss it."

When were we going to discuss it? "Alright."

Lizzie smiled. I tried to pull my fingers away but she snapped them back. These old habits of ours, the receding and taking, Lizzie the perpetual winner.

"You should rest."

"Yes."

She pushed me away, turned her back and fell into sleep. I watched her for a moment before walking out of the room through to Father and Abby's bedroom. At the back window I recognized the stoop of a man outside. John.

I gritted my teeth. He stood near the pear trees with arms on hips. He had a small crook in his spine, a tilted smile and he took a handkerchief from his suit pocket and wiped it across his face. He looked into the sun, wiped his forehead once more. John went towards the front yard, towards the crowd. It was a shock to see him. John's visits to the house had lessened since Abby arrived, only coming a few times a year rather than every month when Mother was still alive. Each time he visited the household stiffened.

"Good day." John would shake Father's hand, strong-wristed. The men stood on opposite sides of the front door.

"Good day," Father would say, wiping his hand on his trousers.

John would look him over, smile like he had ginger in his mouth. "You look well."

"Likewise." Father, a nod of the head.

The script of loathing. Strangers remembering a past. Once, shortly after Mother had died, I caught Father shaking then stroking John's hand as if it were hers, as if by doing so she would walk out of John's body and back into the room. A moment passed. John said, "That's quite enough," and Father broke away, returned his hand to his pocket and kept it hidden for days. "I forgot where I was for a moment," he said.

Distance longs to change people. I saw it each time John came: every few weeks, every few months, a year. Mouths became thick with lost conversation. I knew that John only visited to stay in our lives. "Darling girls," he said. "I'm most happiest when I see you." As a teenager I relished the visits, but as an adult I soon lost interest in his theories of industrialization, of hunting and butchery and sea travel. "You've got to let the animal come to you, Emma, always to you." There was a meanness to his voice. He stopped bothering to ask me what I was up to, what I liked, as if I was past the age of being enthralling. Not like Lizzie. She was golden all the time.

Lizzie loved our uncle more than ever, held on to him like a prize. They belonged to each other, Lizzie always the delight. Every now and then they would make fun of me, of how quiet I was, how plain. "If she were an ornament, nobody would even notice if I knocked her from the mantel and smashed her!" Lizzie would say, made Uncle laugh. In those moments I wanted Lizzie to die, never to have existed. But I reminded myself that Mother had given Lizzie to me to love. I would always have to accept Lizzie without hesitation.

I watched John eat a pear, take bite after bite. His trousers were hitched tight, his long legs creeping out towards the dirt and hard ground.

"Tall like Father." I said it without thinking.

John stood still, inspected the yard with little head snaps before turning his head towards the window. He squinted and smiled at me, waved.

I pulled away, walked downstairs towards the kitchen. People spoke:

"Are there known family enemies?"

"Claims she was outside. Preparations for a fishing trip."

"Apparently he was still warm when Miss Borden found him."

"Looks like a hatchet, the way his face took the blows."

"Mrs. Borden tried to take shelter under the bed when the attack began. Too big to fit."

Bile swamped my throat; here were some answers. I thought of Lizzie finding Father: skin peeled to bone beyond bone, the place of nothingness, the place beyond death.

From the dining room, Dr. Bowen brought a chair for me to sit on, placed it near the stove. "They're going to move your father and Mrs. Borden into the dining room shortly. Best you stay in here."

I didn't want to sit. "Yes, alright." I tried to swallow, tried not to think of their bodies.

"How is Lizzie?" Dr. Bowen said.

"Asleep. I think she's still very frightened."

"Lizzie witnessed some horrible things. She'll need extra attention and affection from you." Dr. Bowen pushed his round-rimmed glasses up the bridge of his nose.

"Yes, of course." How much more could I give her?

My heart groaned and I thought of Father's blindness to all my sacrifices for Lizzie: as a teenager devoted to her scholarly pursuits of God while my own diminished; giving up my bedroom; the constant attention; the lullabies at night; the tiring days of listening to her rants; abandoning the life that might have come with Samuel. All of it for Lizzie. My flesh heated. How could Father not have noticed? Always putting Lizzie first, always taking her side, never asking my opinion. It felt wrong to think of these things, to hold grievances while he lay in the sitting room.

The dining room door opened: feet shuffled, a grunt. My skin flushed then cooled to goosebumps. I was empty. I had wanted to tell Father so much. Maybe I should have been honest with him, told him my real reasons for going to Fairhaven.

———

The side door opened. John stood in the doorway, said, "Emma," and walked slowly towards me, his hands clasped. "It's a tragedy. Just a tragedy."

"Hello, Uncle." I braced myself for his touch.

John placed his hands on my shoulders, didn't notice the jump in my muscles, the drag of my feet. He smelled of sweat and chewing tobacco, of sticky pear, of a slight medicinal smell.

"Emma, my condolences." John's voice high-pitched.

"Thank you." I began to tire of being the polite one.

"You'll be staying on, John?" Dr. Bowen said from behind me.

"Of course. I wouldn't dream of leaving them alone."

I was no child. "I could manage . . ."

"Nonsense. I intend to stay as long as I'm needed. This is all beyond comprehension." John's head, back and forth in disbelief.

"When did you get here?" I caught the accusation on my tongue.

"Last night. I thought I would visit your father and Abby while I attended to some business nearby." John was a pendulum on his heels.

"Where was Lizzie?"

He was quick with answers. "I saw her at dinner and then she went to visit your friend, Alice. She seemed to be quite upset, actually."

"Why did you think so?"

"I didn't think it important to ask. She came home after I went to bed." John eyed me, a hawk.

Nothing was said for a time.

"To think we all had such a lovely time together last night. Now this." John shook his head, his voice thick with quiver.

"Yes, it's hard to believe." I wanted to run away. Bile swirled. I was beginning to sink, waited for it all to be over.

"I'm going to check on Lizzie," John said. "See if she's alright."

I straightened. "No, she's sleeping. I'll check her later."

"I insist. I need her to know that I'm here to take care of things."
He ran his free hand over hair, smiled.

I bit my tongue until blood nearly burst. I didn't want him
anywhere near my sister. John headed for the back stairs.

Dr. Bowen said, "I'll leave now and come by tomorrow morning.
If anything should happen during the night, send for me."

"Yes, alright."

The sound of men leaving.

Upstairs slow-moving feet sounded across floorboards, the low
rumble of John and Lizzie filled the house. I heard the clock on
the mantel, the ticking slower than heartbeats. What was the last
sound Father and Abby heard? I sat for a moment and listened:
the house seemed to forget that they ever existed.

The sudden emptiness of bodies, the way the air felt cold, a void.
I stood in the kitchen, wondered what I should do next, but all I
could think about was what happened that morning: Abby struggling to hide as she was repeatedly hit; the sounds she made as she
cried for it all to stop. Lizzie finding Father and then Lizzie calling
me home. The police had told me to take comfort in knowing that
the house remained a fortress.

"Nobody is coming back for you." A voice in my ear. "We'll
make sure the house is locked right up!"

I looked at the officer. "Alright."

"And we have officers guarding everything."

"Alright."

And then the officer walked away.

I stood still for the longest time, waited to hear Lizzie's movements. I wanted to speak to her, to go over the events, to understand
what it was that Lizzie had seen. What was the best way to console

the unknown? I looked at my hands, flipped them over and over and I wondered what I should do next.

———

There was a time in my life when I believed I could have a place in the world, that I deserved bigger things than the average young woman because I could imagine an existence outside of Fall River, outside family life. Then I turned twenty-five and everything I knew about myself all but ended. It was the year Father tried to marry me off.

"It's time you became a wife," Father had said one morning, adjusting his black cotton bowtie in the mirror. It was as if the notion had only just occurred to him, that he had become aware that a daughter my age should be palmed off to another man. Up until then Father hadn't shown a sense of urgency in the matter. Neither had I. I had liked the idea of marriage, liked that it would take me away from the family, from Father, but I wasn't sure I wanted a husband in the way that I was meant to: living side by side, day in day out, having to abide by what they wanted versus what I wanted. I already had that with Lizzie. I needed something more. If I were to take someone I wanted to do the choosing.

Father would not allow it. "I know who is best for you. You need to wait until you've matured to make those decisions."

"You want me to wait until I'm thirty-six, like Abby did? By your own admission I'm old enough now."

He shot a finger at me. "Your mother has nothing to do with this, Emma. You mind yourself."

Father and his changing. Just like those times he wanted me in school then out. I could see through him, could see that he wanted me around to keep Lizzie in line, to make sure I didn't live a life he did not approve of. I hated him.

Father put the word out that I needed a suitor. "We're a fine family to join," he said. "There will be many fine men to choose from." We waited. As it turned out, nobody wanted to marry a Borden. Men didn't come knocking at our door, did not bother talking to me at social engagements. I hadn't realised how lonely a heart could become. I put all that behind me, concentrated on how I could make myself happy.

But Father became impatient. "I've made contact with associates outside Fall River who have eligible sons."

He made me feel diseased. I suspected I would not have much say over who my suitors would be. The more he searched the more I disliked the idea of marriage. Months went by. Then replies to Father's letters began to arrive, made him smile. "Emma! We've found someone. A wonderful young man from a respectable family like us. I think it would be good for all involved."

I wondered if love would play a part in any of this. "What if we don't get along?"

"You don't have to. These arrangements are straightforward, Emma." According to Father, the marriage would be a business decision. Just like him and Abby.

Soon the suitors arrived. There was: John, a banker's son, horrible breath; Isaac, farmer's son, loved hunting; Albert, doctor's son, too fascinated with blood; Thomas, too uninteresting to recall; and Eugene, a military son, thought art was a waste of time.

Months of having to put on a happy face for boring men. I had not liked any of them, could not bear to have them touch me in any way. The only thing I liked was when I was able to get out of the house for outings. Father made them leave a deposit behind each time they took me out to ensure good behavior and that I would be home on time. The money went into his pocket and the outing would begin.

Once, Albert took me to Rhode Island to see the Atlantic Ocean, paid Father thirty dollars. A cool, rain-filled day, Albert viced his arm through mine, led me to the water's edge. I looked out at the ocean, smelled salt and dead fish, thought of taking my clothes off and throwing myself in, for the water to wake me up from this boredom. I tried to think of ways to tell Father that, like the others, this man too was unsuitable.

Disappointed fathers. The world was full of them. Was I too picky?

Then there was Samuel Miller.

Samuel came for dinner, was tall, reeded, had a closed mouth. He presented at our front door, brought with him white, smooth hydrangeas. Petals drooped from the heat. I despised hydrangeas.

"How lovely and thoughtful," I said. He smelled of peppered musk, made my knees second-guess direction.

He smiled, wide beam, sincere. Something I hadn't anticipated.

Abby made a dinner of boiled potatoes, swordfish and white sauce, and roasted purple carrots. We all sat down to eat, Lizzie making sure she sat next to Samuel, and Father got down to the business of knowing the young man.

"What do you do with yourself?"

I cut a potato with my fork.

Samuel pushed his dark hair out of his eyes. "I've just finished law school."

Father smiled like a child on Christmas Day.

"What are you interested in, Emma?" Samuel asked.

My heart pushed against my chest, felt like it would jump out of my throat. Nobody ever asked me a question like that.

"She likes boring things," Lizzie cut in. She smiled, eyed me like a jackal.

"Now, now, Lizzie," Abby said, calm, a note of happiness. "Let Emma answer for herself." She winked at me. I wondered if she had only interjected to save me because she liked the idea that this time around, I stood a real chance of moving out, would be out of her way.

Lizzie didn't let up. "Do you like dancing, Samuel?"

"On occasion. With the right person." His eyes my way.

"Maybe you can teach my sister to dance. She has arms for legs." Lizzie chuckled to herself, thwomped a chunk of swordfish into her mouth.

I reddened. "Don't pay attention to her. We usually keep her in the attic."

Samuel laughed, pointed his fork at me. "Your father neglected to tell me about your sense of humor."

What else had been neglected?

Later, days later and beyond that, there was talk of books, of the wonders of walking for hours to clear one's mind, of our favorite art.

"My father pushed me into law," he told me. "I would have preferred to study music."

"What do you play?"

"Violin. I can't find the time for it anymore." When Samuel took my hand, he made my skin collapse under bone, bubble back to the surface, lava flow. I could not let go, a twin soul for me.

I wanted more from this person. The things we could achieve. I was willing to live side by side. I imagined a new life with him, let myself be in that possibility. Then I let the words escape: "We should marry one another."

I rushed through decades in my mind: us traveling, me painting in a room filled with violin concerto, us in bed, limbs still knotted together even as our bodies became old. I had to live that life before Samuel had a chance to refuse me.

But he leaned in close. "Alright." Then his lips on mine, a first kiss. I wanted more from this person.

We told Father. Abby held me in her arms, smoothed her hands over my shoulders, made me warm.

Later that night I told Lizzie she could be flower girl if she wanted. Her folded arms across her chest. "I don't care."

"I would really like you to."

"I don't want to talk about it." Lizzie sulked out of my room into hers, slammed the door. I went after her and said through the door, "You'll be able to have my room when I move out."

Lizzie was the sound of bricks, throwing books onto the floor. I hoped she would get over it.

The engagement continued. Samuel visited and Father sat in on our appointments, the three of us in the sitting room together, the three of us in the parlor, the kitchen, a stroll down Second Street. "I want to make sure Emma doesn't do or say anything to make him change his mind," Father told Abby.

What had I done to make my father think so poorly of me?

Then a rare opportunity presented itself: Father and Abby went to our Swansea farm. I invited Samuel over, sent Lizzie off to play with a neighborhood friend. He arrived, that same peppered musk, and I took him upstairs to my room.

Once there, Samuel touched my white and gold brass bed, noticed the lilac-colored ceiling rose above us. "I like that you've only got one fleur-de-lis in the center. It's very refined."

I sat on the bed next to Samuel.

I reached out to him, stroked his stubble cheek, traced my finger over his thick, dark brow. Samuel smiled. I had never touched anyone like that before. The amazement of someone else's body. He was a tremor underneath my fingers, excitement in the blood.

We kissed. The way our tongues touched, warm. Hands travelled across each other, made me prickle. I was an expert of self, wanted more. "Take my blouse off," I told him.

He nodded, he did. Samuel stroked my neck, my shoulder blades, made me feel like the sun had risen inside. He unhooked my corset and I breathed deep and full. The windows rattled. I wanted more from this person.

I removed my linen undergarments, sat bare-chested, took Samuel's hand and placed it against my breast, my heart. "Get to know me without my father."

Samuel undressed, skin brushed against skin. When Samuel kissed then licked my breast, when I stroked the inside of his leg all the way to his groin, felt how warm he was, felt the direction his blood travelled, I heard the opening of a door, pulled away from Samuel, turned.

Lizzie stood there, her eyes scorn, cheeks deep anger, lips becoming white. She said, "You're not meant to be doing that." Lizzie backed away, thundered downstairs.

"You need to go after her," Samuel said.

"I know. I know."

We dressed in silence. Samuel kissed me and I told him to leave the house through the side door. "It might upset her to see you."

I found Lizzie sitting on the sofa in the sitting room, kicking her foot into the carpet.

"Lizzie, you should've knocked." I tried to be gentle.

Lizzie kicked in time with the clock on the mantel. "You've sinned, Emma."

What was sin, exactly? "No, I haven't. Samuel and I . . ."

Lizzie kicked faster. "I'm going to tell Father you were giving yourself away before you're allowed to."

I pulled tight on her legs. "Stop it, Lizzie!"

We glared. Then Lizzie said, "Are you really going to marry him?"

"Yes. And I can't wait."

"For what?"

"To get out of this house, to get away from you all." My voice rising from the pit of my stomach.

Lizzie's cheeks ballooned, reddened. "You'll never leave if you don't get married."

I took her wrist and held it tight.

She tugged, tried to escape my grip. "Don't you think you can go live without me. You're breaking your promise to Mother. You're selfish, Emma."

It hurt. "Don't you dare say that."

Lizzie ripped free. "I'm telling Father."

I boiled, slapped her across the face. "Don't you even try. It's not yours to tell."

Lizzie cried. "I'm telling everyone. Then no one will want to marry you."

To be shamed by your sister. I lost control of the situation, lost control of Lizzie. All that freedom was slipping away. Father couldn't find out. I was afraid of what would happen if he did. I sobbed that night, my body ached. I thought of Samuel, of growing old beside someone, our knotted limbs, the places we could go. Then I thought of family, things that could be lost. It was my experience that life doesn't let you have both. I had seen it with Mother, her joy of having two daughters bounce around together, her heart full of love and safety, only to have one of her girls die when the universe had decided Mother had had too much of a good thing. Her family destroyed. Best be cautious.

When I told Samuel it was over, I could barely get the words off my tongue. I listened to him whimper, as if something twisted from his heart, was killing him, and everything in my body felt as if it were being dragged out of me, set alight. We kissed one last time, blood pulsing underneath flesh, and Samuel left me. When I told Father the engagement was off, he said, "What happened? I tried to give you a good one." He shook his head, a dismissal. The way that made me feel: defective.

I thought of Lizzie, thought of Samuel. I knew I had made the wrong decision.

EIGHT

BENJAMIN

August 3, 1892

THE TRAIN PULLED into Fall River, smoked the platform with thick steam, made women's skirts billow, reveal the tops of their boots, their stockings. My leg had stopped bleeding but it was difficult to move, like there was a steel rod under my skin. Passengers stood, stretched and cracked their bodies, gave me their camphor smell. I stood too, pressed my head against the window, felt the burn of the sun into my forehead along the top of my head, made my head lice critter. I gave myself a scratch. I saw John standing underneath a large white platform sign, realised that he had no luggage. His family visit was going to be quick. He nodded at men in top hats as they walked by. I heaved myself down the aisle and stepped off the train, went over to John.

"Enjoy your trip?" A smile so wide it made me want to punch him.

"It was cramped," I said.

"Ah well, we're here now. Let's move on."

Off he strode and I took after him. We got out of the station and onto a wide bluestone street. The loud sounds of horse-car drivers calling, "Take you up to Main Street, take you all the way." There was a deep silver clang of tram bells, of a baby cry-hollering like a sick animal, mewing for its mother, of shopkeepers sweeping their storefronts, bushy mustaches swallowing their faces. It was too much noise for me. "Will we be here long?"

"Have patience."

We began walking up the street, my leg thump-dragging behind me and John said, "We ought to get that looked at before you do anything."

Delays. They were no good. "I'm alright."

"Nonsense. It's part of the payment, isn't it?"

I had no say in the matter. We walked on, were smacked in the face with a stench pumping from factories and cotton mills. John led me through street after street of close housing adjoined to shops, our shoes echoing like small hammers on the sidewalk, and soon we came to a white storefront with a chipped enamel doorframe, peeled black letters V T SUR E N, a mutt-colored cat curled in the shop window.

"Where are we?"

John swifted his head along the street, on a lookout, and said, "I know a surgeon who can help you. Just keep to yourself."

We went inside, a doorbell chime, and John told me to sit on a leather-covered stool by the wall. Antiseptic smells stung, a wet fur smell surrounded me. John disappeared down a hallway and I wondered how he knew this surgeon. My leg started on its bleeding again. Time passed and John returned with a doctor.

"This here's your patient," John said.

The doctor wore a leather apron, leather waders, pushed his glasses up his nose when he came close to me, coughed into his hand. "I see." He came at me, bird-dived towards my leg and poked. "I can clean this, sew you back up. What do you say?"

John grinned and the doctor grinned and another cat came lurking from the hallway, wrapped itself around the doctor's legs. A cat cannot be trusted.

"So be it," I said. I'd never been stitched up before, had always let my body do its will.

"Well now. You get fixed and I'll be waiting around." John thwacked my back, hit my ribs hard. The doctor led me down the hall into a bare-bone room. "Sit there," he said, pointed to a daybed. "Remove your trousers."

I did that, exposed bruises and scars, my chicken knees. The gash on my leg had opened me up good and I wanted to put my finger inside to see how far down I could go. The doctor went over to a bench, fished around some amber glass jars along the wall. There was a large wooden table in the middle of the room, tiny drops of blood on it, and from somewhere I heard the rattle of a cage. The doctor got a jar, then got his medical kit and brought both over to me. Inside was a large brass syringe, long, sharp objects that looked like thin chisels, a pair of heavy scissors, tweezers. He took out the scissors and the tweezers, lifted the amber jar, said, "Right then, I'm going to pour this on you. It's a type of acid. It'll sting but it'll do wonders."

I took a quick glance out the door, saw a black cat limp past. The lid came off the bottle and liquid poured onto me. My leg twitched like I had fire ants marching. I gave a howl and somewhere in the back of the building, another howl rose, met mine.

"That should do it," he said. "Now for the stitch-up." He came at me like a fisherman, a little hook and catgut line, threaded my leg together, pulled through skin tags. My head, thick and hot, made me want to fall into deep sleep. I closed my eyes and later John was shaking me awake. "Right now?"

I wiped spittle from my mouth. "It's over?"

"Easy, wasn't it?" The way he eyed me, an owl at night.

My leg had been bandaged, trousers pulled up and John helped me from the bed, said, "Time to move on." I looked around for the doctor, looked around for other patients, didn't see him, didn't see them. We left the shop, went into the street.

"I think you'll be much improved," John said.

"So what do we do now?"

"We'll be parting. I have to see my niece then take care of some business. I'll meet you back at the station at six o'clock and we'll make our way to the house."

"Alright," I said. "But I'm hungry."

"Sorry. I'm afraid I've nothing to spare at the moment." He gap-toothed a smile. "Until then!" John legged off, left me in the street. I did not care to be left like that. I should've gone after him but thought better—get money, get Papa.

Downtown. I sniffed the air. A draught horse pulled a mill cart. Two dogs nosed each other and ran up an alleyway. People stood on the sidewalk, spoke to one another about the weather, all the silly-chat that bore into you, made you grind teeth.

At Main Street, a police officer talked to a junk man. As I neared them, the officer made the man remove his bag from his back, empty contents on the side of the road, tin plates crashing. The man's back hunched as the officer went through his things, inspected the plates before tossing them back on the ground. I closed in on the men, heard the officer say, "I don't believe these were given to you."

"People are kind. Those church ladies really did give me their old wares." His voice brittle.

"You looking to jail?" the officer said.

I stopped next to them, stared at the officer, at his insect limbs folded across his chest, at his stupid menace face, and he said to me, "Can I help you?"

I could smell his fists, the way he readied himself to bruise the man. I knuckled myself up, got a feeling inside me that wanted to punish. "You're all the same. Making nothing but trouble," I said. I swayed side to side, stone crunch under my boots.

The officer clicked his tongue. "Is that so?"

Knuckles hardened. "Yes."

"Maybe you should mind your own business."

That made me laugh. I filled the street with myself.

"This place is full of crazies," the officer said, dug his finger into the man's chest, pointed hard. "Like you."

The man said nothing, tried to pick up his belongings, put them back in his dirt-greasy bag.

"Put them down," the officer said. It was just like Papa telling us what to do and so I took a swing at him, cracked him in the eye.

The officer covered his face. "Shit," he said.

"Get your things and go," I said to the man. He nodded, kept packing. I cracked the officer again and I took off down the street, heard him blow on his police whistle, make it shriek. I kept going, ran through leg pain, laughed and laughed, felt alive. The whistle shrieked again and voices called out, "Stop him! Stop that man."

I went down a laneway, went down parallel streets until I was near the train station. My leg throbbed but I kept on, got to the station and went looking for the urinals. Some sweet smell, some stench smell. I got myself in a stall, locked the door and huddled onto a toilet seat, porcelain under boots. I waited there.

———

Town bells dinged six. My leg throbbed and I uncurled myself from the toilet seat, stretched out and felt along my thigh. No new blood. I waited outside the station for John. He was late. I didn't care for this. Time passed. He came lanking along, a whistle on his lips. "Ah! Benjamin." John patted me on the back. He smelled like he'd been near a woman.

"Are we going to the house now?"

"Let's hold on for a moment, let me tell you some things." He stood too close to me, made me feel his sweat and heat. "I was hoping to get a key for you to use tonight but their maid wasn't forthcoming. You may have to do the job tomorrow."

"But you need to get me in. I can't do it right if I don't know my way around the house."

"Now, I don't think I can do that, Benjamin. It's all about tact."

I've found some people never properly think through their needs. I'd have to do the thinking for John. I said, "You need to let me in if you want this problem solved."

John shook his head. "You're going to have to find your own way in."

"Leave a door unlocked."

"Andrew likes the house locked tight. Then you have the maid to contend with."

An unexpected quantity. Things should not be kept from me. "This maid. Will she be a problem?"

John tapped his lips. "Bridget might get in the way, but then she's a little daft. She may not cotton on that you're in the house."

There was a train whistle.

"Does your niece know I'm coming?"

"The less she knows the better."

I should've told him that wasn't necessarily the case but no matter. "Have you decided how you'd like me to solve the problem?"

John creased his crooked lips. "I'll leave that up to you. But I worry that he'll know who sent you. And that's going to be a problem for me."

"What are you asking me to do, John?"

He clicked his tongue.

I had thought of so many ways for Andrew. I would come in through the side door, catch him in the middle of tying his shoelaces. I'd glove his hands in mine, take a shoelace and tie it around his wrists, slap him a few times around the ears. "Listen good," I'd tell him, and he would. Then I could take a carving knife, swing it around, scare him until he lost his bowels. I could take a worn and wooden baseball bat, break legs. I could punch him good, I could call him names, I could make him weep for God, I could treat him like my papa. That's when the real problem-solving would begin.

"I'll make it discreet," I said.

John looked me up and down, a study. "Good. Because at the end of it all, I just want my nieces to be happy. I'd hate for them to be frightened in their own home."

"Of course."

"Don't let me down."

I stared at him. "Don't let me down, John."

John looked away from me a moment then rubbed his hands together. "Splendid. Shall we get going? I'd like to show you the house now."

I let him get a few feet in front of me before I followed. We made our way along Main Street past houses with large lawns, towards houses that were short of space, short of privacy. Every now and then I looked for the junk man, looked for the officer, but saw neither.

John whistled as he walked. I was already sick of his tune. We walked to streets that counted down to the beginning of Fall River: Fifth, Fourth, Third. We got to Second Street and John stopped, said over his shoulder, "This is us." The street was lined with full-green trees camouflaging windows and doors, was littered with men and women taking early-evening strolls, a horse-drawn cart carrying empty wooden boxes, dirt-gray moths fighting lamplight.

"See that dark-green two-story? That's the one."

I hadn't anticipated the place to have layers. I was used to flat-dwelling, nothing but bare façades and a few rooms. There was no light coming from the front windows like the other homes, nothing to suggest there was life inside.

"Go to the backyard," John rushed.

"And do what?"

"At some stage I'll come to you."

For the first time since our meeting, he seemed nervous. I couldn't have that around me. I nodded, even smiled at him, to put him at ease.

He crossed the street, made his way to the house and knocked on the door. An elderly tub of a woman wearing a blue bonnet opened the door, filled the frame with her hips and stomach and John took her hands, kissed them. He was loud when he said, "Good evening, dear Abby." The wife. She looked away from him, like he was wearing a vulgar mask, and John burst in, shut the door.

I counted to three, crossed the road, jumped over a small white fence, made sure no one was passing by and got close to the house. I smelled a flood of kerosene snake out from the door gap. I put a hand on the door. The wood was warm and at the top of the door were brass numbers: 92. I turned the handle. Locked. I ran to the side, slid my way to a window. The sun dropped. Through the window I could see inside, could see the top of a black-shine sofa and, above that, a painting of a horse in a field, the muscular beast kicking its legs behind, all its anger. I saw John reach out to shake a tall man's hands: the way they eyed each other, the way the tall man grinned and bared teeth. I knew that was Andrew. I sized him up best I could, took stock of his balding head, the liver spots on top, his cranky arms and thin frame. My papa had been shorter, sturdy-shouldered, weak in mind. And I could take on Papa. Andrew wouldn't be a problem.

John and Andrew shook hands, shook hands, shook hands, let go. In between them came the maid. "Bridget," I said. The thick dark hair of her, her broad shoulders, her hard-knock chin. Maids always came near the things they shouldn't. Bridget looked right at the window. I bobbed down, hit my elbows against the side of the house. I moused into a ball on the ground, tried to disappear into darkening night. Ants crawled up my arm, bit me good, and the grass underneath me was summered, dry and upright, prickled. I waited and waited, then looked through the window again. The room was empty, as if what I saw before was ghosts.

———

I went to the backyard. Along the fence was a full-bloom pear arbor, the sickly-sweet smell of half-eaten fruit thrown to the ground. I thought of the worms underneath churning earth, climbing over each other until their soft jelly bodies rolled into one. I pulled a pear and ate, juices on fingers and chin. There was a sharp twinge towards the back of my mouth and I reached my index finger inside, felt another loose tooth. I took hold, pulled and twisted, threw the tooth under the pear arbor.

All around me crickets thrumped their little throats and the moon started to show, covered grass with a balmy sheen. There was a barn to the left of the yard and a large rug hanging over the clothesline. My leg began to itch and I scratched, enjoyed the way my skin came under my fingernails, the way I piled myself up. I watched the back of the house, watched windows light and dim with kerosene lamps, watched Bridget move from room to room. When she was upstairs in the attic she removed her bonnet, pressed herself against a window, looked out into the early night. I wondered if I waved my hands, would she see me out here in the shadows? I bet she knew about Emma's and Lizzie's father problems. I had a mind to ask her about them. The conversations we could have. How easy my task would be then. Bridget stood up there in the window and I moved towards the house. I tried to lift the windows on the first floor, all locked, and then I tried the basement double doors, twisted the handle back and forth. Locked. I twisted the handle again and felt resistance. I let go and the handle rattled. Someone behind the door. There was a key in the lock, some grunting, and I ran to the pear arbor, flattened myself along the ground. The basement door opened like an earthquake and there was a kerosene glow. A woman stood there. She held the lamp high, watched a moth swarm the light before sweeping it away with the back of her hand.

The woman came outside, came right into the yard, and I could hear her breath, shallow and nervous, something bubbling inside her. She wiped her fingers across her eyes, like she'd been crying, and she put the lamp on the ground, let out a deep belly-sound of anger.

I lifted my head a little, hungry for her noise. This was a feeling I knew. The things you could do with it. She did it again and said, "As the Lord liveth, there shall no punishment happen to thee for this thing." I lifted my head higher, started to raise my chest off the ground. I realised then that this was Lizzie. She had problems indeed. Somewhere around us I heard, "What on God's earth was that noise?" and Lizzie covered her mouth with her hand and scanned the yard, made me bury myself back into the ground. Crickets hammered, Lizzie shined the light on the rug, went close to it, picked up a wicker slapper that was leaning against the house. Lizzie, with her back turned to me, started beating the rug with the slapper, over and over, grunting from effort, her shoulders round and fierce.

"I am not those things. I am not those things," she spat out, a freight train across country, no slowing it down.

I pulled myself onto my hands and knees, slowly began to crawl towards her, wanted to get close to her to smell anger, find out just how much problem-solving I would have to do. Lizzie cried out, made the rug swing like a dead man. I was halfway to her when John appeared in the basement doorway. He lifted his lamp high, caught me on all fours. He sneered, shook his head and I stopped still.

"Lizzie, what's going on?" he said.

"I can't do this anymore." She beat the rug.

John walked to her, put his lamp on the ground then took Lizzie by the shoulders. "Now, now," he cooed. "You can do anything."

"Why does he always have to put me down?"

"Why does anyone do anything? Don't listen to him." John looked over towards me and I slowly crawled back to where I'd come from. I flattened into grass. He armed her tight, hushed her, told her, "I'm going to help you feel better. Do you like the sound of that?" John held her tighter, nuzzled into her, made Lizzie narrow into him like a cat. "Yes."

They stood for a time and then Lizzie asked, "Am I a good daughter?"

"The very best, I'm sure."

"What do I have to do to get Father to see that?" The strain in her voice.

"Just continue to be yourself. He'll learn his mistakes soon enough."

"Maybe he will," Lizzie said. Crickets hammered the yard. "I'm surprised to see you today."

"I told you I'd be coming."

"I thought you were arriving tomorrow."

"I had a change of plans, had things to attend to. I thought I'd come earlier, perhaps see Emma in Fairhaven."

"Did you?"

"No. She wasn't where you said she would be. She'd gone out."

Lizzie wrenched her head up. "Where was she?"

"Her friend didn't say. I got the feeling she didn't trust me." John palmed Lizzie's forehead, a soothing.

"Helen's always overcautious. She's no fun," Lizzie said.

They sat on the step of the basement door and John swung his arm around her.

"Everything alright around here? Abby seems stranger than usual. She's a bit too quick in wanting to leave rooms." John whistled the words out.

"Is she? I haven't cared to notice."

"Has she been causing you heartache?"

"Mrs. Borden is as bad as Father. Sometimes I think she deliberately sets Father against me."

John shook his head and rocked Lizzie back and forth. "Fancy pitting a parent against a child." John had a strange way with his niece, all that holding and stroking. I didn't like the look of it.

"She always has. And now she's gone and got Father to deed a house to her and her sister."

"I can't fathom why he would agree to such a thing."

"It should be for me and Emma to have. It's our money too."

I imagined Abby whispering into Andrew's ear, like Angela into Papa, whispering how he should leave his children. I'd have to speak to Andrew about women like that.

"What would you say if I told you there would be no more problems?" John said.

Lizzie looked at him. "In what way?"

"I'm going to arrange a man-to-man talk with your father, remind him to treat you and your sister properly."

"That could work." Lizzie brightened.

"I suspect it will, Lizzie."

"When will you speak to him?"

"How about tomorrow?"

Lizzie dug her fingernail under fingernail, wiped the debris on her skirt. "When?"

"How about when he comes home from work to have lunch? I'd make it discreet so as not to embarrass him in his own home. Perhaps you could persuade Bridget and Abby out of the house?" John was making it easier for me.

Lizzie rubbed her temples, closed her eyes. "That could work. That could work," she said quietly.

John smiled. "Well, it's settled."

"It's settled."

He tightened himself around Lizzie, kissed her on the forehead. "You try to relax tonight."

"You know, I'm thinking I'll go see my friend Alice."

"Splendid idea."

Lizzie stood, said goodbye and went into the basement, left her lamp behind. The door closed.

Time passed. John raised his voice. "Did you catch that?"

"Yes," I said, remained in the shadows.

"You can see how distressing this is for her."

"Yes."

"Please do your best."

"Yes."

John stood, dusted himself. "I'll be off now."

"Will you let me in the house tonight?"

"No. It's too risky."

"Where will I go?"

He pointed. "The barn's over there."

I was no animal. I pulled myself up, stood tall and meat-cleaved towards him. Noses almost touched. "I don't like how you're speaking to me."

"That's not my concern."

"I could easily make it so." I wanted to put him in his place.

He pulled away, patted me on the back. "That's the way. Be just like that." He laughed, opened the basement and went inside. Crickets hammered the yard. There was no point staying outside getting bit by insects, those hate-filled things. I picked up Lizzie's kerosene lamp, turned it to half-light and went to the barn. There were stacked wooden boxes, wooden crates of broken plates, odds and ends of discarded household items, an empty bird aviary. I made my way up the barn stairs to a small loft, got myself settled under the window. I turned off the lamp, looked out at the house, watched the comings and goings of shadows. I would become one of them.

NINE

LIZZIE

August 4, 1892

IN THE DINING room, Father and Mrs. Borden, stiff and straight on undertaker's boards, were waiting for the coroner, waiting to tell them what it was to be dead.

The police had gone out for a moment, had left the inside of the house unguarded. Neighbors retreated back to their homes. Emma was somewhere. At the tip of my mind I heard Mrs. Borden call to me, "Come and see us, Lizzie. Come see a secret." I didn't want to let them down. I crept the stairs towards the dining room. I made sure I was alone. I opened the dining room door and lifted an eye into the room. I held my breath. There under white sheets, frightened and silent, their bodies held each other like first-time lovers. I closed my eyes while Father reached his arm around his wife and told her, "It will all be over soon."

I walked into the room. A thick stain of heat and blood, of broken muscle and bone, dug under my nose, *critter critter.* I walked slowly to the dining table and stood at the end. I touched the edge of a crisp sheet. I lifted my head towards the ceiling. Underneath the light fixture, paint crumbled into tiny flakes of yellowing white, summer snow falling on top of the sheets covering Father and Mrs. Borden. Father would hate such a mess.

I hid a smile underneath my palm and tasted salt. On my wrists there was a spatter of blood, tiny droplets that were still finding their way under my skin. I licked my finger and wiped at it, erasing Father, erasing Mrs. Borden from my body. I lifted the sheets. Underneath, like an echo, I could feel Mrs. Borden hum, her vibrations jumping through my body, humming the songs she sang when I was young and couldn't sleep. I wanted to shout at her, "Stop it! You are not that person anymore," but instead I thought about what she was now: the beginning of carrion. Soft skin opened like a rock; hard underneath hard underneath cold. I lifted the sheets higher. They weren't wearing any clothing. I poked Mrs. Borden's thigh, *so cold,* quickly pulled the sheet down.

I thought about Father, stretched out like a bone xylophone, one arm stuck to his torso while the other reached towards mercy, towards Mrs. Borden. I went to Father's side of the table, lifted the sheet again. His hair was matt and thin. He looked like he was in pain. I leaned in, *just a bit,* and kissed him on the side of his face where there had been a cut. The clock on the mantel ticked ticked.

"Poor Father," I said. "Can I get you anything to make you more comfortable?" The walls around me hissed. They weren't wearing any clothes. I wondered if I would miss him. I pulled the sheet down and I saw them wriggle closer to each other, hands caressing each other.

I gritted my teeth, *No more touching! No more make-believe love!* and I stepped back from the table towards the door. In the corner of the doorjamb a flower petal clung to the wood. Three days before, the dining room was covered in violet bloom, Mrs. Borden having filled vase and vase and vase with those sickly flowers she liked having around so much. I watched her breathe in those small petals, watched her smile and sway her hips. When she exited, I walked in and ripped off the petals until there was nothing but stem and glass. I did it to all of them. For a moment, my small violent impulse had felt restful. And then, after a time, it didn't. I felt just as I had before. I picked up as many petals as I could and left the room. I said nothing.

I took the petal from the doorjamb and stuck it into my pocket. I walked out of the dining room into the sitting room and left Father and Mrs. Borden behind. Outside someone yelled, "I can see her," as I passed the parlor window towards the front stairs. I smoothed my hands over my hair. I walked up the stairs, made the wood yell.

I ran my hand across the hot banister and it melted into my palm like taffy. Everything slowed and the walls pulled themselves away from their foundations. There was no more silence. Everything was loud and thunderous the closer I got to the top of the stairs. On the landing, the heat was a tyrant of rage and pushed my mouth open, forcing my breath to be shallow then big. I heard myself scream then laugh.

I walked into the guest room where they found Mrs. Borden and saw that the police had opened all the drawers and cupboards, spreading our life across the floor until it was dirty and soiled. Father would be angry at the mess. I thought of how he would demand I clean it and how I would turn to him and refuse. There would be a moment when his eyes would snap, his neck becoming thick and superior. He would knot his fingers together and shout, "You will do as I say," and I would smile at him sweetly and press my palms over my ears. I would watch his mouth open open shut, open open shut and pretend he was saying, "I am wrong, Lizzie, and you are right."

On the floor the police had laid out an old towel. It was covered in bloodied boot prints, *invisible soldiers*, and I thought of the time when I was eight, when Emma and I became ghosts leaving flour footprints all over the kitchen, *I was so small, small, small.* So long ago.

I had tiptoed around Emma's bed and whispered, "Make me laugh, Missus Chatter!"

Emma rolled over, wiped dribble from her mouth and asked, "What do you want to do?" and I told her, "Let's be naughty," and we walked downstairs, me a jumping jack and Emma a mouse, into the cold kitchen, waiting for the sun to warm us. We went through the cupboards telling each other:

"We could eat sugar!"

"We could hide one of the knives."

"We could hide in here until someone opens it and we jump out."

"Let's eat all the food except for the horrible stuff."

And then Emma spotted the flour tin and asked me, "Lizzie, would you like to be invisible?"

"A ghostie?"

She nodded, like a jump. "Yes."

I said I would if it really meant no one would ever see the naughty things I would do, and Emma told me, "No one will ever, ever see you, not even when you're old and spotty."

We stood in the middle of the kitchen with the flour tin between our feet and took off our nighties, bent over the tin and dove our hands into the flour, made fistfuls of clouds onto our bodies.

"Make sure you cover my face," Emma said, and I threw another handful at her, into her eye. She yelled at me in the voice she knew scared me, yelled and yelled until she heard Father walk down the back stairs and unbuckle his belt. We listened to the leather slither its way through loops of material, his boots whipped into the staircase. Then it became quiet. We closed our eyes and became invisible.

———

I opened my eyes. My shoes were drifting along the bloodstained carpet, the last pieces of Mrs. Borden's life licking at my heels like an ocean. *I'm in the sea.* At the bottom of the ocean, I saw fine strands of gray seaweed, saw little fish swimming through it, hoping to hide from sharks. I crouched into the water and let the blood sea salt cleanse my face. I waded across a wave. I fancied myself an explorer, a deep-sea diver. Floating in the water I found a hair comb, a cameo necklace, a piece of lace from a pillow sham, a little scrap of bone. Signs of sunken treasure, a bounty stolen from pirates. I tried to put treasure into my skirt pocket, careful not to let it sink me. I let out a deep breath. Something made me feel like crying. I left the ocean, left the room, felt fresh air sweep my face.

Downstairs a thud sounded and echoed through the house. The heavy boots of a police officer thumped up the stairs. I quickened across the landing into my bedroom and locked the door.

My room was tight with heat. I looked at the silver crucifix above my bed, reminded myself that He had suffered too. My body ached and all the blood rushed to my ears then forehead making everything black and solid. I stood in front of my mirror and pulled at my clothes, *when did they become so tight?* peeled away the layers until I was naked. My skin was pale and opaque, *this is not what thirty-two should look like.* Everything hurt. I wanted to feel better. I forced my fingers onto my arms and ordered them to march like ants. They trounced over hills and mountains, digging trenches under my arms and breasts, *I'm beginning to feel better,* and the army advanced down my rounded stomach to view my groin and thigh. I filled with tingles, good things. My skin cooled and the house dimmed its heat. With a one two left right, the army continued towards my toes, taking with them my webby skin until it became liquid, beautiful. I pressed myself against the mirror.

I layered my clothes back onto my body and straightened my hair, *perfect.* I peeked out my bedroom window at Second Street, took in the bright whites and purples of front yard glory, took in the dank layers of grit and rot that clung to houses. Below me was Irish Mary hanging out clothes. She scratched her head, that lopsided thing, and then she looked at the basement for a time. I knew what she was thinking. Bad things do happen.

I wanted Emma to come up, but I was afraid she was angry with me for letting Father die. There were many things I needed to explain to Emma but I didn't know the words. I thought of her coming upstairs, running for me. I would open my door and she would pick me up from the floor and cradle me in her lap and I would tell her, "It was so terrible, Emma, so terrible. I thought they would never stop with their questions," and then she would look at me with those loving eyes and kiss me on the forehead and tell me, "I will take over from here now, Lizzie, you go away and disappear and leave this behind you."

I wanted to tell Emma something. I sat on the floor by my bed and thought about things I'd never told her. There had been the times Mrs. Borden had told me I was a disappointment to Father, of her slapping my face and me laughing back at her; of the time I saw Mrs. Borden through the keyhole, naked and shivering. I thought about the night after Emma had gone to Fairhaven. The shameful thing I did.

Nightmares had grabbed me in my sleep, bruised me to screaming. The things I had dreamed. I woke to a morning that was half awake. I looked around my room, had that feeling that someone had reached inside my body and pulled me out backwards, had left me with nothing but animal noises dripping from behind my ears, loud then louder until I couldn't hear myself think. Sweat broke me, made me flood salt into my bedclothes, *the day is already too long*, and I got up, stripped the bed, stripped myself, made heavy cotton piled in the corner of my room for Bridget to clean. My heart beat and beat, galloped into my throat and exploded. I couldn't help but shake. I needed Emma, needed something like comfort. I put a dress on, tried to calm myself, but every time I blinked, closed my eyes longer than I should, the flash of night was there. Behind the wall, I heard one of them—Father or Mrs. Borden—toss and writhe in bed, *I have been in there before*, and I wanted to feel safe, wanted to feel small again. I went to Father and Mrs. Borden's room, let myself right in.

Shadows played through curtains. There in the bed lay Mrs. Borden, *Father already gone*, her lump of body, barely moving.

Emma would've said not to go to her but I couldn't help myself. I walked towards her, the floorboards creaked, and Mrs. Borden sounded her heavy in-and-out breath, little tornado, and I got close, my fingers stroked the bedclothes then the wooden bedframe. I kneed the bed, shifted all my weight forwards, leaned over her head. She didn't even know I was there. The side of her face was wrinkled, was not the face I remembered from my childhood. I leaned closer, touched the creases around her eye, her paper-loose skin, *peel her away, peel her back*, and my heart slowed and, for a moment, I was calm. What touch can do. Fingers slid through gray hair and I stroked and stroked. Mrs. Borden looked restful in that sleep, like she used to, like she always would, I stroked, hair like horses, and I leaned even closer, smelled her skin, old moth wing and saliva, and I kissed her forehead, felt the tip of my front teeth press into skin and bone. Mrs. Borden moved underneath me. I pulled back, saw her stare at me.

"What in God's name . . ."

"I'm feeling funny. I had such strange, awful dreams."

Mrs. Borden pulled the covers to her chin. "What do you want me to do about it? Your father isn't here." A spit.

I sat on the bed close to her. My heart thumped, made me lick my lips. I told her, "I want the bad dreams to stop but Emma isn't here to help."

Mrs. Borden let out a little moan, pulled herself onto her elbows and sat up. She stared at me, the longest time, and I looked at her, the way the corners of lips drooped and flattened. Then I looked at the space in the bed next to her, the space where Father had been, *it's probably still warm*, and Mrs. Borden followed my gaze, shook her head and shook her head. "No," she whispered. It made me feel like I was thirteen, like the day Father and Mrs. Borden hadn't wanted me in their bed anymore. "You can't keep coming in here after you have a nightmare, Lizzie." Father and his mean words. It took me time to get over it.

I stared at her, stared right into her center and waited. It was quiet in the room. And then she pulled the covers down, pulled them across, showed me the space beside her. If only Emma had been there: I wouldn't have had to crawl into bed beside Mrs. Borden, wouldn't have had to treat her like a mother.

TEN

BENJAMIN

August 4, 1892

THE SUN HIT me like a cannon. The pigeons danced on the roof. Time passed and the barn door opened. There was movement below, a woman trilling like a bird, saying, "Morning, sweet ones." It was Lizzie. Then she screamed.

"My birds!"

I lifted onto hands and knees, was a secret crawling to the top of the stairs. I looked down, saw her hands in a deep waste drum. She screamed again, pulled out a dead pigeon, wings tipped and stiff, without a head, like all dead things. She pulled out another and another, let them pile at her feet and yelled, "I hate him! I hate him!" Lizzie held the birds against her chest, made them listen to her heart. The sun cracked across the barn, the breathing of wood. I remembered Papa: moving through the house, bare feet slapping the floor until he stopped at my bedroom. "Boy. Boy."

"Yes, Papa?"

"Open."

I opened the door. The smell of musk and burnt tobacco, of old mud. Papa smiled a browned tooth. "Get your coat."

I got my coat and followed him out. We moved quickly. "Where are we going?" My feet marched like rats.

"You're going to hold some things down for me."

We reached the family chicken coop. "You hand them to me while I take to the ax."

Papa stormed the chickens. I was holding the birds upside down, their scaly legs rubbing the inside of my wrist like an itch.

"Give," Papa said.

I handed a chicken, watched it writhe, watched its eyes bulge. When the ax fell, the chicken was thrown into the air, blood dropped on my skin, its head oddly animated on the chopping block. I picked up another, tried to hold it steady as it squabbed with fear.

"I can't hold them. They're too flighty."

I handed a chicken. Then another. A chicken, a chicken.

When it was all over, I was told, "Collect them heads and take them to your mama."

The heads had stacked on the ground like kindling. I was afraid to touch them. One of the heads moved, eye blinking and beak gasping. "Papa, it's still alive."

"It's all nerves."

I slowly picked the heads off the ground and placed them in a bucket. Blood stench. I was covered in it.

Outside the barn Andrew's bellow voice called, "Lizzie! Lizzie, come here." Lizzie turned and I receded from the stairs. Andrew stood at the door, his shadow filling the open space.

"Get away from me," Lizzie said.

Andrew sighed. "I hoped you wouldn't find them before I . . ."

"You killed them!" Lizzie threw a pigeon at Andrew. The bird hit him in the abdomen, slumped to the ground. A wing snapped.

Andrew stepped inside the barn, slapped Lizzie across the face. "Stop this nonsense."

Lizzie sobbed, stamped her feet, wooden toy soldier sound, and said, "Why?"

"They are vermin, Lizzie."

"They're my pets. I cared for them."

"They were bringing disease into the house."

Lizzie bent down, picked up the bird and held it. "Why did you have to be so cruel? You could've just let them fly away."

"You know they wouldn't. Some things are better off dead." Andrew moved towards her, lifted his hand, the gold ring on his pinkie finger shined. Lizzie hit him.

"I don't want you to speak to me anymore." A tear stuck in her throat.

"Lizzie, please be reasonable."

She pushed past Andrew, held on to the dead bird. I crawled to the window and looked out. Lizzie stood in the middle of the yard, swung the bird back and forth, back and forth. Andrew came beside her, attempted to stroke his daughter's hair.

"Don't touch me."

He took his hand away. "You'll get over this," he said. "We'll talk this afternoon."

Lizzie turned to him. "You think you know everything. God will punish you." She dropped the bird to the ground and left him alone in the yard.

Andrew rubbed his hands over his face. The sun cracked over the barn roof, made a crack through my bones. Now was the time to go to him.

He began to walk away from the yard like an echo; slow, defeated. I downed the stairs, opened the barn door. Fresh air kissed my lips, glare made small haloes in my pupils. Andrew went to the side of the house, his lean frame drowning in his dark-gray woolen suit. A pigeon flew above his head. He reached for the bird, missed. He smoothed wrinkle-hands over his forehead. I wanted to rush forwards, ball my hands against his face, make him see sense, but he was gone then, had disappeared inside the house.

I stretched my arms wide, reached for the pear arbor. I pulled on heavy fruit and squeezed, let juice dribble between my fingers. I ate. I pulled another, ate, tossed the pear cores onto the dirt and wiped my mouth along shirtsleeve. I smelled terrible.

I walked to the middle of the yard, stopped at the dead bird, bent down and picked it up; lead feathers. I snapped off a wing, made that bone twig sound, and held it against my face before tucking it into my trouser pocket.

A door opened and someone moaned. Then there were feet. I didn't want to be seen, and I hastened towards the barn and pressed against the outside wall. Bridget came into the backyard, cloth and bucket in hand. She wiped her arm across her face, stood still. She placed the bucket on the ground, doubled over and vomited into grass. The sound her body made. She vomited again, again, emptied contents, heavy liquid, brown, spoiled. She lowered onto her hands and knees, rested her forehead on the ground. The sun was gold light against her white cap and apron. Birds sounded off.

Bridget vomited once more, pulled herself up, and took off with the bucket to the far side of the house. She moved like tar. When she began cleaning the windows I waited, ran across the backyard. I went to the basement doors, quietly turned the handle. Locked. What was so precious in this house that everything had to be locked? I ran to the near side of the house, to the side door. Unlocked. Bridget had made a mistake. I slipped inside. There was a narrow hardwood staircase, brass clothes hooks along the wall. I went further in, into a kitchen, shutters were half closed, cast the house in shadows, smelled of baking, of old meat, of skin, of people overheating. My stomach begged. I walked over to the stove, large enough to put someone inside, burn them good, and took the lid off a deep, blackened pot; an acidic smell. I scooped my hand and dunked it into the soup. It was warm. I raised my hand to mouth over and over, dribble-dribble down chin, down neck onto shirt and onto the floor. There was the taste of something sweetened, like marzipan. Meat shouldn't taste like that. I shouldn't have been so eager. I put the lid back on the pot, saw a plate of johnnycakes on the counter. I picked one up, inhaled, a hint of sugar, and placed the brick-heavy dough to my tongue, licked before biting, swallowing it whole. I brushed crumbs off my shirt, heard footsteps above me. I looked up at the ceiling, noticed sooted cornices. "Might be Andrew up there," I said.

———

In the room with a large sofa, a dark-wood clock sat on a mantel. I slid my finger across the wood, slid across to photos of Andrew and Abby, to a photo of Lizzie, to a photo of a woman I could only assume was Emma, her dark hair, stone chiselled nose, high forehead. She looked nothing like her sister, Lizzie with the round-puff cheeks and plum-fat lips, the top of her ears bent like a little sail. Such ordinary-looking women.

My finger slid from the mantel, across the wall, across a bookshelf, and to the window. It was covered with a thick lace curtain, and peeking through the other side of the glass was the top of Bridget's bonnet. Her head bobbed up, bobbed down and I snuck fingers behind the curtain and pulled them back, watched Bridget on her knees rinse her cloth in a metal bucket.

Someone above the ceiling hammered long strides across floorboards. I went to the sofa, sat down, spread my hands over the smooth horsehair upholstery. The dead animal had a nice gloss. From there I could see straight through to another room with a piano inside, through to the front stairs, to the comings and goings. This house was bigger than anything I had known. I could have my way with Andrew anywhere. I rested my head against the sofa, felt my stomach cramp and boil, hooked my fingers through the rip in my trousers and felt along the surgeon's line. I thought of Papa. Being in the house made me want to revisit him, tell him all the ways he did wrong, the way Andrew was going to be told. I got up then, went to the dining room, circled the long table, gave its hard wood a knock-knock, tugged at the heavy, floor-length lace tablecloth, tugged on it like I would Mama's skirt. I missed her. The window shutters were open, a clear day in front of me, a peek view of a next-door neighbor fixing the collar of her blouse. I pressed up against the window, enjoyed the sun on my head, on my eyes. Time to search for Andrew.

I turned around when I heard someone begin to walk down the front stairs. I bent down a little so I could see who it was. I expected

Andrew, expected that he would come through to me, let me take him by the shoulders, jostle him some. "You know why I'm here, don't you?" I'd ask him. Andrew would shake his head.

"You've been unkind. You've not listened." I'd pull him towards me, get right close.

I saw dark trouser legs, a spindle body, heard, "You ensure you take care of yourself in this heat, Abby. We wouldn't want you to get worse." John was on the stairs. He came into full view, palmed his hair then smoothed out his shirt.

"I don't plan on doing anything but stay inside," Abby said.

This would be difficult for me. John made it to the entrance of the house when we made eye contact. "You!" His eyes widened, face dropped, and he shot a look up the stairs.

Abby came in to plain view then, her head down, concentrating on each step, heavy-handed on the banister. I quickly pulled a chair out from the table and curled underneath.

"What were you saying, John?" Abby asked.

"Wouldn't you know it? I've completely lost my train of thought."

"That's happened to me more times than I care to admit."

John gave a weak chuckle, the kind that made shoulders rise to ears. My stomach cramped, head swooned, eyes watered.

"Now, shall I tell Bridget to make enough dinner to accommodate you today?"

"You know, I think you should. I'll stay another night. I'd like to spend more time with Lizzie."

"Very well."

"I imagine after I tie up a few loose ends downtown that I will be quite exhausted."

John had said nothing about staying longer. He'd promised to help me out of Fall River. I didn't take kindly to liars. We would have to have words.

Abby opened a cupboard, handed John his jacket.

"What time is Andrew due home?" he asked.

"He usually pops in for a short time around one o'clock."

"Splendid. I'll be back early afternoon."

Abby opened the door and he left. She shut the door, turned a key in the lock, sighed. Andrew gone. All this unexpected news. I'd have to hide in the house until he came home. I thought of options: a bedroom upstairs, the basement, the cupboard under the stairs. There were chances I would be caught, that Abby would even find me there under the table. She'd see me and scream, try to claw my face. My knuckles would bulge into fists and I'd smack skin with skin, tear Abby's mouth wide open, split lip and tongue. I'd keep her quiet about me.

Abby stood in the middle of the sitting room, stared towards the outside. My stomach cramped. She went to the window, pulled the lace aside and tapped on the glass. "You're rushing, Bridget," she yelled. "I expect you to do this properly." She dropped the curtain, walked towards the dining room and stopped. Abby cried, little shaky tears, everything to herself. The ceiling began a crack sound. It had to be Lizzie. My stomach cramped. I'd eaten pear, eaten mutton broth.

The ceiling cracked again and Abby looked up, went to the kitchen, her stomach in rumbles as she neared the counter. She took a johnnycake, held it like a paperweight. She bit, debris falling into the collar of her blouse. Abby brushed herself off, glanced at the floor, down at the mess I had made. "Where's this coming from?"

she said. Crumbs led her to the broth spill at the stove. I heard her stomach. She bent over, stuck her finger in the broth. I noticed her wedding ring tight on her finger. I could suck at a finger like that. How she grunted about.

Abby stood, shook her legs out, shook her worn leather boots and thick ankles. She had a tear at the bottom of her skirt. I thought women like her spent money on themselves.

"Bridget can't even keep the floors clean," she spat.

The ceiling cracked again and Abby looked up, followed the creaking above into the dining room, right close to the table and her legs quavered. She sniffed the air, said, "What on God's earth is that smell?" She went back to the kitchen. Sniff, sniff. She went into the sitting room. Sniff, sniff. I was giving myself away.

"Lizzie," Abby called out. "Lizzie, come down here."

A door opened upstairs and Lizzie descended the wooden stairs. She came into the sitting room, stood a distance from Abby, wore a blue dress underneath a long-sleeved white apron. My stomach cramped. Fruit doesn't do this to you.

"What?" Lizzie's voice a lick.

"Do you smell that horrid stink?"

Lizzie sucked in the air around her, exhaled. "I don't smell a thing."

"It's more in the kitchen, I think."

Lizzie entered the kitchen, took a breath. "I don't smell it."

"It's a smell of rotting or urine or . . ."

"You're probably smelling yourself."

"What a vile thing to say." Abby crossed her arm over her heart.

Lizzie shrugged. "I have no idea what you want me to say when I don't smell a thing." Lizzie had a snap to her.

For a time Abby said nothing and Lizzie took slow steps towards her, closed the gap. They watched each other. Then Abby said, "Why are you wearing an apron?"

Lizzie smoothed her hands over white, smiled. "Cleanliness is next to godliness, Mrs. Borden." She took a step closer and Abby's stomach rumbled.

"You been eating the mutton?" Lizzie asked.

"I've had some, yes." Abby was almost a whisper.

"Did you manage to leave me any?"

Abby scratched at her temples. "I assumed you'd already eaten."

"Why?"

"Someone's left mess all over the floor."

"Sure it wasn't you?"

I pressed my face hard against the wooden chair leg, smelled thick wood polish.

"You little pig." Abby was a reflex, slapped Lizzie across the cheek and mouth, drew blood.

Lizzie gave a small lip bite, tasted herself. She folded then unfolded her arms, pulled herself close to Abby, leaned in and kissed her on the mouth. Lizzie pressed hard into Abby, pushed her head slightly back. For a moment, Abby took it. Then Lizzie stepped away, wiped her lips on her apron, left behind a bloodstain. The women said nothing.

Lizzie walked away from Abby, went towards the front stairs. Up she went. Abby cried out, made a red-fox vixen scream like something being dragged from her, pressed her hands into her face, shook her head, no, no, no. She straightened herself, dried tears on her sleeve. I heard the buzz of a fly in my ear.

Abby walked to the front stairs, walked until I could hear her overhead. My stomach cramped and I rocked forward, gave a heave, had the mutton soup come out of me and onto the carpet. How it made my eyes water. The fly buzzed, landed in my vomit. I heard Lizzie and Abby speak, heard Abby say, "If you're going to stand there . . ." I heaved again and Lizzie spoke. The room spun, everything hot, and I held on to myself, and everything turned to dark.

———

I woke to blinding sun, tasted salt carpet on my tongue. How long had I been out? Outside, two children screamed on the sidewalk past the house, long echo laughs chasing one another. "Don't do that to your brother," a woman called. That way of being with a sibling. My lips turned a smile.

I was about to crawl from under the table when I saw Lizzie in an armchair in the sitting room. She slumped, sat leg-wide, made her skirt stretch into a tug of war, was lifeless-looking into the carpet. She'd removed her apron. Lizzie whispered to herself, little lisps of tongue over lip. How long had she been there? Had she seen me? Lizzie rubbed her forehead, tugged at her hair, kept quiet in a quiet house. My leg began to ache, tired from curling. Soon I'd have to move through the house. Lizzie reached into her lap, got out a half-eaten pear and sank her teeth into flesh. Sloppy-mouth. She bit again, pulled her feet together. Bite, she sat straight. Bite, she cracked her neck. Bite, she licked her lips, slurped herself into a smile.

Lizzie stood, went to the kitchen, and threw the pear into the sink. I crawled slow to the other side of the table, my hands dived into my own vomit. Cold, gravel-thick. What it took for me to stay silent. Lizzie pulled a spoon from a drawer, stuck it in her mouth, disappeared from sight. I could smell the deep pit of myself on my palms. Lizzie came back to view, raspberry jelly jar in hand, scooped her spoon deep into syrup fruit, made glass tink. Where had Abby gone? Lizzie ate jelly, emptied the jar and left it on the counter. She stretched her arms above her head and, like that, she left the kitchen and sometime later the side door opened, slammed shut. Lizzie was a strange little creature.

I crawled out from under the table, could hear Lizzie and Bridget speak in the yard, a mumble rush. With things the way they were, I couldn't stay in that part of the house. I'd be caught. Getting to the backyard without them catching me wouldn't be easy. I'd have to hide somewhere else in the house until Andrew came home. I headed to the front stairs, climbed up. Heat ate me like a crow. There was a dollop of syrup-red on the banister. I touched it, let it spread over fingertip then brought it to my mouth. I tasted fresh blood, the kind that sings. There was an open door to a room and I went inside, saw another red dollop on the doorjamb. I touched, brought fingers to mouth, tasted again. My cheeks recognized the tart metallic. I had tasted blood like this so many times before.

I stepped further inside, noticed something white lying by the radiator. I went closer, knew before I picked it up what it was. The underside piece of skull was colored blood, its flesh still holding on to strands of graying hair. I lifted it to my face, inhaled; a tiny scream inside my nose and mouth. Someone had been dealing out punishment without me. I looked over my shoulder, heat slapped me across the face and I dropped the bone to the floor. "What is going on?" Outside, the two children screamed, laughed.

I saw the bed then, a small spatter of blood on the white duvet cover, two neatly ironed pillow shams covering feather-down pillows, a chunk of plaited hair in the middle of the bed and, beside that, another piece of skull. The taste of metallic sulphur on my tongue. I slowed towards the bed, picked up the bone and held on to it. "My, my. What a treasure trove we have here." I leaned on the bed, felt the mattress depress underneath me. That's when I saw Abby lying face first on the ground, her body caught part way between the dressing table and bed.

Her body was shaped like an S, face buried in folded arms, legs straight, stiff. Blood haloed around her head, a thick red honey-stick in the carpet. I crawled off the bed and kneeled beside Abby, rocked her shoulders. My fingers sank into flesh and I stared at the back of her head. Thick cuts like tree roots led all the way to the beginning of brain. I stuck a finger inside one of the incisions. The cuts were ferocious, and I moved my fingers in and out of bone track, and wiped them on my trousers. Papa always said not to waste spilled blood.

I looked around the room, looked for clues as to who had sorted Abby out. I didn't like the idea that John might've asked someone else to help solve the family problem. Did Lizzie know Abby was there on the floor? I stroked Abby's back, thought of Mama. I looked at the bed, at the small piece of skull bone, and reached for it. It weighed the price of gold in my hand. I held it to my nose, breathed it in, smelled a hint of violet flower. I placed the skull bone inside my trouser pocket for safe keeping, to show John what had happened while he was gone.

———

I was at the top of the stairs when I heard Bridget and Lizzie speak.

"Miss Lizzie, have ya seen this? There's a terrible mess in the dinin' room." Bridget was quick.

"What are you talking about?"

"Someone's been sick all over!"

"Show me." Lizzie, like she was on a deer hunt.

I needed to find John, needed to find Andrew. I headed downstairs, through the banister caught sight of Abby, under the bed. I heard Bridget say, "I'm worried 'bout Mrs. Borden. What if this is her vomit?"

I wanted to call out, "She's here. She's dead." But I couldn't get myself caught.

"Perhaps it is," Lizzie said. "Perhaps she's been very sick."

"Let's go check on her."

"Oh, we can't. Mrs. Borden left. She had a note from an ill relative and she's gone to help."

"I didn't see anyone come," Bridget said.

"They came." Lizzie hesitated.

Voices trailed, a door opened.

I went down the stairs, my shoes, echoes, only to find empty rooms, no one in the piano room, no one in the sofa room, the dining room. No one in the cupboard under the stairs. Someone had made that blood upstairs, had made things complicated for me. It wouldn't be long before Abby was found, before police arrived. The time to deal with Andrew was running out.

The clock struck ten. Andrew would be home at one. I couldn't chance hours in the house. I'd have to stay in the barn. I headed for the basement, descended, and when I touched a foundation post, I felt something wet, slightly sticky. I tasted. It was Abby. Someone had taken her blood underneath the house. There was an itch inside me, one that wanted to hunt. I made calculations—police would arrive and would search the house, would search down here. I took towards the double doors that led to the backyard, grabbed and pulled. My luck—they were unlocked. I let them open a crack. I peered an eye outside. Lizzie was by the pear arbor, picking, eating, letting pear flesh fall to the ground. Time passed and she dropped the pear core, came towards the basement, made me quick-step behind the doors, push myself up against the wall. She walked by me, wiped her hand across her mouth, brought with her the smell of grass, of hard sweat, and didn't notice me at all. Lizzie went up the stairs and into the kitchen. I got myself out of the basement to the barn. I needed a good hiding place. A pigeon on the barn roof sounded and I looked up. That's when I saw the crawl space above the loft. Coffin length. I climbed the stairs then jumped up, pulled myself into the little space and rolled against the wall. Abby's skull piece dug into my leg.

———

I heard a woman wail morse code in the backyard. Scream, scream. Something unexpected. I wasn't sure I was hearing things right. Then a short time later there was brute panic outside. "Make them all stand back on the sidewalk. Don't let anyone onto the property."

"Yes, sir."

I writhed to the edge of the crawl space, saw the barn door was open. Someone had come in. I hunched myself down, took a look out the loft window. A crowd was gathering on the street, police paced up and down the side of the house.

I gave the window a little push, pigeons sounded in trees, and Bridget was escorted into the middle of the backyard by an officer, his hand a rock on her back. Bridget cried and the officer said, "Please take your time, but do tell me if you saw anyone follow Mr. Borden home."

She shook her head. "No, sir. I just let him in and then Lizzie called to me a short time later that someone had killed her father."

Someone killed Mr. Borden. This unexpected thing. What was going on in the house? John better not have changed his mind, done this by himself. I moved away from the window. I noticed the changes to the barn floor below—a lady's journal strewn on the ground, large boot prints, sections of dust wiped away. Someone had definitely been there. How had I not heard anything? The barn was the heat of sun-fire, and an officer yelled, "Stand back. Stand back."

I noticed small blood droplets patter along the floor of the loft towards an old, heavy blanket. I followed the trail and lifted the blanket: an ax head, blood-thick, was covered in tiny gray hairs, human moss. The metal had been snapped away from the handle, the piece annealing from use. "My, my, my." Underneath blood, underneath gray hair, two long strands of auburn hair. I picked up the ax head, smelled it. That caramel static stench. "My, my, my." Someone killed Abby. Someone killed Andrew. I'd have to keep the ax, take it to John, demand answers, demand my payment. I put the ax head in my trouser pocket.

Outside, voices. I took another look from the window, saw two police officers. One kicked the dead pigeon in the yard, the other helped himself to a pear from the arbor. He turned around. Blue-purple eye. I knew him, knew my work. The officer from yesterday. None of this was working to my favor. I jumped up, pulled myself back into the crawl space, lay on my stomach, found it hard to breathe. I thought about John. We'd have to have words. I listened to them all, listened to pigeons on the roof.

ELEVEN

BRIDGET

August 3, 1892

LATER THAT DAY I was sweeping the kitchen floor when I heard voices trail from the back stairs. Mr. and Mrs. Borden. I wondered if she had told him about me leaving, what he might think. It would be nothing for Mr. Borden to replace me. I was a girl among girls who had replaced a girl. But he would care about the money, would care that I had been receiving more than my worth.

I swept the floors, hunkered the broom underneath the stove, forced the straw bristles as far as they could, collected soot, collected black-green rot food scraps over the white-painted tiled floor. Out came a small piece of orange skin, hard and dried. I put the orange peel under my nose, bitter citrus. Someone had been feasting and I hadn't noticed. Eating in secret, burning the remains. Lizzie. This was something she would do. I sniffed the peel again. A memory of fruit.

Last summer when Mr. and Mrs. Borden went to the Swansea farm, Lizzie and Emma bought southern fruits from a Boston market. Orange, peach, apricot. The eating that had been done on the side steps. The smell of orange, burst juice tang, a dance for the tongue and nose. The way peaches wept down fingers, wet lips. The sisters bent over their parted knees, sat a way Mr. Borden would never allow. They slobbered the fruits, suckling babies. Emma had asked that I keep watch, make sure nosy neighbors wouldn't drop by for a visit. Oh, how I was happy to be outside, to be near deliciousness. Emma and Lizzie sat close together, their elbows hitting. They didn't seem to notice how their bodies knocked against one another.

"This is as good as the orange I ate in Rome," Lizzie said.

Emma rolled her eyes. "How many times are you going to bring that up?" They laughed, like sisters do. Like I had done with mine.

"Until I'm tired of talking about it." Lizzie grabbed another orange from the basket, dug her nails into the skin and ripped it open. Peel to the ground. It was a color rarely seen back home. Lizzie split the orange in half.

"Bridget, would you like some?" Juice, fingers.

"Are ya sure?"

Emma nodded. "Have you eaten one before?"

"Not really." In another house I worked, the lady there went through a southern mourning, wanting to go back to her Florida childhood. She got herself some oranges and I made her marmalade, made her Madeira cake. I licked orange peel and juice from my fingers, the closest I got to eating the fruit.

"Let us treat you," Lizzie said, the way you would to a guest at your manor home.

I took the orange and my teeth went in. It was like sour sugar. My fingertips were sticky. I ate it all.

"Have you been to Rome?" Lizzie asked.

"Lizzie, don't be rude." Emma wiped her mouth.

Lizzie gaped her mouth. "How is that rude? I'm making polite conversation."

"No, miss. I've not been anywhere 'cept home and America."

"Well, you could one day." Lizzie matter-of-fact.

"Lizzie . . ."

"She might marry a rich man." Lizzie grinned.

"Where do I meet 'em? Not in the kitchen." I laughed at that, at how Lizzie believed that someone from her walk of life would notice me.

The sun came through the tree canopy, was only a whisper on the shoulder. A small white dog ran past us down the street. The cotton mills steamed in the distance. The smell of fruit, a secret feast. I didn't question how they got the money for it. I licked my fingers, let the afternoon be.

There would be no summer fruit for me this time. The girls had kept it for themselves. Mr. and Mrs. Borden kept up their talking and I scooped up the dust and the mess in the dustpan, put it in the bin, threw the peel on top. The clock struck three thirty. Borden voices continued from upstairs and so I went towards them, one step at a time, quiet. It was Mr. Borden speaking as I neared their bedroom door.

"I dare say she won't keep another flock of pigeons again."

"When will you tell her?"

"Before long."

"Andrew, you should do it sooner. She'll be upset."

"They're pigeons! She can see them all over Fall River if she really misses them."

Lizzie had started collecting the dead flock in the fall, when she'd found a pigeon with a broken wing in the backyard. She'd asked me to fetch a small wicker basket and so I did. The bird was placed inside and she put the basket in her room. She cut long strips of her bedsheet, bandaged the wing.

Lizzie asked the father of one of her Sunday school pupils to build her a small aviary. Mr. Borden was not impressed. "You're inviting trouble. Get rid of it."

"No! Don't be savage. It'll be eaten alive out there."

The bird healed and the collecting began. It seemed easy to do: offer up food and wait to close the cage. The pigeons fattened and I thought about them in a pie. Every now and then she sang the morning to them, sang, "As the Lord liveth, there shall no punishment happen to thee for this thing," and she cooed and tweeted, cooed and tweeted.

"I don't want to even think about what she'll be like if any of them escape," Emma had said.

"It wouldn't be that bad, would it?" I asked.

Emma looked at me, like she was seeing right inside. "You don't know my sister."

Back behind closed doors Mrs. Borden told her husband, "I just don't think you should let it be a surprise."

"Like finding out John is visiting."

"I hadn't a clue, Andrew." Mrs. Borden's defences were up.

"That child has a nerve sometimes."

"You can't stop them from seeing family."

"He doesn't feel like that anymore."

"Being angry won't help."

I waited on the back stairs a little longer, waited to hear my name, waited to hear Mrs. Borden's anger, but there was nothing more and so I gave up, headed back to the kitchen. A turning of a key, the sound of a shoe kicking the bottom jamb of the front door as it opened. I stuck my head around the corner, saw Lizzie come into the house, remove white gloves, hang her parasol in the cupboard under the front stairs. I moved to the sitting room, said, "Hello, Miss Lizzie."

"Hello." Not a smiling face.

"Somethin' the matter, miss?"

"Nothing. It's hot is all." Her cheeks were red, rounded like apples.

"Would ya like me ta fetch ya water?"

"Sure." The way she said things, all dour. Lizzie was on the down. I got her water, got her a slice of fruitcake for extra. I handed her the water, held onto the plate. "Are Father and Mrs. Borden here?"

"Yes."

"Where are they?"

I jerked my head towards the back of the house. "In their room."

"Now I'll have to listen to them all afternoon while I'm in mine." Sweat beaded along her hairline. Where had she been?

"Maybe ya could go in Emma's room?"

"I'm not going to be cooped up in that shoebox."

"Sorry, miss."

She looked at me and gulped her glass of water, didn't stop for breath.

After she finished she said, "Bridget, do you have by any chance any prussic acid?"

"I'm thinkin' I don't, miss. Why?"

"I need some for my seal-fur cape. I was thinking while we've suitable heat I might clean it, dry it outside."

Lizzie wasn't great at cleaning such delicate things. Oh, she'd ruin it, then I'd have to fix everything. "Ya should see the pharmacist."

Her eyebrows laced together. "Don't you think I would've thought of that already?"

"Yes, miss."

Lizzie snatched the plate of cake from my hands. "You're no use to me."

She took herself up the stairs, slammed her bedroom door.

The door opened again. "You've left your garbage in my room."

The rags, the bucket. I'd forgotten. "Feck," I whispered. I ran up the stairs.

Lizzie filled the doorframe. "Why were you in my room?"

I took a step in, thought she would move. Our shoulders touched. "Mrs. Borden asked me ta dust. I knew ya'd not like it but she wouldn't listen." I hated being this close.

"She's impossible." Lizzie stood her ground. We shared breath.

"Then yer uncle knocked while I was up 'ere and I forgot all 'bout it."

Lizzie brightened. "Uncle's here?"

"Earlier, while ya were out. He said he'll be back this evenin'." The sun moved across the roof, cast a shadow in the room.

Lizzie shoved me away from her, clapped her hands. "Oh, goody." She smiled too wide for her own face.

She let me inside and I got the rags and bucket. I looked at the white aprons on her swooning sofa. She saw me. "I've got many things to do."

"Okay." I looked at the aprons again, couldn't help it. What was she going to do with them?

"Tell them I shan't be down until much later."

She pushed on my shoulders, got me out of the room, shut the door.

———

Evening. I went about my night-time jobs. Mr. Borden sat on the sofa, talked of how his neck and shoulder ached. "It's like a long cramp," he told Mrs. Borden, rolled his neck from side to side. She sat next to him, put her hands on the sore spot. "Does it hurt when I do this?"

"No."

She kneaded him, her fingers in the dough of his skin. "Does it hurt when I do this?"

"A little bit."

She kept kneading and Mr. Borden said nothing, closed his eyes and grimaced. I could've told him he had wood-chop neck, the pain from felling birds, the pain like my daddy would get from working farms, chopping wood for fires, the pain like my brothers had from blacksmithing. The way you fix that pain is to never begin in the first place. Oh, but the things that are done.

I kept at setting the dining table, polishing cutlery extra careful till I could see myself in the back of spoons, the pitches of forks. I'd catch the sight of Mr. Borden with his hand on Mrs. Borden's knees. It almost hung there, like a mistake, but Mrs. Borden didn't shoo him away and she kept kneading. "It might be time for you to see Dr. Bowen," Mrs. Borden said.

"Perhaps you're right. Perhaps I'll see him tomorrow morning."

They agreed into each other, Mrs. Borden murming, murming, Mr. Borden clearing his throat and nodding. I was done with everything in the dining room and came out to tell them so.

"Ask Lizzie to join us," Mr. Borden said.

I thought of his slapping her, did not want to bring anyone down to that again.

He cleared his throat. There was something about his eyes, something that made him look like he wasn't there. It put a chill in my back. I got myself busy then, went to the kitchen and took a pot of mutton broth off the stove, ladled into earthenware bowls. It was when I was about to head upstairs to fetch Lizzie that there was a knock at the front door. My stomach dropped and I prayed that I wouldn't be asked to answer it. I heard the knock again, and Mrs. Borden said, "That's him."

"Perhaps he'll have had a busy afternoon and not care to talk all night," Mr. Borden said.

"I hope so."

I heard Mrs. Borden pepper off to the entrance and open the door.

John's voice filled the house and after they were done with niceties, the door closed and they came into the sitting room.

"Andrew!" John stuck out his arm for a handshake.

Mr. Borden was slow to take it, said, "John."

"It's been a while."

"Yes."

"I trust you're well?"

"Yes."

They kept the handshake going.

"Let us get your coat, John," Mrs. Borden said before asking me to come out from the kitchen.

Out I came and John smiled at me. I saw his teeth, something caught between them, and he kneeled down to my height, made me take his jacket from his shoulders. They kept speaking while I hung the jacket up and on the way back through the sitting room, from the corner of my eye I thought I saw something outside. I looked towards the window, saw the evening begin to black through the glass, saw all four of us reflected, saw Mr. Borden step away from John and wipe his hand along his trousers. I went to press against the window, saw nothing out there and so I stood about, waited to be told what my next move would be.

"I trust you had a pleasant afternoon, John?" Mrs. Borden asked.

"I always do. Although, sadly, I didn't get around to carrying out all my business."

"What exactly are you doing in town?" Mr. Borden showed his teeth.

"This and that. You know how it is."

"Man of secrets, are you?"

John laughed, Mr. Borden stared him down.

"You must be famished, John. Come and have supper," Mrs. Borden said.

"You spoil me, Abby."

Mrs. Borden blushed.

"Just like my sister did." John smiled at her and she eyed the carpet, shrank into herself.

"Yes, well, come along and let us feed you."

She looked at me then, said, "Bridget, take care of everything, will you?"

"Yes, marm."

They moved into the dining room. I heard a thump against the sitting room window, cupped my hands against the glass and looked out. I half expected to see a ghost. I saw nothing. "Pshaw," I said. "Mind's playin' tricks on me." Into the dining room I went. Not a one sitting close to the other. John was all elbows on the table.

"What took you so long?" Mrs. Borden asked me.

"I thought I saw somethin' out the window."

"What was it?" Mr. Borden asked.

"Nothin', I don't think. I couldn't see much."

"You're imagining things." John smiled, the way he did.

"No, I don't think I was." It came out strong. I know what I see, what I hear.

Mr. Borden cleared his throat, like he was scraping the sides of it with a knife.

"I'm sorry," I said. I went about serving what they wanted. Mr Borden, mutton broth, bread; John, mutton broth, bread; Mrs. Borden, a slice of cake, two butter biscuits. All of them a cup of tea. The slurping, the chewing, digging into my ear. I stood against the wall, waited.

"Business doing well?" John asked.

"Yes," Mr. Borden said.

"How so?"

Mr. Borden took a mouthful of broth, was red in the face. "Don't be crossing lines, John."

"Dear Andrew, I wouldn't dream of it. Simply making conversation." John gripped Mr. Borden's forearm. "We're family. I'd never want to upset."

Mr. Borden pulled away. "All the same, my business is my business."

"Of course."

They went about their eating. My underthings clung to my sweating places. I did not care to know any of this. I looked at Mrs. Borden, wondered where she had put my money tin. Mrs. Borden breathed out and in through her mouth, the way she does when she stands by my side as I cook, when she doesn't like how I go about adding too many herbs, makes me get that uneasy feeling. Mr. Borden dug his spoon into the broth, clanged it against the earthenware bowl, clanged so loud that I thought he'd dig on through to the table, dig a hole big enough to throw John inside. I pushed myself into the wall harder than before, my feet cracking the floorboards. The three of them slowly eyed me, as if I had just told them that I'd laced their meal with poison.

"Don't you have something better to do? Go fetch Lizzie," Mr. Borden said.

"I thought she could stay on, help us with our dinner." Mrs. Borden scratched her temples and Mr. Borden made knuckles, rocked them back and forth on the table, and I said, "I can wait close by if ya need me."

She frowned. I couldn't tell anger or sadness. I did not care to find out. I was out the room then, almost skipped out, closed the door behind me. I heard them talking a little, closed my ear to them, and I went to the parlor, got the idea that perhaps Mrs. Borden had hid my money there. I lighted an extra kerosene lamp, coughed away the fumes and began searching. On hands and knees I crawled the room, checked under the low sofa, saw nothing but a taffy wrapper. I fished the wrapper out, rubbed my thumb and finger over the wax paper, held it against my nose. Butter, molasses. The soft comfort. Lizzie had been treating herself again. I put the wrapper in my apron pocket, kept searching. There was nothing under sofas, nothing behind the calico and velvet cushions, nothing inside the upright piano, nothing in this room they kept for appearances. I moved to the cupboard underneath the stairs, opened it, shined the lamp right inside and spread apart the coats. There was no tin and I started to feel a shame for looking, that Mrs. Borden had made me act like a gutter thief, had made me feel that wanting to leave was the most traitor act. I spread the coats back to rightful places, took a little feel of the first Mrs. Borden's fur coat that Emma and Lizzie still kept in the cupboard. The brown fur was coarse, reminded me of stray dogs. I shut the cupboard, heard Lizzie's bedroom door open, heard her feet huffing right down the stairs, all the way down to me at the bottom.

"What are you doing?" She pointed a stubby finger in my direction.

"I've lost somethin'. Just lookin' for it in places."

"Better not let Mrs. Borden see. She'll think you're stealing."

"I'm sure she already thinks it."

Lizzie smiled. "Oh, Bridget. Aren't you her favorite anymore?"

"It's nothin'."

She came towards me as if she were creeping about. "Where are they?"

"They're in the dinin' room. Yer uncle is with 'em."

Lizzie looked past me, suckered her lips tight. "What are they discussing?"

"I tried not listenin'."

"Come on, give me something." Her dull blue eyes looked right inside me, like she could wrench it out. I didn't want her to touch me and so I told her, "Yer uncle asked 'bout yer father's business."

She clapped her hands. "Ha! That ought to start things up." Lizzie was bright, seemed to lighten in her body.

We headed through the sitting room and Lizzie asked me to fetch her a bite to eat. "I don't want broth. Anything but that dirty old mutton you've been reheating all week."

"Yes, Miss Lizzie." Nobody should have to eat that dirty old mutton.

She pulled at herself, straightened her skirt, fixed her collar, ran her tongue over teeth and went into the dining room, made the room break into welcome.

"Darling Lizzie!" John said.

"Hello, Uncle."

A chair was pulled out, legs dragged on the carpet, made me cringe, and I went to the kitchen and set about making Lizzie supper. I could hear them talking, mostly Lizzie, all her daily travels.

"I bumped into Mrs. Hinkley today, Father."

"Oh, yes?"

"She asked me to read to her."

Cutlery clinked.

"That's wonderful, Lizzie," Mrs. Borden said.

"Anyway, I told her yes and so I'll be doing that of an evening." Lizzie was hoity.

"Who's Mrs. Hinkley?" John asked.

"She's from church. She's an old lady losing her sight," Lizzie said.

"Her father made money from the war. A wealthy family," Mr. Borden said.

Cutlery clinked.

"I see," John said.

"Well, she happens to think I'm good company."

"Has she heard you read?" Mr. Borden said.

"Father!"

"You've been known to stumble on words, be slow." Mr. Borden sounded like he was enjoying himself, like he'd been storing up days of meanness.

"I'm perfectly capable."

I shook my head. Whole bloody family was crazy. I thought of leaving right there and then. But Mrs. Borden had my tin. She'd got me good. I cut bread into thick slices, slathered on butter and raspberry jam, had a teaspoon myself. The taste reminded me of Nanna, her standing in our kitchen at home, her singing "The Rovin' Girl" as she stirred raspberry and sugar in the preserve pot, made jam that got your tongue bursting with happiness. Nanna cooking, Nanna singing, me dancing around the kitchen, bumping into her as I joined in and sang, "And there she came up over that hill, her rovin' heart still beatin' true. I bless the day I got to say, 'My girl came home with the love that once was mine.'"

Before I went back into the Bordens I had another teaspoon of jam. I deserved it. I put everything on a serving tray, held my breath and made my way to the dining room.

They were still talking about Lizzie's new job. "Well I for one think it's wonderful you're caring for someone in the community," John said. "Charity begins at home, they say."

Mr. Borden said, "Of course. As long as Lizzie doesn't become sidetracked."

Lizzie gave Mr. Borden a mighty fine dirty look. "By what?"

"Just remember what does and does not belong to you." Mr. Borden raised his spoon in the air, Lizzie clasped hands on the table. I put her plate in front of her, poured her tea, poured them all tea. It was thick in there, made it hard to breathe. Lizzie breathed rapid hot. She took a bite of jammed bread, dripped a little on the tablecloth. She was always making me clean more. I went to leave the room when Mrs. Borden said, "Won't you stay?" I tensed, my neck pinched, made my jaw feel like it'd been hit with a hammer.

"What on earth for?" Mr. Borden said, saved me from an evening with them.

"We may need extra things," she said.

"It's alright, Mrs. Borden. Ya can fetch me if ya should need me."

Mrs. Borden's face prickled up like a horned melon, her lips tight and pale. She could do nothing but nod yes. Oh, I smiled big at her. I got out of there, left them stewing.

———

I went looking for my tin along the small crevices leading up to the attic. It was hot upstairs, sweat beaded under my hair. I took my bonnet off, fanned my face with it. I thought to check Mr. and Mrs. Borden's bedroom. I turned the handle, knew it would be locked but did it anyway. Some things need proving, some things need trying. Locked. I came out onto the landing, pressed my head against the window, looked into the thick night. I wanted to be out there, wanted the ringing of crickets in my ear, wanted to be walking, going no place in particular, just me on my own, maybe even me and Mary. We could happen across a friend, two friends, their friends, smelling of hot tobacco, of kitchens and yards. We would take to some of Fall River's back alleys, to the places where you could gamble some, dance some like we were in Ireland, back at the crossroads on a Sunday after church. We'd talk about that, how we missed it, a fiddler tickling strings, us being out in the fresh air, the kicked-up dirt road in our eyes, on our tongues, shoes cobbling leather against one another, tap, tap, tap, ankle, toe, ankle, toe, the fiddler mustering the winds to whip us up good, us dancing faster, us laughing, us alive. Mary and me in the alleyways of Fall River. She was the best to dance with, the way she'd hook right under your arm, all tight, and make you feel like you could fly. "Swing me round again!" I'd say and Mary would. I could kiss Mary for making me forget about the Bordens from time to time. Often I would, sloppy on her cheeks, just like a sister.

A thunderclap of doors slamming. Oh, I felt that through the window. I pulled back, put my bonnet back on. Another door echoed and the house shuddered. There'd be no more searching for my tin tonight. Downstairs I found Mr. and Mrs. Borden in the sitting room, all quiet, him on the sofa, she on the chair near the window.

"Where did you go?" Mrs. Borden asked. She looked me over, tried to find a secret on me.

"I took to me room, marm."

She said nothing. What could she? I eased on in, went to the dining room, began to stack the dishes. I got to wondering where John and Lizzie were. Lizzie had left behind more jam, had breadcrumbs on her seat. I brushed them off into my hand, put the crumbs in my pocket. Taking dishes to the scullery, I noticed the door to the basement open, watched Lizzie come, a storm. She looked like she'd been crying and she blew by me and walked into the sitting room. "I'm going to see Alice Russell," she hogged.

"It's getting on," Mr. Borden said.

"You've not worried about that in the past, Father."

I heard her open the cupboard under the stairs, move a hanger, close the cupboard again. Out she went through the front door, made a little earthquake inside.

"You need to talk to her about the way she shuts the door, Andrew."

"Hmmm."

I took a wet cloth, poked back into the dining room and began wiping everything down. The Bordens were quiet, the way they had become. I could never get used to the hot and cold rhythm of the house, could never trust it. Mammy and Daddy, always the chattering kind, always talking of feelings, always knowing where things stood. Good or bad. That's what I was used to. Mr. and Mrs. Borden were so quiet that I could hear John breathe his way up the basement stairs and it was then that I knew he'd been outside and that Lizzie must've been there with him. I did not care to know their conversations. John stood at the dining room door, watched me.

"You've missed a spot, Bridget." He pointed to Lizzie's chair leg.

"Oh."

"Would hate for you to attract flies. They're so difficult to get rid of."

There were many other things difficult to get rid of.

From the sitting room Mr. Borden said, "Would you care to join us, John?"

He moved in and I checked over the chair leg. The tiniest of jam. I went to wipe it down, stopped myself. If Mrs. Borden was going to punish me by taking my tin, I'd leave it be, see what the sweetness would attract. I stopped my head in the door to the sitting room.

"Sorry to be interruptin', marm, but I'll do the dishes and be done for the night."

"Thank you, Bridget."

John sat himself across from Mrs. Borden, stretched his legs and stroked his short beard. She eyed him, pulled her arm across her stomach. "Actually, if you'll excuse me, gentlemen, I'm afraid I'm feeling poorly and need to retire." She stood.

"What a shame, Abby. I was looking forward to having a last cup of tea with you."

"I'm sure we can do so tomorrow."

"Yes, I'm sure we can."

Mrs. Borden called me back in. "Bridget, before you finish, you may like to see Mr. Borden and Mr. Morse have what they need."

"Yes, marm."

She went to Mr. Borden, kissed him on the forehead, the way you do when proving loyalty, and he patted her hand, didn't watch her leave the way John did. I was left on my own to ask, "Can I get you anything?"

Mr. Borden: "No."

John: "I wouldn't mind biscuits for my room."

I nodded, went to the scullery and got what was asked, plated shortbreads and took them to the guest room. The men talked, and I could hear their low voices carry up the stairs.

"Been to the farm lately?"

"I got the chance a few weekends ago."

"The girls go with you?"

"Yes."

"Good to get them that fresh air."

"Yes."

"Might you consider moving to the Hill? Away from the thicker smoke down here?"

"Things are fine here on this side of Fall River, thank you, John. I'm sure they've grown strong lungs over the years."

"Of course."

When I'd finished up for the night, washed up in the scullery, I went to Mr. Borden, in the room alone at that point. "I'm done for the night. Is there anythin' you'll need?"

He smoothed his hands on his legs, stretched out his fingers. "No."

I noticed a gray feather on his elbow. "Mr. Borden, ya've somethin' on ya." I pointed and he looked, picked it off and held the feather between his fingers.

"I thought I got them all." He then stared at me, like a boy in trouble.

"Once there are feathers . . ."

"Yes, yes. They stick around." He looked back at the feather. "Perhaps I shouldn't have done it."

The birds, the ax. He knew I knew. I got a sick feeling. "I'm sure ya had yer reasons, Mr. Borden."

"I'll have to explain."

"Daddy always told me nothin' was ever too late."

He nodded. I left him there, went up the back stairs, heard Mrs. Borden in her bedroom weep a little. I thought of stopping to help her, but she'd made me so mad. I left her alone, kept going to my room. I got in and locked the door behind me, felt the need to do that. I sat on the bed, changed into my nightie. The day I'd had. I didn't care to face another here. I turned my lamp off, huddled down into bed, listened to the night, to the house.

TWELVE

BENJAMIN

August 4, 1892

I HID IN the crawl space all afternoon, heard the rise and fall of voices from the street, felt my skin bubble then melt from the heat. I heard the police walk in and out of the barn like lost children.

"Did we check the loft?"

"Yes, when we first arrived."

"They said she mentioned pears . . ."

"I found a pear core outside, but not in here."

"Chief wants us to find the weapon."

"What makes him think the killer didn't take it with him? Where do you suppose one hides something like that around here?"

"Beats me. I'm still trying to understand how no one heard anything. Not a scream, not a thing."

"Sounds odd, if you ask me."

Their inexperience was almost quaint. I wanted to tell them, "You would be surprised at how little noise can be made at the end of a life."

"Should we take one more look around?" an officer asked.

"Sure. We're not going to find anything, but sure."

The officers were lazy. They limp-scuttled the ground floor of the barn, picked up piles of cloth or wood before throwing them down and declaring, "Nothing spectacular here." They left. I got that electric-feel across the skin, the type that made me want to jump down, run out to the officers and tell them, "You want to see something amazing? Look at this ax head I found." I was bored from stillness. I wanted them to try to take the ax head from me, touch me in some way. As soon as a finger lay on me, my jaw would lash towards them. I would take a bite of flesh and I would hit them. I wanted to do these things because I could no longer do them to Andrew.

Pigeons walked across the roof. A cloud moved overhead, darkened light. I lay and I thought. How was I going to get my money so I could go back south, finish off Papa? I would have to have words with John, like someone had had words with Andrew.

After a time, footsteps filled the barn. I rolled myself to the crawl space ledge, peered an eye. John stood there, a pear in hand, and said in a lowered voice, "Benjamin, you in here?"

I propped onto elbows. "Yes."

John came further into the barn, looked up. "How long you been there?"

"A while."

"Has anyone seen you? Did Lizzie see you?"

"No one saw me. Things got hectic."

John took a bite of the pear, sharp crunch of flesh. "Tell me, when did you decide to kill Abby?"

The way he accused me like that, like I'd break our agreement. "I didn't."

He laughed. "I never suspected you a modest fellow." He laughed at me some more, riled a snarl lip from me. He took a bite from the pear, coughed. I would've liked him to choke.

"There was someone else in the house."

John stilled himself. "Did you get a look at him?"

"I thought you knew who it was."

"No." John went to the barn door, poked his head out, came back in. "I only ever wanted you to deal with Andrew."

"Someone got to them first," I said.

"You know I requested everything to be discreet. There are police everywhere."

I swung my legs over the ledge, sat up as best I could, hunched back and head. "I stayed true to my word."

"Really? Because we have two dead bodies in there . . ."

"See what I found." I held up the bloodied ax head, the piece of skull.

John paled. "The hell?"

"I found the ax in here under a blanket. And this."

"Put that away." John waved his arm, like drowning.

"Abby's head? Don't you want to take a closer look?"

John wiped his eyes. "If you didn't do it, who did?"

"Am I going to get paid?"

He looked at me, rotten core. "I beg yours?"

"I was promised payment."

John pointed a finger. "You've a nerve, you pitiful thug."

"Fair is fair, John. There are a lot of police out there. I could show them what I have."

"No one would believe you! They'd think you did it."

"We've been seen together."

"Is this a threat?"

"Yes." I smiled, showed teeth.

There were two loud voices coming closer to the barn. I swung my legs, rolled myself to the wall, flattened out of sight. The barn door opened.

"Hello, officers," John said. Grimy politeness.

"Mr. Morse. Didn't expect to see you here," the first officer said.

"Simply wanting to stay out of your way." He bit pear.

"We're here to have another search around the barn," the second officer said.

"Is that necessary?"

"Yes. It's part of a crime scene."

There was the sound of metal moving, of things being lifted and dropped.

"A lot of farming equipment here," the second officer said.

"Andrew kept the family supplies here," John said.

"They're farmers?"

"Andrew owns farm land over in Swansea. A hobbyist, you might say."

"Why not keep the tools over there?"

"I suppose Andrew liked to work around the house too."

"An elderly man laboring?"

"He had help, of course."

Objects were moved around.

"Do you know if anyone had any malice towards Mr. Borden? Perhaps the help?"

"You'd have to ask Miss Lizzie. I rarely visit enough to know."

"Of course." The officer paused. "But do you think it's likely?"

"In my experience, Mr. Borden was a solid man."

"Are you aware of any trouble around the house? Anything untoward?"

There were many things untoward.

John was quiet for a moment. Then, "I recall Lizzie did tell me about the daylight robbery last year . . ."

"Yes, that's been mentioned."

"Unfortunately, and given the circumstances today, one might think the family has been cruelly targeted for their money." John bit the pear. I thought of his sliver tongue licking sugar juice. I could taste a set-up. "Nothing like pears in the heat," John said.

"I find them too sickly," the first officer said. "Lizzie mentioned there's fishing equipment in here."

"Oh, yes," John said. I heard the pear drop on the ground, then a rattle of a tin box. "Here you are." The tin was opened, looked through.

"Nothing suspicious here," the second officer said.

They were quiet for a time, then the first officer said, "Tell me, is that a crawl space above the loft?"

Blood pumped through my body, made me shake. If they found me, could I take them all?

I heard John clear his throat. "I'm sorry?"

"Is that a crawl space above the loft?"

"Why?" John said.

"It seems like one."

"Oh, that. It's nothing."

"I think I'll take a look."

"Probably best you don't," John said.

"Why's that?"

"I'd say you'd have a hard time fitting through the hole. Not meant to fit anything in it really." John cleared his throat.

"How do you know?"

"I helped build this barn. Andrew and I were going to make another level but he decided it was unnecessary. I'm afraid in the end all we managed to build was an expensive brooding hut for pigeons." John laughed.

"I think I'll take a look-see anyway."

"Don't believe me, Officer?" John said.

"No, sir, nothing like that. I just think I should be thorough."

"It might be dangerous for you." John on the edge of pleading would make things worse for me.

"How so?"

John was quiet before saying, "Unsound structures. I doubt Andrew paid upkeep on this barn. I'd hate for you to hurt yourself."

There was silence for a time, then the officer said, "Perhaps we'll send for a builder to check over the structure before I climb up."

"Yes," John said. "But wouldn't it take some time?"

"We'll send for someone, ask them to come as soon as they can."

"If you think that's best," John said.

"I just want to be thorough."

"Of course."

"You've been most helpful, Mr. Morse."

"Good. I'm happy to assist with the investigation."

The men left. I could feel the ax head against my skin, the lovely sharpness. I pulled myself up, unfurled ratchet limbs, crack, crack, and it occurred to me that John might have saved me. But I was owed money. I wasn't done asking John questions. I was going back into that house. I wanted to see if the killer had left anything behind.

———

Night carved out the moon. Things became quiet. I crawled towards the barn window and stared out onto a glowing house. A few police officers lined the perimeter and looked bored. One chewed fingernails, spat out his relics onto the grass.

I kept watch on the house, people went in and out of rooms, kerosene lamps dimmed one by one. I waited until the police officers headed towards the front before turning my lamp on. I was out the barn then, night air, an owl hoot, the sound of horses" hooves. Into the basement I went. No need for locked doors now. There was the smell of wet clothing, of urine and fungus. I took a breath, climbed the stairs like a mountaineer. I was back inside the kitchen. The clock on the mantel struck eleven. I walked through the house. In the parlor, a lamp ached, the oily thick smell filled the house from the top down. My head buckled from the fumes. I went to the dining room door, opened it, entered the room limb by limb. A smell of rotting. I lifted the lamp high and there on the dining table: two bodies, solid masses. There were small rounds of dried bloodstains on white sheets, outlines of cavernous skulls. When I was younger, Grandpappy died. Gangrene. Papa had said, "He shoulda let the doctor saw his leg off." I tried to understand how removing a limb could save a life. Papa forced me to stay with Grandpappy's body. "It'll get you used to this stuff."

"But what if he wakes up?"

"Boy, you should know by now that dead is dead. You ain't wakin' from nothin'."

I sat next to Grandpappy's infected body and tasted gangrene on the tongue, foul, rotted fat.

I went to the bodies on the table. I wanted to see what the ax had done to Andrew's body. I lifted the sheet, a set of nakedness, and looked Andrew over, thin-limbed, liver-spotted skin. His stomach had been cut open, loosely catgutted shut, the stitching across his abdomen neater than my leg. He gave off old man stench, unwashed, used up. His time would've come soon anyway. I went closer to him, dragged a finger over his chest. I expected him to breathe in, breathe out. There was blood on his neck, blood in his beard, blood where half his face used to be.

"Andrew," I whispered, "you made someone very angry."

He was a mess of a man. I imagined Papa on the table, him all crushed up. How angry I'd have to be to do that.

I left Andrew alone, went to Abby, placed my hands on her bare feet. Dead cold, callused, rough-skinned. I massaged her feet and in between toes there was a blister, liquid full. I squeezed the blister and it wept.

"You like that, Abby?" I said. Her toenails were unclipped and they cut into my fingertips as I massaged. "Weren't much of a society woman, were you?"

But I liked the way her skin felt around the ankle: Mama-soft. The way Papa never was. "Tell me, who gave you a talking-to?" I was ready to take that person on.

I left the bodies, made my way to the front stairs, through the sitting room with its damp-carpet stench, through to the entry way where I saw a black hat hanging on a rack, walked to the bottom of the stairs, smoothed my hand over the banister. I climbed. I climbed the stairs, headed to the room where I'd found Abby and opened the door, looked in. John asleep in the bed, his mouth wide open.

I went into the room, sat on the bed. "John," I said. "Wake up." John breathed deep, shifted in bed. I heard a noise come from another room. I'd come for John later.

I opened the door to the next room, was hit with the smell of violet and washed skin; a white bookshelf filled with leather-bound and hardcover books; a wooden dressing table, hairbrush, comb, lace gloves; a free-standing mirror; rumple of clothes on the ground; Lizzie sleeping. I watched her chest rise and fall; an ocean tide. I should ask her some questions.

I moved towards her. The ax head pressed against my leg. There was the sound of a bed creaking in another room. Lizzie rolled onto her side and I bent down close. John had been so worried that she'd see me, see what I was going to do in the house. But I'd seen how she was with Abby. Lizzie was no whimper. She'd found her dead father. I wondered if she'd seen who did it.

"Tell me," I whispered. "Did you get a good look?"

"Yes." Lizzie whispered dream-talk.

"What did they do?"

"Father."

I wanted what was mine, I was going to tell Lizzie some home truths. Starting with John. "I saw you today. Your uncle sent me."

Lizzie breathed, a dragon.

"He asked me to talk to your father."

"Father."

"Yes." I leaned closer. "John said there were problems."

Lizzie smacked her lips together.

"But I never got a chance. Now I'm concerned he won't pay me my money. Do you know how important money is?"

"Money," she whispered.

"Get it for me."

I got so close to her face, could feel my breath bounce off her skin. "Tell me who you saw, Lizzie. Was it John?"

Lizzie. "Saw Abby."

"I saw her too."

A bed creaked. Lizzie let out a sore-dog yelp and she opened her eyes, ballooned them wide and turned her face, stared at me. The scream that was made was made again. I stood in a flash, heard someone turn a key in a lock and I ran out of the room. I got to the stairs, saw John standing in the doorway of his room, saw him retreat back inside, and I ran through the house, out through the side door and towards the street.

Somewhere a dog barked. I took off down Second Street, past a police officer, heard footsteps behind me. I quickened, the footsteps quickened.

The ax head thunked against my thigh, made me bleed.

I found myself walking train tracks towards a freight train. My shoes slipped in between the sleepers and track, made it difficult for me to move quickly. A train whistle. I lugged my feet, walked across the thick lines of hard track metal and climbed inside a carriage. The train moved. Everything ached. I wanted to sleep. The train gained momentum. Fall River had been a bust. I put my hand in my pocket, felt the goodies. So many things left unfinished. The train went on and I noticed blood on my hands. I licked my fingers, licked them clean. Someone in that house had lied to me, I thought. One day I'd come back, get what was owed.

THIRTEEN

LIZZIE

August 4, 1892

BY THE TIME night fell, Emma and I had offered a reward for the capture of Father's murderer. Emma had complained that the amount was too much, too showy.

"You sound just like him," I said.

Emma shook her head, upturned a lip. "Why would you say that?"

"I think it shows how much we care."

"Money doesn't prove anything." She was loud.

"Of course it does! The Borden name means something in Fall River. We should do this right."

Emma threw her hands out in front of her. "Enough," she said. "I just want them to find the person who did this and be done with it." Emma's hideous desire for answers made my heart beat faster. She made my teeth want to sink into her flesh and eat her out of my life, made me want to swarm her mind and sort through all the thoughts she had of me, that I was being too stubborn, I was being too secretive, I was being bad, I was, I was. I felt her nastiness crawl over my skin, tiny deaths that made me want to become nothing. Emma sat boulder strong, eyed me like a parent seeing their child misbehave for the first time and not liking any of it. The same look Mrs. Borden gave me from time to time.

Emma tilted her head, mouthed a small-breath whisper then shook her head. "I can't believe no one saw or heard anything."

"What are you saying?"

Emma shrugged, was defeated. "I don't know. Nothing."

A weight dropped through my stomach, perforated holes along muscle. Were other people watching me like this? Thinking like this? My palms ached, became small deserts. I rubbed them together, newly formed calluses bonding. Why was my truth so hard to believe? The police had asked question, question, question, had written my words down like gospel. When Emma came home, the police threw information at her, *I bet that's why she's like this with me*, made her think things. Sitting there, Emma looked exactly the way Mrs. Borden had in the morning, stalking me around the house, shadow of shadow.

I felt like sinking. All day I had made sure I was the daughter Father raised, had answered questions. There had been a moment after lunch when I overheard two officers ask, "How much time would you want to spend alone in a house where you found your murdered father?"

"Maybe Miss Borden didn't run out of the house because she knew someone would eventually come and be with her."

"Or she felt she was in no danger."

"What type of madman would stick around waiting to kill someone else? Miss Borden probably didn't even consider herself a potential victim."

My blood jumped. It wasn't right to make a grieving child feel that way, that somehow they were responsible for death, *does this mean they will come for me?*

Emma rubbed her face. None of this would've happened if she hadn't left me in the house.

"Do you think they're close to finding a suspect?" I said.

"I don't know. I don't know how any of this works." Emma unfolded and folded her hands in front of her, begging.

"What will they do to the killer when they catch them?"

"I guess they'll have a trial."

"And if they're guilty?"

She leaned towards me, let her mouth gorge wide before saying, "They will be hanged."

"Does that always happen?" Heat swamped over my body, made my mind spiral then collapse.

"Do we have to talk about this now?"

"I'm worried, that's all."

"How about you worry about the fact Father died." Her voice a scream.

There was a pop in the middle of my ear. It crawled out and lunged at the walls of the house. A window shook. Emma pulsed in her chair, threw a hand over her mouth and closed her eyes. "I'm sorry," she said. "I don't want to be angry with you."

"Why are you?" I heard my voice sound out like small pebbles across floorboards. I didn't like the way Emma watched me.

"Why don't I get you some tea?" Emma stood.

"Get Bridget to do it."

Emma tied her fingers together, said, "Bridget left us."

"Why? What did you do to make her leave?" I thought Bridget would like it more now things had changed.

Emma gave me a blank, dirty look, went to the kitchen without saying another word about it. The clock on the mantel ticked ticked. I ran my hand over the wallpaper then my chair; felt the sticky coating of Mrs. Borden's cream cake. I rubbed my finger over my teeth, tasted remains of days'-old entertaining.

When I was ten, I used to like it when Father and Mrs. Borden invited the occasional friend over, liked the way I could go unnoticed like a critter, biting off conversation here, sipping mulled wine there. Emma was often invited to sit with Mrs. Borden and friends. I never could.

"It's to make me like her more," Emma spat out.

"It's because you're a grown-up. You're lucky."

Emma pulled at her throat. "It's not that fun."

From the front stairs I'd watch Emma in the parlor drink cups of tea. Mrs. Borden would say, "Emma, dear, tell us about the things you're crafting."

Sip, sip. "I'm sketching a landscape scene." Sip, sip. "Nothing too important."

"Your mother tells us all the time how talented you are," a friend would say.

Sip, sip. "Oh." Sip, sip and Emma would stare at Mrs. Borden before saying, "I still have quite a lot to learn about form and color." Sip, sip. When were they going to talk to me about what I liked? After skin flushed red, Emma would make excuses to leave the table, taking with her a handful of Borden-made cookies and heading for

the backyard. Everyone always chooses the wrong sister. I wanted
to be at the table. I'd make my way down, quiet into Emma's chair
and listen to adult talk.

"No, Lizzie. Not this time." Mrs. Borden rushed her fingers over
my head, made skin dance. Nothing was ever my time.

———

I rubbed my fingers along my forehead, massaged an ache away.
Emma came back into the parlor, placed tea onto the small table
between us and watched me.

"Are you alright?" She stared at me, made me shiver.

"Why?"

"Your head. You keep touching it."

I rubbed again. "Just a strange throb, that's all." The butcher
pounded.

"Let's call for Dr. Bowen again in the morning."

I smiled, and Emma kept her watch of me and I looked around
the room. We were surrounded by ghosts of sympathy. On small
tables, half-full cups of tea and cream had been left by Father and
Mrs. Borden's friends who could no longer handle the stench of
their absence. Underneath the sofa were tiny pieces of paper that
had come away from police officers' notebooks, trailing from sofa
to kitchen like Hansel and Gretel's crumbs, hoping to find their
way home. I rubbed my forehead again. There would be many
things Emma would have to fix to make everything right. I could
see Father's blood on the sofa.

Words slipped out of me then. "I was in here talking to Mrs.
Borden this morning."

Emma seized. "When was this?" Her voice scratched at my ear.

"After she told Bridget to keep cleaning the windows. She said there was a strange smell."

Emma's nose twitched. "What kind of smell?"

The sweet syrup tripped through my limbs. "I don't know. It was probably her." I giggled.

"What time did you speak to her?" Emma said.

My head jerked towards her. "I just told you."

"But you said she had gone to see a sick relative."

I rubbed my forehead. "She did but I spoke to her first." *Is this the way things really go?* The butcher pounded out all sense.

Emma got haughty. "I'm simply trying to understand . . ."

I heard a tiny voice say not to speak anymore, that she wouldn't understand the thoughts swimming inside. But it was hard to keep a tongue still. The clock on the mantel ticked ticked. My body swooned and clothes gripped tight around ribs. This feeling of being held too tightly when I was younger, first by Father then by Emma. The feeling that made you want to jump out of your skin, run like hammers away, away, *I shouldn't be feeling like this now.*

I turned to Emma, saw her stare at me like I was a caged animal. "Why do you keep staring?"

"You look pale," Emma said.

I touched my face, pulled down on skin. "Do I?"

"You should rest."

"There's so much to do. We have to plan the funeral." I parted the parlor curtains, looked out the window, watched people hold hands as they passed and tried to see in. Heads make curious shapes. "Who do you think Father would want to attend for him?"

Emma breathed, curled around my ear. "I can't talk about this now."

"But it's important."

Emma's face drained of color. I leaned towards her and saw light-blue veins along jawbone tighten and pulse, all the little angers waiting to come out and spill. I leaned closer.

"Sit back," she snarled.

"Stop looking at me like that." I pulled at my neck. Emma kept watch until I felt her begin to crawl under my skin, eyes like parasites.

"Like what?" she said.

Her eyes continued to take my skin as a feast, ate the layers until I felt her inside my insides. "You always do this," I said.

"What am I doing, exactly?" Emma burrowed in closer, chewed to bone. All the little strings that hold a body together threatened to undo. How far would she go?

"Nothing," I said. But the more she looked at me, the more I thought things, thought about the time we were robbed last year, how Emma had looked and looked at me for days after. Just like this. "You told Father about the necklace, didn't you?" I folded teeth over teeth.

"What are you talking about?"

"Last year. You told Father I took the necklace, that it was me who stole all Mrs. Borden's jewelry."

She closed her eyes and shook her head. "I can't believe this. It's not that important."

My heart drummed, *strike up the band!* and pressed against my chest, throat tightened. "But how do I know you're not going to tell the police things about me? Things I've said?"

Her eyes pinched into nothingness. "Why are you saying . . ."

"I made one little mistake! I only ever make one little mistake and you always make sure I'm punished. I absolutely hate you sometimes." Heart drummed into my head. The clock on the mantel ticked ticked.

"Lizzie, cut it out right now," her voice spat across the room.

My body lurched forwards then back, forwards then back, the way a body on gallows would swing. My neck ached. I wept. I shook until the floorboards whispered, *no more, no more.* From upstairs I heard Uncle call out, "What's going on down there?" Emma rushed at me, wrapped skeleton arm around me and shooshed, shooshed, shooshed. "It will be alright," she said. Her head curled into mine, magnetic skin, and in we breathed, out we breathed, like children, *we children without parents.*

"This is how you should always be to me," I hummed into her ears. We were warm for a time. Then Emma's fingers crawled over my head, soothed like God and made me electric.

"What's this?" Her fingers stopped sharp at my temple. She pulled away, looked me over.

"What?"

"What's in your hair?" she whispered.

I ran my hand over the spot that had made her break from me; something brittle and coated.

Emma pulled my head towards her and studied. The clock on the mantel ticked ticked. "There's something hard stuck in your hair." Her fingers weaved through strands, pulled gently. "Oh, my," she whispered again.

I studied her fingers, saw a tiny bauble of bone. "No." I said, *no, no, no,* we were quiet.

Emma looked me over then around the room. She wiped at her eyes, strained her neck towards the ceiling. *Mrs. Borden's blood is still up there!* The clock on the mantel ticked ticked. I watched

Emma's ribcage expand and deflate. I wondered what it would be like if she were to die right then. Emma stared at me once more and after a time said, "Do you think you might have hurt yourself?"

My heart skipped a beat. I touched the spot where she had been, couldn't feel blood. I thought very hard. It was all very confusing. "Yes." I touched my forehead and rubbed. "I've been sore all day, come to think of it." I rubbed my forehead again. "I hurt myself a lot when you were away."

———

When Emma was in Fairhaven I sat in my room and picked at my skin. First I picked at the dried skin on my feet, let it fall onto my red wool rug next to my bed, then I picked at skin around my elbows and knees, made myself bleed a little, drip drip onto my white sheets. If she had answered my letters, I wouldn't have felt so empty and lonely, wouldn't have had to force myself to play niceties with Father and Mrs. Borden, to talk to them. Many things wouldn't have happened. I wouldn't have had to sit with them in the evenings. I'd often find them in the sitting room, Father with a book on the sofa, Mrs. Borden with her too-ornate embroidery, knotted color thread lying with each stitch: Home Sweet Home, My Heart Rests Here. One night I prayed for her to prick her fingers with the needle, to sew skin into skin.

"Hello, Lizzie."

"Good evening." I sat in the chair nearest the parlor room and watched them, kerosene lamps burning off that devil-sulphur smell, shading their faces with half-shadows. Father looked up from his book at me, then at Mrs. Borden before returning to the page. Mrs. Borden embroidered, hand up, fingers tight and angular, pull through cloth, repeat, repeat. The clock on the mantel ticked ticked, its tick-tick climbing down over the ledge along the carpet into my feet; little cannons. I thought of jumping up and down, a giant stomp of "Here I am! Here I am!" Instead I coughed. They both said nothing. I coughed again and listened to their breathing, that dragging of air up through aged lung, out of dry mouth and cracked lip.

Mrs. Borden said, "Andrew, did I tell you? Bridget seems to think the upstairs space is attracting a particular smell."

"Is that right?" Father said. "What does she think it might be?" *who cares what she thinks.*

"Perhaps an animal?" said Mrs. Borden.

"Rodent?" Father stroked his short beard.

"Could be." Mrs. Borden embroidered.

"It's the weather that makes it worse," Father said.

"I told her to open the windows." Mrs. Borden embroidered.

"I dare say it'll be trapped in the walls. The damage to the house and the cost to fix it will be enormous," Father said.

"Yes, quite expensive." Mrs. Borden, her fingers around the needle, going in and out, in and out of fabric. She changed the color of the thread from red to purple, in and out. "Suppose we'll have to wait until the end of summer."

"Yes, the animal will have well and truly disintegrated by then and the problem will have sorted itself out." Father smiled, proud of his solution. He returned to his book.

Their conversation made me want to hit walls. They knew nothing. I cleared my throat. "Maybe Bridget is storing food up there and it's become rancid."

"Why would she do that?" Mrs. Borden stopped embroidering.

"How am I supposed to know? Maids do take things. I wouldn't be surprised . . ."

"Don't be ridiculous." Father put the book down. "We all know Bridget isn't the one who takes things in this house, is she?" We locked eyes. His mouth opened. I saw gray tongue poke over gum.

"Unfortunately, Father, there is crime in our beloved Fall River. Many people do many things."

"Yes, they do, Lizzie. They do." Father stroked his short beard. Mrs. Borden put her embroidery on her lap. The clock on the mantel whirled, skipped time. We all turned to look at it. The clock whirled again then stopped. A silence.

"That hasn't happened in a long time," Mrs. Borden said.

We were quiet.

Then Father said, "I'll take it into town tomorrow and have it repaired."

I stretched my legs until my stockinged ankle showed from underneath my skirt, *my, what strong legs you have*, and I clicked my jaw and sighed. Father turned and faced me. We watched each other and in that moment I was small again. I wanted to pounce on him like a kitten and dig my claws into his legs, swipe a paw into his cheek and watch the blood-letting, make him forget about the conversation we'd just had. "Cheeky child," he'd say, "but that is why I love you. What a wonder you are." *I AM the great wonder*, and I'd lick my kitten tongue over blood and cheek, clean him with my fur and preen.

Father and I watched each other. He'd never let me grow, like he didn't trust me. This thing we did night after night after night and I ended up picking at skin because Emma wasn't home. So many times I thought about walking to Fairhaven, thought of stalking into

Emma's bed like the moon and lying by her side, growing tentacles and wrapping them around her until our breathing matched.

A week after Emma left for Fairhaven, I had taken to watching Mrs. Borden trounce around the house, heavy iron-feet walking stairs and floorboards, her puff-puff breath curling around my neck and lips like an infection each time she walked by me.

"Lizzie, you look lost," Mrs. Borden said.

"I'm not that lost. I know that I'm stuck here in this hellhole."

She laughed. "You know that's not what I meant."

My lips gave way to a smile and I tried to suck it in.

"Emma will be back soon enough." Sing-song, sing-song.

"I don't care," I said.

"Oh . . ."

"Actually, I was just thinking that sometimes it's better to stay at home from time to time." I heard myself in the ease of the conversation, the way my voice spread like sweet butter. I knew if Emma had been there she would've said to me, "So what are you trying to get out of them this time?"

"None of your business," I would've answered. Then after a time I'd tell Emma, "I want them to pay for me to go back to Europe."

"You're quite right," Mrs. Borden said. I let myself smile at her, *what is wrong with me?*

The side door had opened and Father came in, stood rigid in front of us. "You two are speaking, I see."

Mrs. Borden raised her eyebrows. "Lizzie and I were discussing the merits of staying home."

"From time to time," I added.

Father looked at me. "As long as one makes oneself useful."

"Don't I always, Father?" Lips gave way to a grin. I wanted to yell out, *Give me what I deserve!* But I kept quiet.

"Have you heard from your sister?" he said.

"Yes. She's fine."

Mrs. Borden moved her head to one side, eyed me, evil, before telling father, "Bridget has been preparing lunch. Some nice roasted mutton . . ."

"It better not be too big. The last leg you allowed her to buy went to waste," Father said.

"I'm sure it's perfectly suitable," Mrs. Borden said.

Father grunted. "I'd prefer people be mindful."

The sun knocked along the sitting room window and came in through the small opening between the curtains, bounced onto my fingers, made my knuckles pop and grow. "Lizzie," Mrs. Borden said, "since you're in the mood to stay at home, why don't you have lunch with us?"

Father smoothed his hands over his chin, his fingers long skin matches, *light up and burn, Father dear.* I heard Bridget in the kitchen blowing over the food to cool it slightly. She coughed and the house whip-cracked above us. Father, his eyes over me again.

"Yes, I think I shall have lunch with you," I said.

Father smiled at Mrs. Borden. My stomach pulsed, churned.

We sat around hard wood and were silent as Bridget served. Father asked her about meat prices and I said, "Gosh, for once can't we just live a little? I know we can afford it . . ."

Father hammered his fist on the table. "It's my money. I ask the questions here, thank you, Lizzie."

I placed the mutton in my mouth, dry hot flesh, and swallowed hard. "I hate that you act like we're poor, Father. You've a building with your name on it!"

Mrs. Borden crossed knife and fork on the plate and wiped her mouth. "Your father works very hard and deserves your respect."

"I was merely pointing out a fact."

Bridget walked into the kitchen and stood without facing us. She rested on one leg and slid her hand back and forth over the kitchen counter.

A clink of cutlery on china. Father cut through mutton, sawed his teeth forwards over his bottom lip, looked over the dining table. I waited for him to yell at me but everything was silent.

"What's the matter, Father?"

He chewed mutton then swallowed. Mrs. Borden wiped her mouth with a linen napkin, her lips red from rubbing. For a moment she looked young. For a moment. "Everyone enjoying the mutton?" Mrs. Borden asked. A little lump of animal flesh was stuck to the side of my throat. It was heavy, made me sweat. I thought of Emma, thought of my boredom. I thought of Europe, how fancy I had been, *I even ate caviar!*

"It's delicious," I said. Father cut meat like a lumberjack, whomped a large piece of mutton into his mouth. The house was silent. Father didn't say another word to me that day. I began thinking things.

———

We made Emma brew more tea and she came back, the clock on the mantel ticked ticked, *seven o'clock.* Uncle came down the stairs, heavy leather, and said, "Girls! This isn't the time to be arguing."

"Were we loud?" I asked, so sweet.

"Just a little. But it's understandable." Uncle kissed the top of my head and said, "I think it's time we eat, don't you?"

My stomach tightened. "Oh, let's do!"

"I'm not hungry," Emma said.

Uncle rubbed his fingers over his stomach, *here kitty kitty*, and patted three times. "Pears don't sustain a man." He laughed. Uncle could be very charming. I caught Emma rolling her eyes.

We sat in the parlor, my hand scratched along the velvet covering of the armchair and right then I was on my Grand Trip in London, a sunbonnet on a mannequin, a store bell ringing, smell of animal hide and molasses from the backroom workshop. I took my gloves off and ran my fingertips over the sunbonnet's dark-green velvet. The stitching was precise, the brim steadfast. Tiny gold diamantés were sewn into the front of the hat, reminded me of sun dreams. I leaned close, took a deep breath, something slightly spicy and prickly had settled into the fabric, made me warm and tingle. The excitement of new things. I leaned closer, quickly licked the hat, wanted to devour it. I wouldn't find anything like it in Fall River.

"Lizzie!" Emma shrieked.

I snapped my eyes wide. "Yes?" I put my palm to mouth. I licked salt, a hint of wood polish, some taste of me.

"What would you like to eat?" Emma was annoyed. Was it wrong to give in to impulse? She made me feel like Father did, ashamed of who I was, a perpetual child.

Cold mutton soup. I smiled. "Anything, dear sister."

Uncle patted his stomach and Emma pushed her boots underneath her chair and dragged them along the carpet. She left the room.

"Uncle, do you think it will take the police very long to find who did this?"

He arched a brow. "Given the strangeness of it all, I'd say it will be some time before there's any resolution."

I rested my head against the edge of the chair, wondered how long it would take for me to feel comfortable, to feel safe.

Emma came with food.

"I'm mighty ravenous," Uncle said.

Stale bread, butter, old mutton broth. Rotting fruit. Fresh milk, apple-spiced cake. Uncle cut into the bread, spread butter thick, the way you do when you know there is no one there to stop you. Emma watched him and sipped her tea. I took some cake and broke chunks, let the deliciousness form soft pyramids in my cheeks. Sugar sang.

"Mighty delicious, Emma," Uncle said.

Emma stared at me. "You should eat something other than cake, Lizzie. Why don't you have some mutton broth?"

"I'm not that hungry." Cake went in my mouth. "You should have some, if you like."

We ate more. I ate greedy.

After a time, Uncle said, "You know, when I was out this morning, I would have accused you of blasphemy if you had told me such a beautiful day would end so violently. To think your poor Abby was attacked so soon in the day."

I drank milk. Emma dragged her finger around the rim of the teacup, made a horrible cling-warp sound. "How do you know for certain that Mrs. Borden died so soon after breakfast?"

"I'm assuming." Uncle stuffed bread into his mouth. "How else would you explain it? I'll tell you one thing, it was rather surprising to come back to the house and find swarms of people out the front."

"I'm well aware of how shocking it was," Emma said.

Uncle stopped eating. "Of course, dear Emma. I should've realized . . ."

Emma stood. "Excuse me. I need to get some fresh air."

"Don't go outside," I said. "The killer might be out there."

"I'll just open the side door."

She left. Uncle and I ate.

———

At the top of the stairs, in the guest room, the heat of Mrs. Borden's blood came to a simmer. Uncle went into the room, sat on the bed. "So strange knowing the horror started in here," he said.

"It had to start somewhere."

He tapped his knees together. "Well, that is true. The police have a few theories."

"They do?" I needed to know them.

"All wrong, I'm sure." Uncle lifted his palm towards his face. His long fingers were stick insects prancing. He smelled his fingers and said, "How on earth did so much dirt get under these things?" He took out his handkerchief and began twisting the cotton underneath his nails, cleaning away the dirt. I smelled it, smelled the earth.

We were quiet. I caught sight of blood by the radiator on the other side of the room, *blood flies, blood soars*, and it made my stomach drop. "Are you sure you want to stay in this room?"

"Of course, my dear one. It doesn't bother me. There's only a little bit of blood." He smiled bright, like Mother had, and it made me feel better again, feel warm inside, like she was in the room with us. My uncle, the gift.

He patted the bed next to him and I sat. There were flecks of blood at the end of the bed. I covered them with my hand. "How long will you stay with us?"

"As long as I can, Lizzie." He smiled, showed teeth. Uncle always knew what to say to make everything better. Then he said, "Did you notice anyone in the house today?

"I've already told the police . . ."

"Don't worry about what you told police. I'm simply curious. Did you notice anyone in the house? A man, for instance?"

I wasn't sure what he was getting at. "No."

He looked at my hands then he looked me up and down. "Are you still upset about last night's conversation with Andrew?"

I began to boil. "I hadn't given it a second thought."

Uncle eyed me. *What was he thinking?* I could hear an early-evening wind knock against the side of the house, wolfish. Something creeping towards me.

Uncle glanced over his shoulder at the place where Mrs. Borden's body had been. "I wonder if she saw it coming?" he whispered.

My forehead ached. I rubbed. "Maybe. You would think yes . . ."

"I suppose so." He studied me some more, made the hairs on the back of my neck stand like wheat in the sun. Then he said, "Did you go into the barn today?"

I nodded.

"I see."

"I went in a few times today. Why?"

A slow smile broke across his face. It made me feel uneasy. "Lizzie, would you like to talk?"

I heard Emma bang her way through the house. How she made my head hurt. I'd talk about anything to make the pain stop. "Okay."

Uncle stood from the bed, closed the guest room door and turned to me.

I unfastened my braids, shook my hair loose. I turned to look at the dressing table and saw Mrs. Borden's blood licking the bottoms of the table legs. There were a few strands of her gray hair stuck to the dresser handles and I wondered how long they would be there before someone had to clean the room and make the mess go away. There were bloodied boot prints surrounding the bed, a map of distress and disbelief. Mrs. Borden had been taken all over the room, from the window to the radiator to the doorway, where the boot prints hesitated before running down the stairs, screaming that she was dead. Now she was placed face up on the dining table.

The strangest of days. "Uncle, I'm not quite sure what is real."

He rubbed my shoulders, like he always did. "Don't you worry about that. I'll tell you what's real if need be."

"What are Emma and I going to do now?" I asked.

"My advice is to stay together."

I looked at Uncle and he brushed the hair off my shoulders. Then he smiled and said, "Have I ever told you how much you remind me of your mother?"

FOURTEEN

BRIDGET

August 4, 1892

THE LAST TIME I tried to leave the house, Mrs. Borden raised me to four dollars a week and took me to Boston. "You know my back isn't what it used to be. I need her to escort me around," she told Mr. Borden when he questioned the expense of a second train ticket.

"Fine."

We would be taking a day trip to visit her aunt who kept forgetting things, forgetting people. Mrs. Borden wanted to make a good impression. The night before we left I washed Mrs. Borden's hair in Castile soap and rosemary, scraped my nails over her scalp, got her under my fingernails. "You won't regret it, Bridget." I didn't stop to ask what she meant.

And so we were packed onto the train, Mrs. Borden in her beige travel coat, me in black, me carrying her red and purple floral carpetbag full of her needs, and she let me sit by the window while she sat right close to my side, and the whistle blew as the train moved forwards, Fall River miled behind us. We got the giddy rush of being away.

"Won't it be nice, just the two of us?" she said.

The way she thought of us. That couldn't be right. We weren't family. But she was easy in the face, had a smile, and she took me by the hand, so cold and fleshy, stroked and patted me like Mammy would, and I told her, "It's good ta be outta the house."

Boston. I helped her out of the train, took her weight as she stepped the wide gap onto the platform, and we weaved through the thicket of people, weaved through women in white-and-navy-striped cotton and silk dresses, and we came out of the station, walked along the stone-tar sidewalk and waited at the edge for a streetcar.

"I always forget how much bigger it is here," Mrs. Borden said.

It was bigger alright, got me thinking that working a house in Boston would get me home quicker.

We boarded a streetcar, rested against the smooth wooden railings and I asked Mrs. Borden, "Where we meetin' yer aunt?"

She licked her lips, said, "We aren't. We're having a day of it."

Another thing I'd have to keep quiet.

The streetcar dinged, took corners and downed street after street and I got hit with city air, that mix of chimney wood and mud and coal, perfume and leather soles, of body smells that came when people walked close together, of that big-time excitement, made me giddy, and we downed street after street and then we were out the front of Filene's department store. Mrs. Borden big-bosomed her chest, made herself seem grander. "I bet you've never come here before."

"No, marm."

She took my arm, pushed me through the wide doors, took me to the dresses, the kind Emma and Lizzie wore to church. She made me change. Dress after dress. Silk and damask cotton too much for my skin. "That is wonderful," she said, again and again. While she made me her living doll, I spied a little parasol, purple lacing, silver embossed handle, and I fancied myself owning it, fancied myself making Mary say, "La-di-da," when I showed it to her. But we bought nothing. When Mrs. Borden was bored, we left the store, and continued the day outside.

We linked arms, and Mrs. Borden daughtered me along Park Street, past Brewer Fountain, water whaling above us, cool splash on our faces, past the church and its too-white steeple, past the red, white and blue draped flags of the Union Club, rosettes curving into the brick façade. On we went and on we went towards Boston Common. We walked through those spiked cast-iron gates, spikes like in the tales Daddy told me, spikes to stick heads on, warn off your enemies. Mrs. Borden took a moment, let me go, stood on her own. She turned to me then, said, "Isn't it beautiful!"

"Yes, marm."

"I love the elms," she said. "I wonder just how tall they grow. Wouldn't it be amazing to be as tall as them?" She raised her arms, made her dress pull tight across her chest.

I looked up into their fat, green canopy, watched the breeze twitch rough leaves, saw a wild rabbit come up to a gray, split-bark trunk, rub itself against it, shed its fur. "It would."

We spent an hour sitting in long grass, an hour guessing the smells caught in the air.

"That's roasted coffee."

"That's the harbor."

"That's fresh horses."

"That's a shucked clam."

Our stomachs begged for food. "Come on," she said. "I know somewhere." I took her paper-thin hands in mine, pulled her up off the ground. We walked through the Common to School Street, went a little further till we came to Parker House hotel. I knew about this place. "Misses Lizzie and Emma eat here," I said.

"And now you do."

The hotel was all brick and limestone, like a manor house I'd once seen in Dublin when Daddy had to take work on the Liffey. We went in, took a seat in the dining room, listened to the rabble talk of people who knew people. We were brought fresh, crusty bread rolls, dark-yellow salted butter, a bowl of cream-gray clam chowder thickened with oyster crackers, a sprinkle of parsley. I dug my spoon in, slurped like a Borden. I'd never seen Mrs. Borden smile so much.

We left in the afternoon, headed back to the cotton-mill fog of Fall River. Mrs. Borden patted my hand all the way and when the train slowed, pulled up at the station, Mrs. Borden said, "Staying has its benefits, Bridget."

She soured me then, made me remember that I wouldn't be going home anytime soon.

———

I woke, a new morning, same as all mornings. The heat itched me awake and I rolled over, felt my head swoon as I moved, my stomach flip. The day ahead would not be good. I turned on the lamp, looked at my family on the wall, told them, "I'm askin' her today ta give it back."

I lay in bed. The morning was quiet, like it hadn't been in a long time, not anyone walking around, not the sound of a pigeon. "Alright, I'll get up," I said, and I unlocked the door, came out onto the landing, noticed how light it was getting outside. I'd overslept. I heeled down the stairs, didn't stop to listen to Mr. and Mrs. Borden. I got the mutton broth on the heat—God, it stunk—had to taste it to add more salt and I noticed the wall by the stove shined, had two long streaks of a silvery wetness. I wiped my apron across the wall, smelled the cotton. Butter and fat. I wiped again and the streaks started their dripping. I heard someone come down the back stairs, took a look behind. Mrs. Borden. She came towards me, said nothing at first, and I stirred the pot. She stood and watched and finally she said, "You're starting late."

"Sorry, marm."

"Don't let being sorry stop you from working."

I went on getting some johnnycakes started. She watched and soon Mr. Borden came down the stairs, carried with him his slops pail, and I heard his urine swirl inside it, heard Mrs. Borden grind her teeth. The smell was sharp and fungal. The kitchen got hot, got crowded. Mr. Borden went outside, emptied the pail. I stirred the pot again and Mrs. Borden watched me, scratched her temples.

"Go get Mr. Morse," she said. She gave me a look, tuttled her hand in my direction, and I did what I was told, did what I had to do to make the day go faster.

I knocked on his door, heard him clear his throat on the other side, his morning thickness coming up, being spat into the slops pail.

"Mr. Morse. It's breakfast."

He rushed to the door, opened it. We were face to face, too close for the morning. "Good morning, Bridget."

"Mornin'."

"Isn't it a wonderful morning?" His breath like old socks.

"Yes."

"A good night's sleep always puts a spring in my step."

I nodded. "Breakfast is ready." I left him there, went back to the kitchen and began to serve up the mutton broth and johnnycakes.

John joined the Bordens in the dining room, and he and Mrs. Borden talked about how they'd slept, the dreams they'd had. I took in food, tried not to smell the broth, tried to steady nausea. I left them alone, went and sat on the side door steps, put head between legs, felt like I was on a ship headed home, up and over waves, my head north and south. I listened to morning foot traffic along the street and closed my eyes, counted to ten and zero, zero to ten, again, again, waited for nausea to pass.

Lizzie was calling my name, got me to come back inside.

"What are you doing today?" She said it without blinking, looked at me in a strange way.

"I don't know until Mrs. Borden gives me orders."

"There's a fabric sale. You should go buy yourself a few yards so you can make yourself a new uniform." She'd sugared her voice.

"I'd not be doin' that. I don't have the energy."

"But it's only for today. Mrs. Borden will be going." She rushed along, sounded pained.

"I'm not well, Miss Lizzie. I'd not . . ."

She eyed me, said, "Fine, suit yourself," and left me alone, went to her father in the sitting room.

"Good morning."

"Good morning."

"How are you today, Father?"

"Remains to be seen. Still somewhat unwell." He said it slow. I wondered when he'd tell her about the pigeons.

I went to the dining room, collected the dishes and took them to the scullery, started to wash them. Mrs. Borden came in then, was thunder, said, "Once you've finished you'll be washing the outside windows." The way she said it, like we'd never known each other before.

I rubbed cloth over a bowl, said nothing to her. Mrs. Borden stayed, watched, then said, "Are you still leaving?"

I rubbed. "Yes, Mrs. Borden." I looked at her, her eyes a-droop, glassy, and she seemed so worn down. I thought of my mammy. "Marm, I was hopin' for me tin."

She shook her head.

"Mrs. Borden, it's all me money in there. I cooked and cleaned. I stayed."

She rubbed her temples. We looked at each other, heard Lizzie and Mr. Borden talk and talk, the way they did, and she said, "Do those windows properly and we'll see."

"Yes, marm." I tried not to be sour, so I told her something true. "I still think 'bout our trip ta Boston." I smiled.

"Oh?" she said. I couldn't read her.

"Thank you, Abby." Her name slid from the tongue, was easy. I was close to going home.

Mrs. Borden took steps away from me, wiped her eye, went to speak but said nothing. Instead, she went up the back stairs, left me with the dishes, left me to hear Lizzie tell Mr. Borden, "I'm going to feed my pigeons."

I finished the last dish, came into the kitchen to see Mr. Borden stand there, his shoulders rolled forwards. I wiped my wet hands on my apron and he said, "Excuse me," pushed me out of his way and tripped through the side door.

I went to the basement, got my soap for the windows, heard Lizzie scream. The pigeons.

———

Outside in the heat, my face like a fire, my stomach churned a terror, made my head bounce, had me on all fours letting myself go, all that vomit into the grass. After, I thought I heard a tapping from the barn, thought it must've been pigeons, must've been Lizzie, and went to the left side of the house, started cleaning the windows. Along the bottom of the glass were finger smudges and I wondered when they'd got there, when it was that Lizzie decided to grubby my hard work. I tipped the bucket out, headed to the house to refill, thought of telling Mrs. Borden what I had found.

With clean water I went back to the windows, noticed half-eaten pears leading from the pear arbor to the side of the house. John and Lizzie had been out there the night before. What strange games had they played? Sweat dripped down thighs and I let myself go again, vomited at my feet.

"Bridget?" Mary's voice behind the fence.

"Yeah?"

"Are ya alright?"

"Never better." Oh, I wanted to sleep then. I leaned into the fence.

"What's gotten into ya?"

"Me own cookin'." I paused, waited for nausea to pass. "Or maybe Mrs. Borden's punishin' me."

Mary laughed.

"I'm meanin' it. Probably rather see me poisoned than leave."

"Lordy. Wait there." Mary scuffled behind the fence, limped away, and soon enough she was in front of me, her cherub cheeks rosed, her skirt hiked up so that it showed the bottom of her knickerbockers.

I looked her over. "I interrupt somethin', did I?"

Mary punched me in the shoulder. "Shut up. I've been cleanin' floors."

"Ya'll cause the scene, runnin' round like that."

"Bet not as much as you did when Mrs. Borden heard yer news."

"She's got me tin." My stomach groaned, a little devil.

"Ya've been held ta ransom!" Mary hobbled closer to me, put her hand on my forehead. "Bridget, yer bloody boilin'."

I gently pushed her hand away. "Keep that up and ya could be a detective."

"Ya shouldn't be out here."

"I've got no say."

Mary shook her head. We both looked up at the house, at its little chips of green paint falling, at a spat of dried pigeon dropping next to the sitting room window. A spider spindled its legs in a web. Mr. Borden never bothered doing anything about the sides of the house.

Then Mary looked at me, said, "Reckon ya'll be well enough to play Irish switch on Sunday?"

"Not a worry. I'll beat ya even if I'm still sick."

She grinned. "Well then, I better get back, get to practising after I wash them floors." Mary touched my forehead again, her hand cool and soothing, and she turned to leave.

"Mary," I said, "what am I gonna do if I can't get me tin?"

She shrugged shoulders. "I bet ya'll think of some way ta go."

That was my some way. I looked up at the house, could hear wood cracking in the stove, coming up through the chimney. I went back to washing windows. There had to be some way.

Mrs. Borden knocked on the sitting room window, was cross-faced, told me to do it properly, like I never cleaned a window before, like I'd never done this job before. I washed, my hands working the glass in smaller circles, and Mrs. Borden squinted eyes, scoured mouth. My wrists cramped. She disappeared and I stopped. I didn't feel like doing anything after that. I sat awhile, heard my stomach hiss like a demon, heard people thundering up and down Second Street. Everything was getting too much. "I'm not doin' anythin' more," I said, and when I went into the house, saw no one about, I noticed someone had been sick near the dining table. Not even the decency to go outside. "Bloody typical." I went to take a closer look and Lizzie came up behind me. I told her about the mess, that I was worried about Mrs. Borden. "She's too old ta be sick on a hot day like today."

Lizzie patted my shoulders, I didn't like her touch, and she stood too close, looked red-cheeked, like she'd been running. "Don't worry about a thing, Bridget."

"Where's Mrs. Borden?"

She cocked her head to the side, looked at me like I was a little stupid. "She's had a note to see a sick relative."

I'd not heard anyone deliver a note, not heard her leave. Lizzie kept looking over her shoulder and I wondered if she was expecting John.

"No, he left a while ago." Lizzie chewed her nail, spat it onto the carpet.

I hadn't heard him leave either. I wasn't hearing anything properly. I really needed to rest. Lizzie broke her own vow then, offered to help me clean the dining room mess. "You finish the windows and I'll take care of it."

I hesitated. If it wasn't cleaned properly Mrs. Borden might not give my tin back. But the thought of having to do it myself . . . "Alright."

Lizzie was up and down, made banging noises, made throat noises, little grunts. She darted into the barn and out again and I couldn't help but feel she was up to no good. I went to check on her. Lizzie was using a broom handle to pile the vomit into a brown slime hill before picking it up with a cloth, throwing it into a pail. Lizzie and her dry-retching. I wanted to laugh at her. Lizzie only cleaned when she wanted something. I walked away.

The morning kept on, got hotter. I washed a window by the basement, damned Mrs. Borden to a fiery pit for making me do this, and Lizzie came to me like a saint, said, "Why don't you come inside and rest."

In we went. We drank water together. She stared at me. The hairs on the back of my neck stood.

"I'm going upstairs now," she said.

"Alright."

When she left, I stuck my head in the dining room. She'd gone without cleaning the sick from under the table properly. I took my water into the sitting room, sat awhile on the sofa. The house made no sound.

The clock struck ten and sometime after there was a rattling at the front door, someone trying to get in. I stood, waited. There was a knock, another knock, and Mr. Borden yelled out, "I can't open the door."

I ran to him, fumbled my keys—'Pshaw!'—and opened the lock, saw him all pale and sweating.

"Mr. Borden, ya alright?"

His eyes rolled, like they didn't mean to. "Unfortunately not. I've been sick at work, can't quite stomach the day."

He came in, gave me his hat and coat, and I heard Lizzie laugh, saw her standing on the stairs, halfway up, rocking a bit, side to side. Mr. Borden went to sit on the sofa in the sitting room, rubbed his hands over his face.

"Let me make ya comfortable," I said.

"No, Bridget. I'll look after Father." Lizzie was there behind me, hands clasped in front of her. "Why don't you go upstairs and rest?"

"Okay," I said. "Call out when ya need me."

I left them talking in the sitting room, Lizzie telling him that Mrs. Borden was out, and I went up the back stairs, my head and body aching, went up to my room, shut the door a little, and lay hot on my bed.

———

Last winter, we had snow and wind, right up against the house all night like a ghost knocking to be let in, like it wanted to bury us. I'd gone down the back stairs, my ankles clicking, and I knocked on Mr. and Mrs. Borden's bedroom door until my knuckles purpled. Mr. Borden opened the door. "What is it?"

"I'm worried about the snow. It's soundin' like a blizzard's comin'."

He crossed his arms. "The house is secure. It will pass."

"Yes, but I'm wonderin' whether . . ."

"Bridget, leave us be. The house is secure."

He shut the door, Mrs. Borden calling to him, "What's wrong with Bridget?" She should've come to the door, talked with me. They both should've listened to me. I went back to my room, and in the morning I woke to Mrs. Borden yelling, "The door will not open! Andrew, it's blocking us in."

I ran down the stairs, found her at the side door, frantic. "Bridget," she said, "something terrible has happened." We looked at the door. I'd tried to tell him. The house wouldn't let us out.

Later Lizzie opened a shutter. Feet of snow compacted against the window. She pressed her hand against the glass, sweaty print on my clean window, and said, "It feels like it's inside with us." The snow wasn't white but was muck-sleet soot, pebbles and dirt, had little twigs from trees.

"Close the shutter," Mr. Borden said.

"But I want to see how long I can keep my hand on the glass." A whine.

He sighed, said, "I told you to close the shutter." His voice a boom. Lizzie did what she was told.

"Tea ta warm ya up?" I asked.

Mr. Borden turned to me. "Fine. Be sure to check all the windows are shut. I don't want a drop of heat leaving this house."

"Yes, sir." I nodded, did what I was told as well. The house was closed up.

The beginning of days together. Lizzie and Emma kept to their side of the house, up in their rooms like mice. They would call for me, say, "Bridget, come and take our plates away."

"Bridget, bring us tea."

"Bridget, is there any cake left?"

They called out and called out, never left their rooms, made me work until I got a stitch. I'd have to fetch their slops pails, fetch their dirty underdrawers, fetch them news of what their parents were up to. Often they would fight among themselves, sister spats, fill the house with yelling and slammed doors, and I'd try to close my ears to them, block them out and get on with the day.

Then, after four days of snow, Lizzie and Emma were forced downstairs with Mr. and Mrs. Borden when the upstairs radiators gave out. The four of them in that sitting room, with that ticking clock, with their mouths shut tight, with Mr. Borden sucking his pipe sliding between his teeth, with me bringing plates of leftover sliced meats, carving with dead cold hands, having the knife slip, my blood rising to skin surface every time, their body heat hitting each other, making them yawn. With that, my nerves were shot.

Lizzie and Emma plaited each other's hair, Mrs. Borden crocheted. They read, and I did what I was asked. One afternoon when we were all in the sitting room, rugged in blankets and the snow still thick, the Bordens fell asleep, their mouths wide, air coming in and out like an ocean tide, smelling of old meat and butter. I sat and bit my nails, thought of dropping my clippings into their mouths to see what would happen. The only thing for sure would be that they'd send me back to the agency, tell them I should never be hired out. I put the clippings in my apron pocket, watched them sleep, wondered what they dreamed. Oh, but I was bored.

I went to the photos on the mantel. There was Emma, there was Lizzie, one year to the next. In Emma's photos, she always looked in pain, like she'd been told nightmare things. Then there was Lizzie, an opposite. I'd always thought they never quite looked related, instead like one little girl had been plucked from thin air and placed in the bedroom of the other. "Here you are," someone would've said. "We've found you a sister, someone to keep you company." Emma, as if she'd never been happy with the sisterly arrangement.

The blizzard kept on for five more days and we kept on in the house together, all close, all hot, until the weather broke, until the snow melted, and when it did, I was the first to open a window, let in the cold air.

———

I was thinking of the winter, wondering when Mrs. Borden would come home from visiting her relative, wondering how soon I could leave the house, go back to my family, go back to best feelings, when I heard a chock, chock sound come from the bottom of the house.

I thought of Mr. Borden and the pigeons. Chock. There was no bird sound. Chock. My heart got to beating fast and I gripped onto my bed, turned to look at my family. Chock, chock. A sound of grunting, like an animal eating. Chock.

Where was that coming from? Chock, chock.

A horse cart rolled down the street. Chock, the air was still, chock, the city bells struck, was much too loud. I gripped onto my bed, couldn't move, couldn't breathe, couldn't think. My bladder felt like bursting. The house went quiet. For a moment I wondered if I was in a dream. I didn't want to open my door, didn't want to go downstairs, didn't want to know what was down there.

Then I heard Lizzie call out, "Bridget!"

PART III

FIFTEEN

BENJAMIN

May 6, 1905

I NEVER FORGOT Fall River. Roaming town to city, puncturing faces, setting things straight, I never forgot that I had unfinished business. Over a decade and I never forgot. It was only ever a matter of time before I would go there again. On and off I'd think of Andrew and Abby, wonder who had broken them, wonder if I had got to Andrew first, would I have been gentler? Who could say what anyone would do in the heat of the moment? A few months after Fall River, I helped someone else with a problem, leaned in hard, broke a face, broke a neck, a twig, collected payment, then I helped another, and another, kept on helping until I raised enough to help myself, take care of my own problem.

I arrived at Papa's house at dawn. More than thirteen years since my last visit. I slipped in through the back door, sniffed my way through the rooms until I was in a girl's bedroom. Small musical boxes on a dressing table, a pile of clothes next to the bed. I watched her sleep, went in close. "Guess who?" I whispered. The girl was lost to light snoring. I touched her hair, liked the way it felt against my palm, and as I leaned closer, I could see my sisters in the patterns of her skin. "It's your brother."

There was a creak-crack from somewhere in the house. I hunted it down. In another room, two sleeping bodies. I walked in, watched Papa sleep. His face was leather, deep-lined. There was something about him, something soft. Something I'd never seen before. I caught soap scent on his skin and I wondered, had he always smelled like this and I'd forgotten? Papa horse-kicked his legs underneath the sheets, like I'd seen him do so many times before, and Angela sleep-hitched her arm across his body, rubbed him to stillness and dreams. They slept peaceful and I did not care for that. He should've been like this for us. What those years might have been like. I'd still be at home with my mama, with sisters, with some love. So I readied my hands, placed a palm over his mouth. He opened his eyes. There's a strange feeling when you look into the past. It's like dreaming. Papa watched me, his breath on my skin. He dug his teeth into my hand. He looked like he might cry. I pressed hard and Papa's hand covered mine, pulled it away, and after he took a breath he said, "You came back."

I nodded. A bit of me wanted to crawl against his chest, get warm.

"I never forget, Papa."

He stared at me. "It ain't time." He elbowed his way up to sitting, grunted as he pushed into me, old man anger. I pushed him down, made the bed rattle. Angela rolled over beside him, her face scrunched in sleep.

Papa tried to paw me, made me boil inside. I cracked my knuckles. I wouldn't give in. I was here to finish things. I put my hand back on his mouth, took a look at Angela before staring Papa down.

One thing I'd never understood from all my years of helping people was why they were never completely satisfied with the ending of things. Was it because they never got to have a final conversation? Was it because nothing would ever get them to feel right about the past? There I was with Papa, and so I asked him, "Do I still disappoint you?"

He tried to say something but I shook my head, pushed my hand harder onto his mouth. I looked into his eyes, watched them dart around, felt his lips tremble under my palm. His frightened eyes. For a moment I thought of letting go. Papa tried to push against me, but I was stronger and I finished the job, felt him become still under my palm. When I stepped away from him, I heard movement from down the hallway, a bed squeak. I ran out of the room, bolted from the house into the morning. I ran and I ran. But it was odd. I didn't feel relief, didn't feel different this time. Something was missing.

I wondered if it had been the same for Lizzie when Andrew died. I'd kept track of her, kept newspaper articles in a little oil-coated rucksack on my back, kept the ax, kept the piece of skull, kept thinking I'd get back to her and John when time allowed. I collected the first article a week after I'd left Fall River. Accused of murder. What a devil daughter, to kill her father and mother. I thought about her in the house that day, her coming and going, her strange little ways, her anger. Maybe she had been the one, surprised us all, had been the one who took my money, took my fun.

I stole newspapers from shops, collected Lizzie for almost a year while she was awaiting trial, and then I put her away, only took her out when the mood struck. That whole time I was collecting. I wanted to see if there were any clues as to who did the crime, wanted to keep tabs on John, wanted to know what happened to all that family money. I looked at the illustration of Lizzie dressed in black in a courtroom, a headline reading: LIZZIE BORDEN PLEADS NOT GUILTY TO MURDER.

That made me laugh, the pleading. She had city doubt stacked against her. Two days after Andrew and Abby were killed, whispers skipped up and down streets. Lizzie did it, she hated her mother, the maid said she heard Lizzie laughing when Mr. Borden came home. There's nothing like neighborhood finger-pointing.

Not everyone accused Lizzie. Family friend Reverend Buck declared that "Fall River couldn't afford to have a vile creature, a butcher like this one, roaming at large. Lizzie told me that she saw someone loitering inside the family home that fateful night." She had remembered. What fun that must've been for her. Police checked and rechecked the house, went over the stories that Lizzie had told them. When the police realized how much sedative she had been given, they put her loitering man down to sleep phantoms, and I was in the clear. It was during these reexaminations that police made discoveries, a blood spot on one of Lizzie's petticoats, Alice Russell letting slip that Lizzie burned a stained apron and dress in the stove the day after the murders, that Emma had encouraged her to do so, that when Alice had begged, "Lizzie, please think about what this will look like," Emma stoked the flames, made sure the cotton burned quick.

And then, on August 11, 1892, it happened. After the burials and after the inquest began, the police came for Lizzie. She was sitting in the parlor, windows open, the way Andrew and Abby would never allow in the evening. Emma was by her side when they came in. She wouldn't let Lizzie go willingly. Some say they held hands, others said Emma wouldn't let them begin the arrest until the windows were closed. The charges were given, arrest was made. "Lizzie, you did this thing." Lizzie tremored, Lizzie almost cried, Lizzie bent like a reed. If I were there I would've told her that she wouldn't have been in this situation if she'd just showed emotion, gave them what they wanted to see. But I knew, you can't play along and strategize at the same time. She should've disappeared like I did.

They took Lizzie to the police station, made it official, and readied her to be taken to Taunton jail. Emma sat with her while transport was arranged. An officer told the *Boston Herald*, "The sister held Lizzie like a babe. I guess that's what women do. I don't know, I've never been around when one's got arrested." It made me think that he didn't know women at all.

I never liked reading the parts that came next, reminded me too much that I never got my payment. Inflated by their father's $300,000 inheritance, Emma told Lizzie not to worry. "I'll save you. However much it takes, I'll save you." There was an illustration of the sisters holding each other before they took Lizzie away, put her on the train to Taunton.

Fall River drew lines—guilty, not guilty. While Lizzie was locked in a cell, urinating humiliation in a slops pail, Emma hired her father's lawyer, Jennings, and they prepared for trial. You read the usual things when friends are called as witnesses: "I've known Lizzie for years. She'd not ever do a thing like that;" "Nothing but love for her father." Horse shit. The good bits came when, one after the other, friends and acquaintances told reporters, "Well, Mrs. Borden and Lizzie never did get on well."

For ten months she was held in jail. I liked to think it's because they didn't trust her to stay put. But she got special treatment, was allowed to eat home-cooked meals, was allowed to grow strawberries in her cell. Spoiled and rotten. Then, finally, on June 5, 1893 the trial began. For thirteen days newspapers sent their reporters to the New Bedford superior court to take stock.

Day one. The trial began. Day two, the jury was taken to the scene of the crime. I could've shown them around: Here's where Abby tried to save her own life by crawling under the bed. As you can see, she was just too big. Here's where I found blood. Here's where Bridget vomited. Here's where Lizzie filled with anger. These are the doors that were locked. Over there is where Bridget washed windows and Abby yelled at her. This is the table where the bodies were laid out. Here's where, here's where, here's where. The jurors would poke their old fingers in everything, pretend they were investigating the facts when really they wanted to touch the spaces dead people had been.

While in the house the jurors were told that Emma still lived there, despite it all. One of the men said they noticed Borden family photos spread throughout the house, on the mantels and side tables, on walls and dressers, on bookshelves and in cupboards. Emma always had company that way. Another juror said it was very sad, "The way she was alone like that. I'd imagine she wouldn't take well to having her own thoughts day in and out." Another, "Miss

Borden made us tea while we were there. Seemed to have made her happy to be useful." These different truths.

As the trial days continued articles always mentioned Lizzie's clothes, her black-black drab, a missing button, her provincial face, sour-white cheeks, her New England stride as she walked into and out of the courtroom. The way jail was making her plumper. Lizzie sat, stared at her hands, stared at witnesses as one after the other testified about her relationship with Abby. What would people say about my relationship with my papa if I was ever caught and put on trial?

On the third day, John told stories of his whereabouts on the day of the murders, told stories like he believed them. "I was in the sitting room and Mr. Borden and his wife came in and out of the room all morning. At some stage Mrs. Borden came in with a feather duster and cleaned."

"And then what did you do?"

"I left the house, went to the post office."

"And then?"

"I returned to the Bordens' in a horse-car."

"When you got to the Borden house, did anything attract your attention at first?"

"No, sir. In fact, I ate a pear."

"But you were informed of what had happened?"

"Yes." John would've been smug.

"Did you see Mr. or Mrs. Borden first?"

"I saw Lizzie."

"No, Mr. Morse—which victim did you first see?"

"Oh, I saw Mr. Borden."

John went on and on. I thought of that day, how police were there in ones and twos after Andrew was found, how fistfuls of people gathered out front of the house. It was hard not to notice something amiss, but John had simply wanted pears first, would investigate why the police were there second.

It was on the fourth day that Bridget, that fire bubble of secrets who everyone dismissed as stupid, told the court that after she found out Andrew and Abby were killed, she took three officers down to the basement where the Bordens kept a box of hatchets by the furnace.

"I didn't touch the hatchets but the police took three of 'em," she said.

She wasn't believed. "Why did the police take three?"

"I'm not sure." Bridget would've shrugged.

"Did you touch them?"

"I left 'em alone."

"Now, tell me, when Miss Borden got you down from the attic and told you her father had been killed, what was she doing?"

"Standin' at the door. She was excited." Indeed. Lizzie had been excited that day, all her movements. I could still see her in the house, could still see all of them in there, moving around like strangers to each other, not noticing the blood that was boiling up from inside. Andrew and Abby on the dining table. The smell of rotted pears, rotted meat. John standing in night shadows watching me.

"Excited?"

"More excited than I'd ever seen her before." Bridget's eyes would've widened.

"Was she crying?"

"No, sir." Big shake of the head.

"That's not what you said at the inquest. You said, 'The girl was crying.'"

"I didn't say she was cryin'. I couldn't've said it. I know what she was doing."

The more people spoke the more Lizzie found herself in trouble.

"She didn't get along with her mother."

"There was tension."

"Sometimes Mr. Borden would be yelling at her."

"Miss Lizzie can be temperamental. Or so I've heard."

"When I questioned Miss Borden on the day of the murders, her story kept changing. I got to thinking something was a lie."

On day seven, a grand miracle happened, the kind that only people with the money to talk their way out of danger can do. Lawyer Jennings successfully argued that Lizzie's inquest testimony should be inadmissible. "She was never counseled about her rights. She didn't know that what she said could be incriminating. She was in great shock. She wasn't under arrest at the time."

The judge accepted. Her father's money had been put to good use. Lizzie had a second chance, had her words cleansed. Reading that always made me heat and rage, made me shout at the paper, "Some of that money belongs to me." What I would've given to have that kind of money, make rights in my life.

It was talk of riches that brought Emma to the stand on day eleven. She was forced to publicly acknowledge the problems of the family, to talk about property, the bloodlines that owned it. Emma, laying out Borden puzzle pieces for me to fit together. It was the closest I ever got to hearing her voice, this mysterious sister who perfectly timed her vacation. I imagined how her voice sweated tension, dripped onto the courtroom floor whenever the subject of Abby came up.

"Why did your sister stop calling Mrs. Borden 'Mother'?"

"I don't know." Eyebrows would've come together.

"How did your sister address her then?"

"As Mrs. Borden." That cold-hearted way of relating.

"When did your sister start calling her Mother?"

"Early on, when she was very young. Before I even called her Mother."

I could've told them for certain that's not what Lizzie was calling Abby on the final day together.

Emma was dismissed. She wasn't giving them anything. I wondered if Emma was like me, a protector of sisters, willing to do anything to keep them happy and safe. In the illustrations, it always looked as if Lizzie tried to make eye contact with her sister, and Emma was always looking away. It made me think she knew something about her sister that nobody else did.

I got a kick when Lizzie was made to look at her father's broken skull. "This is what an ax can do," the prosecution told the jury. I knew what a lot of things could do. I had seen Andrew and Abby's heads, had smelled the heat coming out of their skulls. I'd always wanted to see what their heads were really like once the skin had been peeled back. Were they like plaster dolls? I read and reread these articles like it was breathing.

A black box was brought into the courtroom, placed on the prosecution's table and was opened. Out came Abby's skull, out came Andrew's, chiselled white-yellow bone. The courtroom gasped, Emma snapped a cry, Lizzie lost control, fainted where she sat. Imagine how they would've reacted if they saw that firsthand, all fresh, like I had. But I knew the score—the prosecution was doing this in the hope they would find a weapon to match the injuries. They would never find it. That made me laugh good and proper.

"This is an outrage!" Jennings said. "Absolutely no consultation was made with my client and her sister to do this to their parents."

Why would anyone ask the sisters whether they could decapitate the bodies after the funeral service? The medical doctors would've waited until the last horse-drawn carriage had left Oak Grove Cemetery before bringing the coffins into the women's quarters near the cemetery gates and opening them up. The sight that must have been. Like all dead things, the Bordens would have slipped from their skins, bodies bloated before returning to size, their heads a mess of summer hate. The doctors would have held their breath, readied themselves to remove the decomposing heads so that the bodies could be put back in the ground, covered up and mourned over.

The prosecution made the scene sound warm, a family-friendly vacation—the heads took a trip to Boston, rode train carriage comfort, and arrived at North Station, made their way over paved, horse-browned mud roads, past multi-story sandstone buildings and down sidewalks to the Harvard Medical School. Squirrels climbed oak trees as the heads neared, streetcars dinged greetings, welcomed them to Boston, power lines zapping as electricity pulsed like blood. A grand city show for the sad New England heads. Andrew would've thought it all too much.

I learned what it took to boil human skin from bone. First, a vat of water was brought to the boil, then the heads were taken from their box, and a thick fluid spilled from the underside, soaked into the velvet lining. The medical doctors said, "We realized then that their brains had begun to liquefy. Mrs. Borden's brain had

evacuated out through the large hole in the right of her skull."
Evacuated. I liked that, just like the image of water boiling and
the heads being dropped in like mutton legs, bounced around the
pot in a dance until skin bubbled like animal fat, floated to the
surface in a mess of hair.

There were illustrations of the skulls being held high in court.
The Bordens, what was left of them, had kept well, and it was easy
to see how much the ax had destroyed. But Jennings didn't like it.
"Your Honor, it would please us if the heads were put away this
instant. This does nothing to solve the crime. Poor Miss Borden is
a mortified mess. Look at her." Everyone would've looked at poor,
pale Lizzie, just as they had done all throughout, and Jennings said,
"I'd like to take this moment to state the obvious. Her demeanor
proves she couldn't have committed the crime. The very sight of
the heads is making her ill."

The heads were put away. Nobody had any sense of fun.

On the thirteenth day, the day I had been waiting for, Lizzie took
the stand, spoke for herself. But it was for nothing. She touched
her forehead, composed herself and said, "I am innocent. I leave it
to my counsel to speak for me." Then she sat down, said little else
on the matter. I remembered her back in the house. She seemed
to have a lot to say then. She had been nothing but a drawn-out
mumble, a repeat of prayer, of know-it-all excitement.

Both sides made final arguments and the jury was sent to
deliberate whether or not they would let a respectable woman
hang from the neck. If she had been someone like me, like one
of my sisters, they would've rushed her out of court and done it
themselves. The jurymen considered the fact that no one found
blood on Lizzie, considered the fact that the house showed no signs

of forced entry, considered the fact that Andrew could be a very hard man, considered that there was no murder weapon found. If I'd been there, I would've given them so much more. When the twelve men decided Lizzie was not guilty, because, "We believe women just don't do this type of crime," the courtroom broke out like cannons, cheers lasted for three minutes and could be heard almost a mile away. It reduced Jennings to tears, reduced Lizzie to an ecstatic. Emma sat with her sister, and waited for Lizzie to regain her composure.

I got thinking that if I had been there, I would have shown them the ax head and Abby's skull, told them that thanks to John, the Bordens would have died regardless. They needed someone to tell them that it's family you need to worry about, not an outsider. I knew what people were capable of.

———

"No murder weapon found." I'd been keeping a big Borden secret for a decade. I'd saved Lizzie. And now she owed me, John owed me. I liked the idea that one day, this little thing might show up, bring her what she deserved. Give me what I deserved. Maybe I'd feel right about things, could search again for my mama and my sisters after I'd finished with Fall River, go and belong to a family once more, tell them that they no longer had to worry about Papa.

I stole onto a train to Fall River. When I arrived I walked through the same streets that John had shown me. There was the same sulphur-river smell, the sounds of church-bell booming like an ache. My gums bled and I went in close to a shop window, opened my mouth. A tooth hung. I gently pushed the tooth back into the gum line, and pushed on to Second Street.

There was the algae-green tiled roof of Lizzie's house. Pedestrians weaved in and out of each other, children laughed and poked each other's arms, legs. Near the house, people crossed the street, crossed their hearts, zigzagged briefly from one side to the other. I quickened towards it. A small boy darted out in front of me, yelled, "Karoo-karoo, I touched it! I touched the murder house!" and raced away to a group of children waiting down the street. They took his hands and rubbed them. The boy looked back towards the house he had escaped from, saw me, and said, "Don't do it, mister. It's cursed."

I stopped. Ninety-two Second Street: a small green fence, two half-leaved trees on either side of the pebbled path. A lamp. Overgrown grass. The front door had scratched-away dark-yellow paint. Brass numbers 9 and 2 hung loose. A pigeon walked tight lines across the roof. The smell of aged animal flesh and rising damp drifted from underneath the house. I stepped towards the door, felt a tug on my jacket.

"Mister, what are you doing?" the boy asked. His face was freckled, was brown, was too concerned.

His voice ate at my ear. I growled.

"I'm sorry, mister." The boy ran.

I walked around the side of the house and into the backyard. The barn was termited wood and broken window—the way Mama's house had been when I'd tried to return after I punished Papa. Overgrown grass hid a rusted shovel. The Borden sisters had really let the place go. I went to the pear arbor, pulled fruit and ate. Sweet juicy. I threw the pear core to the side, hit the fence, made it pop. As I headed for the basement double doors, there was a black cat crittering around the edges of the house. I bent down to pat fur and the cat hissed. I hissed back. Papa would've liked to skin a cat like that.

I pushed against the doors, could see that they were still locked, like they had been all those years ago. But I wanted in that house. I pushed again, was hard-bodied, and like that, the doors gave way, a flooded dam, and I went into the basement, smelled mildew, saw piles of old cutlery stacked in a pile, saw a rat run across the floor, claws sounded like little beads dropping.

I made my way to the kitchen, saw that everything was dust. On the counter tops, more plates and pans were stacked like monuments. I thought of Abby, tasting foul soup, her last meal. She should have treated herself to something better.

I went to the sitting room. It was filled with furniture stacked against walls, a light scent of camphor. At the mantelpiece I ran my finger across the wooden ledge, looked up and saw myself in the mirror. I checked on the tooth, dead fruit hanging, and pulled on it, yanked the tooth free, sucked away saliva and placed it on the mantel.

There was the sofa where Andrew had been. It was brittle, moth-eaten. I lay on it, heard the crunch of wooden slats underneath me as I lowered my weight and rested, the back of my neck scrunched into the armrest. The smell of trapped musk and tobacco. I thought of Andrew, the way his head must have rolled to the side while he was dying. It takes a lot to swing an ax into flesh and bone. The ax would have been heavy in the hand as it was lifted up and down. The wooden handle would have slid between palms, tearing into skin, bringing blood to the surface. Halfway through, the killer's arms would begin to ache and they would stop for a moment or two. The killer would look down at Andrew's face, amazed at the way bone could splinter exactly like forest wood. Then they would take a deep breath, work the ax again, that chop and swing, chop and swing. To think Lizzie might've had it in her to do it.

I decided to go upstairs, went to Lizzie's bedroom. The last of the late-afternoon light streamed through the windows, moved across her paint-chipped bookshelves, her stale-wood dressing table. Her bare, single, wooden bed broken against a door. The full-length mirror I'd stood in front of years before was cracked at the bottom, a spider web. Half-ripped wallpaper hung over the right-sided window, yellow and brown at the edges. I looked outside, out onto Fall River. This dirty place.

I laughed, my voice echoed through the house. Nobody called this place home anymore. Certainly not the sisters. I'd have to find them.

———

The next day, I headed downtown; the clink of bone souvenir in my bag made heads turn. A father told his son, "Stay close to me." I walked, tried to figure out how I'd find Lizzie.

I went along Main Street for hours, watched people come and go, noticed dogs seemed fatter, noticed there were more buildings, more reasons to spend big and waste time. But there was no sign of Lizzie. I walked on, even visited the surgeon that had fixed my leg but the shopfront was empty. I was headed back to the bowel of town when luck landed my side. On the opposite side of the street Lizzie stood in the sun like a saint. Emma stood next to her, disdain, folded her arms like tinder in front of her chest and said, "Lizzie, let's go."

"I'm not done yet." Lizzie's voice slow, aged.

"I don't want to keep waiting. People will look," Emma said.

"Good. Why shouldn't they? We're Bordens. We've done a lot for this city."

Emma stepped away from her sister, stood in the shadow of a shopfront. Two children ran up the footpath, made their way towards Lizzie, and she turned to watch them, gave them a smile. "Hello, children," she said, her voice a witch. "Have you thanked the Lord for this wonderful day?" The children stopped, shook their heads. One was close to tears.

"No, Miss Lizbeth."

"You should always think of the Lord."

The children looked for their mother, ran away. Lizzie laughed.

"I wish you'd stop doing that," Emma said.

"I'm only having fun. Lighten up, Emma." She continued to stand in the middle of the footpath, forced passers-by to walk around her, brush up against her like they were dancing. Nobody made eye contact with Lizzie. Emma began to walk away, acknowledged a man as he came towards her, both politely nodded heads, and Lizzie was slow to follow. I quietly slunk behind them.

"I want to host a dinner party," Lizzie said.

"We had one last week." Emma, pained.

"But I want to gather different people." Lizzie said it like a pout.

"I think it's ostentatious."

"Is that so, Father?" Lizzie laughed.

Emma quickened her pace, her hips rocked from the effort of it.

"I didn't mean it to come out like that." Lizzie tried to close the gap between herself and Emma. I continued behind, kept some distance, waited for my moment.

The sun opened. Birds sounded. Lizzie flat-opened her hand and lifted it towards the sky, clicked her tongue behind teeth, waited for a bird to land. When none came, she tried to slip her arm through Emma's. Emma pulled further away. We walked through wide streets, houses grew into mansions, the spaces between them plains. Little dogs yapped across lawns, cocked legs against rose bushes and goat's beard shrubs, dug around yellow and clotted-blood-colored hollyhocks. We rounded the corner onto French Street and the sisters headed towards a large white house. This is what inheritance brings you—money, life.

"I'll take my lunch in the front room today." Lizzie was sweetness.

"Excuse me?" Emma straightened her back.

"It's your turn to do the lunches."

"I'm not your house girl."

Lizzie hooked her arm through her sister's, leaned her head against shoulder. Lizzie thumbed at Emma's skirt. "Play nice, Emma dear. I'm just the baby . . ."

"Yes, Emma, she's just the baby," I said, put my thumb in mouth. I didn't expect to announce myself to them so quickly, but the timing.

Emma was the first to turn, sucked in all the air around her when she saw me. "Good grief." Her cheeks sank, showed hard cheekbone.

Lizzie looked me over, studied my face.

"It's been a long time, Lizzie," I said. "But I've returned, like I told your uncle I would."

Emma rubbed her hand over her chest, massaged her heart. "Lizzie, do you know this man?"

Lizzie tilted her head. "I'm not sure," she whispered.

I came closer, said, "As the Lord liveth, there shall no punishment happen to thee . . ."

Lizzie touched her forehead. "How do you know that?"

"Lizzie, who is this person?" Emma said.

I came closer, opened my bag of goodies. "I thought you might like your items returned. I was going to hand them over to your uncle but things got complicated." I smiled at them both. "Actually, I'm glad I kept them. Because now I can get what is owed. Directly from you."

"What are you talking about?" Lizzie was a puzzle.

"My payment. John asked me to help you both. I held on to a secret. I realise now that John won't uphold his end of the deal."

"I don't speak to Uncle much anymore." Lizzie said it like she was in a daze.

Emma pulled at Lizzie's shoulder, tried to get her away from me. "I'll call the police."

The sun was hot, made skin itch. I reached into my bag, pulled out Abby's skull piece, placed it on the ground. Lizzie touched her forehead. "I found this in the room," I said.

Lizzie reached for the skull and Emma covered her mouth, went white. "I had a strange dream that night," Lizzie whispered.

"And then I found this." I pulled the stained ax head out, placed it next to the skull. I looked up at Emma, said, "Did you know she was going to do all this?"

The sisters stared at what lay in front of them. Emma stiffened, a coffin stance, and she watched her sister, took a look at me. Something caught in Emma's eyes, like she was working things out. "Is this real?" Emma choked.

Lizzie turned to her sister and Emma stood back. Lizzie began with, "It can't . . ."

Emma pointed to the objects, was calm. "Take all of this away from me." For a moment everything was quiet. There was a light breeze. Then Emma's body began to tremble, a landslide of feeling. A strange noise dribbled from her throat. I would've laughed at her had I not wanted my money from the sisters so badly.

Lizzie tried to wrap her arm around Emma's back. "I knew," Emma whispered. "I knew." Emma pushed Lizzie, ran as fast as she could towards the house.

I looked at the skull and ax head. "Lizzie," I said, "I've been wondering: are you happier now that your father is dead?" A part of me wanted her to say no. I didn't want to be the only one who felt unfulfilled after they'd punished their parent.

Lizzie let out a scream, spat at my feet. "You wicked, you evil," she stuttered, looked as if everything was draining from her.

"That's how you thank me for taking the weapon? I helped save you. I kept it secret for you. I want my money."

She touched her forehead, stared at me dirty. She reached into her little purse, took out a coin and threw it at my feet. I did not care for that. Lizzie took off rickety towards the house, left me thinking all manner of things. There was some commotion coming from houses, neighbors sticking heads out of flyscreened doors. If I wasn't careful, I'd have a crowd. I could not let myself be caught, not now when I was so close. It was because of Lizzie and her uncle that I was in this position. I picked up the objects and put them back in my rucksack.

There was only one thing to do. I'd have to punish her, just like Papa, just like I did to make things right. I could taste sweet blood. A bird sounded loud in tree branches, front doors opened, voices flowed from them. My legs were leather as I walked towards Lizzie and Emma's house, whip-crack, whip-crack, hands thick, made of knuckles. I got to feeling that Lizzie owed me an explanation of exactly what happened that day.

I could tell the house had been freshly painted, white on white, and there was a small, drooping rose garden of pinks and white. The concrete steps leading up to the door were thick, primitive, a good place to crack a skull. A sweetheart seat swung in the wind on the front porch and as it swung, from the corner of my eye, I saw a man walk out from his house, hedge clippers in hand, and I gave him a nod of the head, good neighbor.

"What are you doing?" the neighbor called.

I turned my head. He cleared his throat, watched me. I ignored him, figured I could deal with him later if need be, went back down the front steps towards the side of the house. That voice of his called out again. By the side of the house there was a small dip in the ground and above that an open window. I searched around for something to stand on, saw a wicker chair near a pear tree. I lumbered the chair over, sat it under the windowpane and looked into the house. I heard Lizzie and Emma down the hall, their voices broken ceramics.

"You can't do this to me," Lizzie said.

"I've believed you as long as I could."

They came closer, Lizzie's back faced the entrance of the room. She stomped her feet. "You promised you'd never leave me."

"And you promised me that the past would stay there."

I licked my lips, pushed against the side of the house and leaned closer through the window. I was helping to destroy them.

"That wasn't my fault. That was a madman."

"I don't want you in my life anymore."

"You don't mean that." Lizzie's voice was beginning to thin, to die, like it did when she found her dead pigeons.

"I'm tired, Lizzie."

Lizzie's fingers grabbing, moving across Emma's hands.

"I've already called Mr. Porter. He'll be here soon to pick me up."

"You're breaking Mother's promise."

"Don't you dare." Emma gave a little push, made Lizzie stumble, and she went down the hall, left Lizzie screaming guttural, "We're sisters! We're sisters!"

Lizzie called after Emma, said, "But I love you." She shouted one last, "Don't make me be alone, Emma."

I thought of Mama, that was how things had ended between us too. No more promised love. I ground my teeth.

The neighbor shouted, "What are you doing?" and I turned from the window, saw him standing across from me in his yard and I knew my time was running out. I jumped away from the window, ran back along the side of the house towards the front door. My teeth clenched. I imagined my hand covering Lizzie's mouth, the weight I'd push into her.

I neared the front door as it opened. Emma came out with two suitcases, had a fraction of a smile. Lizzie called out, "One more chance." Emma said nothing, walked down the path to the edge of the street. A yellow Cameron Runabout pulled up and a man got out, took Emma's bags as she stepped inside the car. The engine revved.

My last chance to make everything right. The front door closed as the car drove away. I heard the neighbor—'I've warned you, now I'm calling the police'—and I took quick, short steps to the front of the house, walked over the word *Maplecroft* tattooed into concrete. The ax head bounced around in the rucksack. I imagined the sweetness of my fist flowing into Lizzie, the bright red she'd be. After I'd finished with her, I'd ransack her house, take what was mine and run away as fast as I could, run until I found my mama, run until I felt better inside. Inside the house Lizzie sobbed and I knocked on the door and waited for her to answer.

SIXTEEN

EMMA

August 4, 1892

JOHN WEAVED IN and out of the house like a specter, made me look over my shoulder more often than I would have liked. I wanted him to leave, to take the police with him, to take the bodies too. But the idea of being alone in the house with Lizzie was too much. I couldn't bear the idea of not having someone to talk to other than my sister, to help occupy my mind.

I asked Alice Russell to move temporarily into 92 Second Street.

"But, Emma, what if the murderer comes back?" she said, her hair thick from sweat.

I tried to reassure her. "We can all sleep in Lizzie's room. Stay together."

When we went upstairs to see Lizzie, she had other plans. She sat plump against her pillows, looked both tired and well rested, the strangeness of a face grieving. "There's no need for us to be cooped up in here. Alice should take Father and Mrs. Borden's room." Lizzie smiled. "And you'll still be nice and close to me and Emma, help us lift our spirits."

Alice knocked her knuckles against her chin. "I don't feel comfortable going in their bedroom."

"I'm sure they wouldn't mind, would they, Emma?" Lizzie chewed on a nail.

I shook my head. "Lizzie, this doesn't feel right somehow . . ."

"Nothing about today feels right, Emma. But we do what needs to be done." Lizzie mimicked the sound of reason. I wanted to shake her stupid.

Downstairs the clock struck three and my thoughts returned to Fairhaven. I would've finished my art class by then.

"Alice is my friend and I think she should stay in the room. It's the only decent room left in the house with space for all of Alice's things," Lizzie said.

For a moment I had the feeling to push Lizzie in the ribs, tell her, "Alice was my friend first. Without me you'd never have her. I should decide what happens." I didn't want to upset things now, not when there was so much left unanswered. Alice stroked Lizzie's hair, and I wished Alice to do the same for me. As girls and young women, the three of us used to sit in a semicircle and draw on each other's backs. "Guess what shape I'm drawing now," I would say.

"A square?" Alice said, missing the finer details.

Lizzie pushed into my fingers. "A hexagon."

"Yes!"

Lizzie always guessed right, made me want to boast, "Look at what I taught her! She's the smartest one in the room."

Alice gasped, like lightning had struck. She turned to me and said, "I just remembered that I was speaking to your father the day before last."

My heart surged, expected divine final thoughts. "What did he say?"

"He asked about my mother and father. He wondered if they might like to stop by for dinner one evening."

"That's odd. He didn't tell me about those plans," Lizzie said. "He's barely spoken to them in months."

"Maybe that's why he invited them," I said.

Alice snaked fingers over her lips. "But I forgot to tell them. I haven't told them. It completely slipped my mind . . ."

A part of me wanted them to arrive for the dinner, for Father's goodwill gesture to outlive him.

"It seems so sad now to remember." Alice continued stroking Lizzie's hair and Lizzie nuzzled into the motion, a mewing cat.

"It is sad, Alice," I said. "My father died. You got to speak to him one last time and you forgot all about it." I was a pain inside, the kind without a central source.

"Goodness, I've said something wrong. I'm sorry." Alice's face crumpled.

I stood from them. "I think it's time to leave Lizzie alone now."

Alice slid out from under the weight of Lizzie's head on her lap, let her land softly on feather pillows. "Of course."

When we were in Father and Abby's room I shut the door. I felt comfort, relief that we were away from Lizzie, that I could have my friend to myself. "I'm glad you're here, Alice."

She ratcheted her head around the room, then stiffened and said, "What's that strange smell?"

I sniffed. A hot room that had been closed off most of the day. I sniffed again, caught the tail end of sulphur, of singed hair.

"It smells like something died." Alice pinched her nose, pinched away the putrid smell. "I don't think I want to sleep in here, Emma."

I wanted her to stay, wanted her near, wanted something familiar. "What if I try getting rid of the smell?"

"I'm not sure . . ."

I searched the room—perhaps a piece of rancid meat from Abby's late-night feedings, a dead mouse trapped behind a wall. I searched, found nothing but a used handkerchief underneath the bed.

As I pulled myself up from the floor I caught a hint of decay in the corner. I took a deep breath and let the smell momentarily take over. "There's something horrid in here," I said, sniffed the corner again, followed the scent up the wall as far as I could reach on tiptoe. It was flooding down from the ceiling.

"I can't believe how strange all of this is, Emma," Alice said. "Nothing is normal."

"I mean, it's so strange to believe that this all happened, just as Lizzie feared."

I turned sharp, a knife. "What are you talking about?"

"Last night Lizzie told me she had a premonition. I feel like this has already happened."

"What did Lizzie say?"

Alice took my hand and she told me about the night before, how Lizzie had come to her after supper and reported that the entire household had fallen ill. "Lizzie was so very upset. It was most unexpected to see her, Emma."

I could imagine Lizzie running across the road towards Borden Street, the way she had many times before, filled her lungs with chalk-dirt air, knees locking from the exertion. She would have rounded the corner, her cheeks rosing like she'd been running a lifetime. By the time she arrived at Alice Russell's house, Lizzie's heart would have been in her mouth.

Alice said, "I heard all this fuss and I opened the door and there she was. I said, 'By God, Lizzie! You look a fright. What's gotten into you?'"

"'Alice, someone is trying to poison the family.'"

The things that happened next: tea was made, cake was cut and Alice was appropriate: she tucked in her ditch-round chin, widened her heavy-hooded eyes, gasped like a canyon when required. "How do you know?"

I could see Lizzie fanning herself with her hand. "Father and Mrs. Borden are very sick tonight, very sick. And the other day, I felt dreadful. We're always so sick lately. I just have this feeling . . ."

"You should alert the police," Alice had said, cupped her hand over heart.

"I'm beginning to think Father has many enemies."

Under kerosene light, Alice Russell heard prophecies of doomed Borden life. Lizzie told her, "I've noticed strangers around the street. Haven't you?"

Alice shook her head.

"After Mrs. Borden's necklaces were stolen in broad daylight last year, strange men have been lurking about. I think whoever robbed us knows there's money inside Father's bedroom. The other day I saw a man standing under the gaslight up by the church and at the beginning of spring there was a man just outside our house!"

"My goodness! What does your father say?"

"I've not told anyone, especially Father; I don't want to frighten him. Poor old soul."

"And Emma?"

"Emma's not paying attention enough."

Alice then reached out and took Lizzie's hand.

"You've not noticed anyone at all? Not even the tall young man with a slouched cap?"

"No. No one. But it sounds like you've got good details of those lurkers to tell the police."

Lizzie fumbled with her teacup. She let cake crumbs fall into her lap. Alice tried to reassure her that everything would be alright, but paranoia stuck.

"I really do think this explains why we've been so sick lately. Even Bridget is sick."

"Who do you think would do such a thing?"

Lizzie shook her head.

I could not begin to fathom what Lizzie's premonition meant. Sometimes Lizzie just knew things. Alice pulled her hand away from me, shuddered from the memory of it all. "I'm sorry, Emma. It's a lot to tell you."

It was what I needed to hear. "If it doesn't bother you too much, I would like to hear more about what she said."

Alice furrowed brows. "I'm not sure I can remember. We kept talking but it seems like a fog. Lizzie went home not long after that."

I thought of Lizzie returning home, whether she had looked to the moon and called out for me, whether her voice bounced off attic windows, carried from one house after the other after the next. Did she hear owls echo in trees, or choruses of crickets throbbing against night heat? Did she hear a creek follow gravity and empty itself into the river? And when she got home, did she do anything to help stop the sickness?

———

My body ached. "Alice, let's try to get rid of this smell."

I opened the bedroom windows and let a breeze filter through.

"I think we need to do more. Will you help me clean the house?" I said.

Alice exhaled, stood still. "I think I should go home and collect some belongings to bring back here. Why don't you get Bridget to do it?"

My back tightened. There would be no more of Bridget doing anything; I thought of the way she had backed away from me earlier that afternoon, the disgust I had seen in her eyes as I reached out to touch her arm.

"Miss Emma." Bridget's voice deep and anxious.

"Was I ever mean to you? Don't pull away."

Bridget had said nothing. I wanted to ask her if she was alright, if she needed a rest from all the questioning. Instead I asked, "Are you able to prepare supper for extra guests tonight?"

The stairs made a cracking sound and Bridget snapped her head towards the back of the house. I touched her arm again and she flinched, brushed my hand away.

"I asked those police if I could leave for good and they told me yes," she said.

"But I need you to stay and help me fix up the house."

Bridget took a breath. "I won't."

"That's ridiculous. This is where you live."

She took a step up the stairs, paused, and took another then another. "I heard her this mornin'," Bridget said.

"Who?"

"Lizzie." Bridget hung her head.

My heart thundered. "Tell me what my sister said."

"She laughed as I let your father in."

"Lizzie's always laughing at something. It's how she is."

"No, miss. She was laughin' like a jackal as I opened the door. No one else was here."

I took a step up to Bridget, tried to close in on her. "This doesn't mean you have to leave. You'll stay here."

"This house is no good, Miss Emma. It's all sick and horror. Ya shouldn't stay either." Bridget pulled her shoulders tight together. "And I heard that noise again."

"What noise?"

"That awful chockin'. Like with the pigeons." Bridget shook her head and left me on the stairs. What on earth had she heard?

Bridget packed her bag and left Second Street without saying goodbye to Lizzie. I wanted to drag Bridget back to the house, the way I had been dragged back. Why should she get to leave?

———

Alice Russell promised to return after seven. It was up to me to clean the bloodied remains. I went downstairs, fetched a water pail and scrubbing brush from the basement, boiled water, poured the water into the pail, added soap. Every moment dragged. When the water had cooled slightly, I made my way to the sitting room. At the closed door that linked kitchen to sitting room, I took a breath, held on to my side where there was a dull ache of dissension.

I took another breath, opened the door. The room was emptied of bodies. The sofa was in front of me and I noticed it had been moved slightly from the wall and a crevasse formed the outline of maleness. I did not want to go into the room. Why couldn't I be more like my sister? She had moved around the house with ease all afternoon. I willed myself to step in, noticed a metallic smell: of heat and of too many voices. I dry-retched. There was a bloodstain on the sofa where Father's head had come undone. The stain had begun to overtake the room, unapologetic, as if it had always been there, and I felt like drowning. Why wasn't anyone there to save me? Lizzie made a small laugh echo upstairs, the way she always laughs, made my body ricochet against the sound. I looked at the bloodstain, took a step closer.

I counted the times I had overheard someone mention the state of Father's face, its new shape, or the way the back of Abby's head was opened and released: one, two, three, four, five, six, seven, eight, nine, ten. I touched the back of my head, felt along the bone that joined the neck. How long does it take the body to realise it is no longer breathing?

Another step.

Outside: the faint sounds of police patrolling the perimeter of the house. My dress suddenly felt too big, my hands and feet too small. There was so much work to be done. I wished I would disappear. I took a step closer to the sofa.

Another step.

I swallowed, caught a forgotten taste on the tip of my tongue, apple marmalade. Abby's marmalade was always too thick, never reached the same consistency as Mother's. Between the three women who made it, mine was the best. When I ate Abby's it always stuck to the end of my tongue, had the taste of slightly blackened apple toffee. Father had developed a liking for Abby's marmalade though, the way he slathered it thick on stale bread, the way he licked sticky from his lips. His enjoyment.

John had said how the men were wiping blood on clothes and towels all day. "You couldn't help but put your hands in it." Now I understood.

I sat at the foot of the sofa and placed my hands in the water. The space where Father's head had laid open was liquid-thick, imprecise. I expected him to walk through the door and tell me, "I had such a silly accident; I cut myself shaving," or, "There was a disagreement but it's all better now." I was surprised by expectation, these things the dead could bring you. The stain would be hard to remove. Along the carpet were signs of how Father had been escorted from the room: the shock of his carved face was signposted by a dropped handkerchief; the conversation as to where best to store the body until the undertaker arrived was marked by small congealed blood spatters by the entrance to the dining room. How long exactly was he lying here before help arrived? I looked at my hands; I should have used gloves. There was a crack and drag along floorboards above my head and I held my breath. Then: a voice. John's low tones followed by Lizzie's sweeping laughter. I gritted teeth, failed to see how any humor could be found on a day like today. I placed the bucket of warm soapy water at the head of the sofa and began scrubbing in small half-circles, looked at the carpet and noticed that there was at once too much blood and not enough blood for the crime committed. Why wasn't there more of him? When we were fourteen and four, Lizzie and I believed that Father was big enough to store the whole world inside his body, that in the center of his stomach was a map that led to a secret world: corners to wait and hide behind, desert mirages for swimming, table upon table of boiled sweets, sugar water to drink, wide gullies full of trees and creatures, ancient ruins, a mother. Then, when I was fifteen, I discovered that Father was no longer a father: he was a person, like all other adults, prone to failure. He couldn't possibly hold everything we wanted. The disappointment.

My wrists were lashed by the warmth of being with Father for the last time, those uncomfortable remnants. What had Lizzie's last moments with him been like?

I scrubbed the sofa, replayed the police officers' conversations:

"And she showed no signs of harm?"

"None that I could see."

"And she told you that she had found him lying down like such?"

"Yes. That is how Miss Lizzie had left him when Mr. Borden had come home."

"And she told you she found Mr. Borden?"

"Yes. She had said, 'Father's been cut.'"

Mrs. Churchill had told me, "I saw your father this morning on his way to work. He looked so nice." She paused. "I keep seeing your mother's body every time I close my eyes. I wish I hadn't gone upstairs with Bridget to get those stupid sheets."

I had stared at Mrs. Churchill's bulbous knuckles. Then she had whispered quick and fast to me, "When I first got here, I asked where your mother was and Lizzie told me she had gone to see a sick relative but then I kept asking her and she said the strangest thing: "I don't know but I think they have killed her too."" Mrs. Churchill began to sob. "I'm not going to tell the police about that because Lizzie was in all sorts of ways. God, to think this was all happening while I was next door. Emma, I didn't hear a thing. If I had, I would've rushed right over."

I leaned across and kissed Mrs. Churchill on the cheek, her ghost-cold skin. "Thank you for looking after Lizzie," I said and my body shook. Why would Lizzie have said such a thing?

Father had once told me, "You have a slow brain for facts." But there I was collecting:

I had asked, "Has the culprit been apprehended?"

I had asked, "Has anything been stolen from the house?"

I asked again, "How long until the murderer is found?"

I scrubbed, blood covered hand. The brush in the water, the brush on the sofa, I scrubbed.

Father's blood was thicker than I'd first thought. It had seeped into the carpet, watered the floral pattern and stained the wood below. I put the brush back into the water and rinsed, all the red, rinsed again. I absent-mindedly wiped the sofa legs with my fingers then wiped my cheek. I closed my eyes, heard a heavy thud upstairs. I gazed towards the ceiling, towards the place where Abby had been found, thought of what would have to be cleaned up there. My knees dug into the floor. I wanted Lizzie to come down and help. Another thud. Laughter.

I scrubbed the carpet, my scalp itched from sweat and heat and I stopped scrubbing, took stock of my work, all that was yet to be done before the funeral. My hands drowned in water, a faded red ring formed around my wrists, the blood that kept coming. I took the bucket outside, past the police lining the perimeter of the house, and threw the water onto the pear arbor. Over the fence I heard Mary and Mrs. Kelly:

"I didn't see a thing, Mrs. Kelly," Mary said.

"Imagine that poor daughter having to come home to all of that!"

"That family . . ."

Why did this have to happen to my family? I waited for the conversation to end and when it did, the women went away and I was on my own. I walked back inside, refilled the bucket with warm water. Back on my hands and knees I cleaned the wall behind the sofa, noticed hair-fine cracks along the skirting board and tried not to think about Father, but he was all around me. I scrubbed harder, knowing that behind the wall, Father's and Abby's bodies were rigid from disbelief. The heat trapped in the room ran across my fingers. I wiped them on my dress, afraid of what the air was carrying.

A strange wind howl whipped from the floral carpet; a lost child, frightened animal, a haunting. I scrubbed, my throat tight and sore, a strangulation, and the howl came again, so loud it filled my ears, stung my eyes, shocked the hair on my arms into tiny needles. The howl. The howl was me. How had I forgotten what grief would sound like? I was no stranger to it.

Then there was movement along the ceiling and a door opened. At the top of the stairs Lizzie sighed and cleared her throat before walking down and I dragged my head towards my sister: arms folded across her chest, head tilted to the side.

"Emma, don't cry," Lizzie cooed, took a step closer.

I pulled back. Lizzie looked at the dining room door. Her fingers twitched, mouth opened and she stared at the mess in front of us. The bucket of blood-water hummed. Watching Lizzie, my strange, strange sister, she became a shadow. I could smell the secrets on her, that mushroom scent. Eyes on each other, Lizzie's hand licked the dining room door handle.

"Lizzie, don't open that door." I wiped my eyes, caught sulphur swim from my fingers.

She looked down at the bucket of bloodied water, her hand across her stomach. "Did all of that come from him?" Like a child in wonder.

"Yes."

"It doesn't seem real," Lizzie whispered.

I wanted to ask her, "How much blood did you think there was going to be?" but thought better. A suspicion shouldn't be acted upon. Lizzie came to me, kneeled beside: her, me, us, like children looking at caught tadpoles. Lizzie stuck her hand in the water and closed her eyes. "Why is it so cold?"

I took her hand out and held it in mine.

"Emma, I think I told a lie. The house wasn't locked all day. The basement doors were open." Lizzie was monotone, a hint of defeat.

I knew there had to be something. "When?"

"I left them open this morning." Lizzie in a tiny whisper.

"Have you told anyone?"

Lizzie was pale. "No. Should I?"

The clock went six. "No. Doors can be opened, doors can be closed."

Lizzie's cheeks flushed color. "Yes, they can." She squeezed my hand. "I'm frightened I might have done the wrong thing."

I stroked her skin, stroked away the blood-water. "It's okay. I'm here."

Lizzie tucked her chin, couldn't quite look me in the eye. "Do you still love me?"

I hardened: ribs ached, fingers tired, shrivelled. It always came down to love. I wanted to say, "No." Then, "Not always," then, "Sometimes I wish you were dead."

"Yes," I told her. "I do."

Lizzie stared at the dining room door, hooked and unhooked the corners of her mouth. She looked as if she wanted to cry but couldn't remember how. When I was in Fairhaven I had thought about the existence of the past, how it hid underneath the skin. At the time it had been difficult to acknowledge that the past was gnawing inside me, that everything—Father, Mother, dreams, baby Alice, a walk along the river, a failed attempt at love, Lizzie, a groaning moon, the death of things, Abby—was stitching together to make a covering, a second skin. It had been uncomfortable. I had even hated it. But now there wasn't much left. The life I'd had was disappearing. Every adult who had ever held me as a baby was dead and no one would ever carry me again. I looked at my sister, looked at blood. That grief inside the heart.

———

I kept myself busy for days, made arrangements for the funerals, made cups of tea for anyone who stopped by the house. They all asked about Lizzie, how she was coping, if there was anything they could do for her. "It must be so hard on the poor thing." This neighborhood chorus that never sang for me. I wanted them gone, to be left alone so I could gather my thoughts. I kept moving and before I knew it, it was the morning of the funerals.

Just after dawn, I went to the basement to wash myself, listened to morning birds fly in and out of nests, the quietness of the house. There was a dull ache, deep and sharp inside, a small death.

I filled a metal tub with water, the sound of rain on roofs, sat on a stool, placed my hands in the water, warm. I washed my body, washed my feet, remembered Father washing Mother the night she died, how he hadn't wanted to look at her face and had, instead, studied the length of her limbs, the width of her heart. When Father had reached Mother's hands, I waited for him to kiss them. Instead he meticulously cleaned underneath her fingernails before gently crossing them over her chest. I had asked if I could help but he had said, "Death is not meant for children," and he made me wait outside his bedroom in case baby Lizzie woke wanting her mother. I went to Lizzie and watched her like a night-soldier.

While I washed, I tried to concentrate on the tasks at hand: family configurations to sort out, the placement of coffins, but all I could think about was everything I still wanted to ask Father and tell him:

1. Why did you ignore me so much after Mother died?
2. Why did you have to marry Abby?
3. Why did you forgive Lizzie for every little thing?
4. It was Lizzie who broke into your bedroom and stole Abby's belongings.
5. I had planned a whole life and you ruined it.
6. Tell me again about the day I was born.
7. There's something you should know about me and Samuel Miller.
8. I remember how your mouth creased when you smiled.
9. Sometimes you are a vile man.
10. I caught Abby praying for a child of her own.
11. Tell me again what my first words were.

12. Did you see who did this to you?
13. I forgive you, I forgive you.

The tub water went cold. The sound of movement upstairs. I dressed in my black mourning silks, patted them hard onto my body until they felt like second skin, placed an oval-shaped silver and turquoise enamel locket around my neck. Inside was a photograph of Mother and Father, finally together after decades between deaths. I emptied the bath water into the sink, looked around the basement: shadows against the walls. Was this where the weapon was hidden? I surveyed the foundations, looked for markings in wood, blood riddles. On the wall by the basement door: a rust-brown handprint. I aligned my hand against the dried print. It was smaller than mine. My hand shook. It's my experience that a man's hand is always big. But this. I didn't want to think about who it could belong to. I noticed a basket full of Lizzie's washing in the corner. I picked through her dirty clothes, days of Lizzie sitting stagnant, that heavy smell, sifted through dresses. I found a slightly hardened white apron, sniffed. Putrid. There was a faded red stain near the bottom of the apron, close to where a groin would be. Someone's time. I felt guilty for looking. I hid the apron at the bottom of the basket, layered Lizzie's dresses on top. The air in the basement was dark and muted and I remembered Lizzie telling me, "The police haven't found a weapon! Imagine not being able to find one!" She had made it seem like a joke.

———

The house was put in order for the funeral and I waited for the undertaker to arrive while Alice Russell made tea. "It's the least I can do," she said. Alice looked at me, saw my armful of Father's and Abby's clothes. "Are they special outfits, Emma?"

"They're clothes they wore," I said. The idea of special things, it hadn't occurred to me. A careless daughter: what would people think? I went upstairs to Father and Abby's bedroom to find them something else to wear.

The last time I had chosen Father's clothes was the day he married Abby. I had carefully picked the necktie and cufflinks, Lizzie chose the brown leather shoes. Before the ceremony we stood in Father's bedroom doorway in awe of our creation. He had looked understated, the way a father should.

Now I had to choose for an ending. Common sense told me that couples should dress in marital cloth, eternity vows going deeper and deeper into the earth. But I decided against common sense. I opened Abby's wardrobe, fingered the drab clothing that had been worn day in and day out. In the back of the wardrobe were silks, blue, red and orange, velveteen capes. Abby had the habit of holding on to past glory: the dresses that once fit her pre-marital body now hid underneath protective covers. She must have believed she would fit them once again.

Abby's wedding dress was there, also under a cloth cover. I paused; weddings, funerals, the same gathering of family. I left the wedding dress where it was, pulled out a simple house dress. I lifted the dress from the hanger and caught the smell of sweat and faded lavender water. How many times had Abby worn it? Had she caught the scent of herself ripening? Had she wondered, "Am I rotting from the inside?" Now the old woman would be buried in the stink. I knew I should find her something else. I was surprised by the detailing on dresses that I had ignored each day:

lace rosettes, fine needlepoint cross-stitch, an owl. I couldn't help but hold the garments close to my body and imagine myself in them, how they would scratch at skin or gather around hips. In the end I chose the blue house dress and a pink silk scarf to drape over Abby's dead shoulders.

It was easier to choose Father's burial clothes: his Sunday best. Black wool and a white cotton shirt. Uniform. I went downstairs and when the undertaker arrived, handed him the clothing. "Dress them gently," I said. The undertaker nodded.

I went to Lizzie's bedroom, knocked on the door before entering. Inside Lizzie sat on her bed, overdressed in mourning: head-to-toe jet black, a crepe dress, long, fat, silk bows around her neck and on her back, a mid-chin-length veil. Over her heart Lizzie wore two thin ribbons of royal blue and ivy green, one for Abby, one for Father.

Lizzie stroked an ostrich feather. "You took your time coming to get me."

Heat crept along my spine, hammered my cheeks. "Everyone will be here soon."

"I'm not quite ready." The feather was twisted around and around, was let go.

"Get up, Lizzie!" I shouted, made my throat strain.

Lizzie slammed her fist into her mattress. "You're mean! I'm doing the best I can."

Doing her best. Not good enough. I strode to her, shoved my arm underneath Lizzie's shoulders, tried to lift her up.

"Let me go!" she screamed, thrashed, and I lifted her a little more, her heaviness, and she said again, "Let me go!"

All the things that could have been said.

———

Mourners began to arrive, told me, "The floral arrangements are lovely." I smiled politely, relieved that someone noticed the finer details of my grief.

Bridget arrived at the front door, wore an ill-fitting, new-looking black silk and cotton dress, gave me a bouquet of violets tied together with a royal blue ribbon. "Could ya put these on for Mrs. Borden?" She'd been crying.

"You're not staying?" I wanted to touch her, to see if she would reveal anything more about what she saw that day.

"No, miss. I'm not family."

"I know, but I thought . . ."

"I'd like to just give ya these flowers. She would've liked 'em." Bridget forced the flowers into my hand, a petal fell onto the carpet.

"That's very decent of you, Bridget."

She looked over my shoulder into the sitting room. "Is Miss Lizzie in there? Is she alright?"

"She's talking to family. Lizzie's been up and down since it happened. Do you want to speak to her?" I should have pulled her inside.

Bridget shook her head, made her cheeks squelch. "No doubt I'll be seein' her around." We looked at each other, Bridget whitening like a spectre. "I'll be off now, Miss Emma."

Bridget backed away from the door, backed out into the heat of Second Street. I stuck my head through the door, leaned into a small breeze, watched Bridget girdle down the street, hold her head high as if trying to look into neighbors' houses to see how they lived. I almost called out, wanted to ask if I could go with her.

There was a tug at my hip. I turned. It was Mrs. Churchill, black-veiled, rouged cheeks. "Emma, are you alright?"

"I needed some air. Bridget was here."

Mrs. Churchill lifted her veil, tried to push past me and look outside. "Oh? Is she coming back? She could be serving everyone tea."

I gently pulled her inside and shut the front door. "I don't think so."

We returned to the small crowd gathering in the sitting room, and I went to the parlor, placed the flowers on Abby's coffin. My knuckles grazed smooth wood. I had been afraid to touch it, afraid that it might tip over, open up, pour her body onto the carpet.

I paced a path from kitchen to sitting room until the service began, made clumsy pots of tea. On each trip, I watched Lizzie, sitting on a black chair, take hands of condolence and say, "Thank you for coming," and "You've no idea of the horror." Lizzie the consummate griever, Lizzie outdoing me once again.

When the service began we sat in front of Father's and Abby's coffins. My legs knocked together, collisions of hard stone knees, and nerves churned through my body, made me want to pass out. I stared at Father's coffin. How was it possible that he could be reduced to hard wood and brass? I quickly glanced around the room: one day this small gathering of friends and family would assemble for me. Lizzie grabbed my hand, trembled, and I squeezed tight until she relaxed.

The priest held his hands in front of his stomach: short-fingered, well-practised gestures of Father, Son and Holy Spirit. He began summarizing Father's life and I expected an historic account of true love between Mother and Father, but all he gave was, "Beloved husband of first wife Sarah, who passed some years before he met

Abby. Many here would agree that marriage to his dear Abby healed the hole in his heart left by Sarah . . ."

This could not be all that Mother was reduced to. I tightened my grip on Lizzie and considered for the first time the possibility that Father had stopped loving Mother, had truly moved on with his life without telling us that we should have done the same.

———

It had rained the day Father brought Abby home to us. I was thirteen-and-a-half years old and they were not yet married. It was cold, fingers prickled from pins and needles. Mother had once told me that the prickling sensation meant that fingers needed to tickle someone. So I went to find Lizzie, pounced on her, drew her close and hunkered my fingers into her ribs, waited for blood to return sensation. Lizzie's mouth opened wide; my triumph of joy.

Abby held Father's hand when she came into the sitting room. She smiled, cheeks pulled tight into soft balls, little cakes. The rain fell. The thick blue vein along the side of Abby's neck pulsated and galloped, linked panic and excitement of impending motherhood together.

As Father spoke, I noticed Abby's hand squeeze tight around his wedding hand.

"Abby is happy to meet you." Father brought her slightly forwards towards us.

Lizzie leaped from my lap and stood next to Abby. Lizzie smiled; disconnected pebbled teeth. Abby's fingers swirled across Lizzie's hair, untangled knots.

"How are you, Lizzie?"

How could she know about us already?

"Goody good."

"Emma, say hello to Abby." Father was forceful, opened his palm wide by his side.

"Hello." It was hard to say.

Abby's lips formed a relaxed smile, the kind that inspired painters. I smiled back involuntarily.

Father told me, "Find your sister's coat so we can all take a walk."

"But it's raining." I was a whinge.

"It's only light rain." Father stroked his dark beard, was struggling to keep himself light-hearted.

"Do you need help?" Abby asked.

"I know where they are."

I went to the cupboard underneath the stairs, my hands fell across lengths of wool and broadcloth: Father's coat, my coat, Lizzie's coat. I let my hands drift further to the back of the cupboard. Wool and fur. Mother's coat. Every now and then, when nobody was looking, I put on her coat and stood in front of the mirror. The coat hit my ankles; sleeves stopped just before fingernails. How many years does it take to grow into someone? If I tried hard enough, I could find Mother on the inside of the coat's neck, underneath two large buttons. Oil of Rose, a sweetness. I would pull the coat tighter around my body and thought of myself inside Mother: how warm it must have been underneath all her skin.

Now the coat waited in the back of the cupboard. I rubbed the neck and closed my eyes. "Today would be a wonderful day to wear you," but thought better: I didn't want to give away this secret in case Abby, this stranger, wanted to wear it. Some things needed protection. I pulled Lizzie's coat down with my own and shut the cupboard. When I turned around, Abby was standing at the doorway and she said, "We thought we'd lost you."

When the rain stopped the four of us walked down Second Street, me and Lizzie leading the way. Behind us: Father and Abby, unified strides. I watched over my shoulder, saw Father look love at Abby. I had seen this type of behavior before—newlyweds at Sunday services.

Lizzie pulled on my hand and we skipped ahead. I was happy to put a little distance between me and the paternal mutiny that was taking place behind us.

"Not so far, chickens," Father called out.

Abby giggled, mistaking his unease for happiness.

There was laughter and small words, little secrets to be kept from daughters.

"I can see the resemblance in their faces." Abby was kind-voiced.

"Sometimes she comes through in their personalities and I don't know what to do."

"Just embrace it," she said.

"I don't want them to be exactly like Sarah. There were problems between us." Father said it serious.

"But she loved them."

"My word she did."

"And I will love them too."

"Good."

I placed my hand over my heart, my breath strangled. What problems? I thought about Father praying over Mother's body the day she died, the way he held her hand. There had been a strange smell in the bedroom that day; it stuck to me. It traveled with me for days afterwards. It had slowly crept into the house a few days before Mother had died; sour and aged, bitter on the tongue. It had stained Mother's hair, made me too afraid to touch. At night the smell took the form of molasses, a hint of sulphur slurping under doors and through keyholes. I had accepted it. A dutiful daughter, I made a hole in my lung and let the smell fill it completely. Then, a week after Mother died, the smell disappeared, leaving the house feeling completely empty.

SEVENTEEN

LIZZIE

August 6, 1892

ON THE MORNING of the funerals, an officer told us that an old man had handed himself over to the police the day before, had told them to hang him for the murders. He had brought his own noose. *Where would you even buy one of those?* The officer described him: sixty-two, thin hair, beard cut short and ragged. "We offered him breakfast but he refused. Said he didn't want to add to his weight and run the risk of breaking the rope." *Swing, swing, swing.* The idea of it made me shiver. The old man's confession took an hour and in the end, the police called for his son to take him home to bed.

"Why did he confess?" I asked.

"Beats me. But, then, we get all kinds confessing to things they didn't do. Maybe he was hoping we would hang him so he could be done with his life?"

I wondered if Father had ever confessed to anything. What would it feel like to do that?

In the dining room where Father and Mrs. Borden had spent two days hidden in the heat, the undertaker placed them in their coffins and opened the door wide, presented them like two debutantes. The smell from their temporary tomb raced through the house, rubbing up against the drapes as it made its way up the stairs towards our bedrooms. Emma opened one of the windows and took a deep breath. "At least this will all be over soon."

For two days every conversation ended with the same wish: at least this will be over soon. When Mrs. Borden's sister came by the house the day before the funeral and asked to see Abby, I told her, *She's dead! She's dead!* "It's best not to go inside the room."

She pouted like a stupid baby. "I wanted to put this on Abby." She held a royal blue silk sash that was frayed at the ends. She paused. "Goodness, I don't even know how I came to have this back in my possession."

"We're deciding what Father and Mrs. Borden will wear." I folded my hands across my chest and she hung her head, looked at her feet. From this angle I could see that Mrs. Borden and her sister had the same hairline, the same bone pattern at the back of the head. I smiled.

"Lizzie, she's my sister. Can't you be kind, just this once?"

I didn't like what she was accusing me of. I gave her a look, made her step back from me.

"Perhaps it could go in the coffin with her," she said, eyebrows raised, meeting thick in the middle.

How much room does a body take in a box? "Perhaps," I said.

She handed me the sash. It was cold, the ends a tickle on fingertips, *this feeling from a time ago*, and there was a tapping in the middle of my spine; fingers crawling over skin making patterns. I closed my eyes and fingers crawled and crawled: Mrs. Borden, Abby, *Abby!* tracing love hearts over my five-year-old shoulders, her fingers warm, palms pudgy-soft. Her sister chases me around their house, taps me on the shoulder and says, "You're it! I'll let you be the queen of the castle." As queen I eat too much cake and my stomach balloons, aches. Abby sends me to her old bedroom to rest. Inside her room, Abby's old dresses hang in the cupboard, all shades of blues and greens that smell like dreams, *dreams I could have!* There is a blue dress full of Abby's happy dreams. I touch the fabric, and under my fingers I feel a little boat in the middle of the widest ocean, Abby at the helm. She moves the boat along a blue sash, and in the distance, around the collar, there is a little island. With all of her strength Abby paddles the boat towards the island using only her hands. She makes it to the shore and jumps out, digs her bare feet into the sand. I take the blue dress off the hanger and hug it, put it over my own dress and Abby comes into the bedroom and tells me, "You can keep that, little darling." She rubs my shoulders and it feels like love. When we go home Emma is waiting for me in my bedroom.

"Look what I got, Emma."

Emma looks. "Where is it from?"

"Mother gave it to me. There's even a dream stitched inside of it! It's about boats and adventures."

Emma folds her arms, pinches her elbows hard. "You should give it back to Abby."

"Why? She said I could have it. You can wear it too if you like."
I turn in a little circle to show her how the dress swirls. "What's
the matter?"

"Don't take things from her."

"Why?"

"Because I said so." Emma walks to her bedroom. "Why do
you have to love her?"

"I won't if you don't want me to," I whisper, *I want to love
everyone.* I sprinkle my hands over the dress, let my fingers slide
down the blue sash.

———

When Mrs. Borden's sister stepped inside the house she said,
"There's a passage I'd like the priest to say for Abby at the funeral."

"It's all been taken care of. We can't change a thing."

She pressed her hand on the dining room door as if waiting for
Mrs. Borden to open it and then she cried.

"It's best not to go in there. It's been awfully hot. We've done
our best to block the door. I've hardly smelled a thing."

She took her hand away. "Why would you say such a horrid
thing?"

I considered answering when Uncle came down the stairs and
said, "Can I escort you home?"

She nodded and they walked out of the room.

"Don't worry, it'll all be over soon," Uncle said and they passed
two police officers guarding the front of the house. *Good riddance.*

A thick haze passed through my body, made me lightheaded.
I rubbed my forehead. Pressure built behind my eyes, tiny flecks
of blood flicked and flicked until all I saw was red and flesh, the

way Father had looked on the sofa, how a finger had twitched, *nerve endings, nerve endings*, the way Mrs. Borden had been on the floor. I pressed hands into eyes. How do I know these things? A yelp crawled out of my throat, staggered. A hand on my shoulder. I opened my eyes.

"Lizzie." Dr. Bowen stood in front of me. "Let me help you relax."

We sat on the sofa in the sitting room, *Father, Father.* I handed him the blue sash. "Could you get rid of this in the incinerator? I can't have it in the house."

"Of course." Dr. Bowen took the sash. "Memories can be painful." He took out his syringe and injected me. Sweet, sweet warmth. It had been like that for two days, this taking medicine. It made it easier to talk to police when they kept pestering me with questions.

"I don't know. I don't know," I had said. "Can't the others tell you what I saw?"

"We need to hear it from you, Miss Borden . . ."

Then I would sleep and Dr. Bowen and everyone would leave. When I woke, Emma would be there scratching at my memory like an old cat. "Tell me," she'd say or, "I don't understand. I don't understand . . ." She was loud in my ear. It made me feel terrible and I'd get scared, begin to believe that she'd leave if I didn't tell her something. I couldn't stand that happening.

"Come and cuddle me in bed," I'd say and she would. For a moment I'd feel safe, feel like I could tell Emma anything. "I had a bad dream the other night."

"When you woke up screaming?"

"Yes. I dreamed a man was standing over me . . . I thought it was Father."

Emma patted me on the back. "It was just a dream."

"But it was so real. What if it was Father coming to check on me?"

"Everything must be very confusing for you."

Emma pulled me onto my side and into her breast, her heart beating into my ear and temple. "Yes, it is. That's why I can't tell you anything more." I would say these things and Emma would cry and cry. It made me mad, *why does she cry? She wasn't even here when I needed her*, and I wanted to crawl inside her and say a prayer so I could make her stop, *as the Lord liveth, there shall no punishment happen to thee for this thing.*

———

Before the guests came, Uncle gathered Emma and me together in the parlor. We sat and held hands and he said, "My poor girls, who would have imagined."

"I'm glad we have each other now," I said. I bent down, kissed Uncle's hand, kissed Emma's hand.

"Not now," Emma whispered. *Always telling me what to do.*

We heard two police officers talk outside the front window. "I bet it is someone they know."

"What makes you say that?"

"No one lets you get that close to whack them."

They laughed.

I touched my forehead. Emma took a deep breath, covered her ears. Uncle patted her leg. She stiffened. "I think I'll go out and get fresh air," he said.

I pulled the curtain open and looked outside, saw the priest walk towards the house, weave in and out of the large crowd that was gathering. I could see reporters slot themselves in between strangers. One of them saw me. I smiled, *so polite I am.*

"Lizzie, pull the curtain back." Emma's voice was hackled.

What else do I have to do to make her happy? I watched Emma, saw her hands and fingers fumble with thumbs. I looked down at my own: quiet, restful. Emma clicked her tongue, crossed and uncrossed her ankles then stared me down.

"What are you looking at me for?"

She took a breath, squeezed her voice out. "Lizzie, I really need to ask you. Are you sure you didn't see anyone around the house?"

"I said I don't know! I was too busy minding my own business to think about keeping an eye out for Father's killer."

"I'm sorry, I'm just . . ."

"You wouldn't have to ask me these questions if you hadn't gone away."

"What are you saying?"

"Maybe no one would have died."

"Are you saying this is my fault?" Emma high-pitched, a nasty.

Yes. No. I want everything to be gobbled up. "It's just that maybe a monster wouldn't have broken in if an extra person had been here to guard the house."

"Nothing makes sense anymore." Emma rubbed her eyes and face.

"Do you think I'm making things up? That I'm lying to you all?"

She looked at me, opened her mouth to speak but nothing came out. I could see her teeth, a few crooked edges, her flat tongue sliding over them. For a moment she was repulsive. "You're a terrible, terrible sister," I whispered.

Emma bowed her head, flipped her fingers in palms. A tiny breeze crawled over my ears and onto my face. Everything still. There was a small creak-creak in the walls of the house and Emma shuddered. Somewhere in the bottom of my mind there was a voice,

She will leave you if you keep secrets. Sweat ran down my temple, came to the corner of my mouth. I sipped it up. Nothing made sense anymore. I lunged for Emma and wrapped my arms around her, sat at her feet, waited for her heartbeat to sync with mine. I held her tight and I thought of her leaving. I cried.

"Shhhh," she said. "Shhhhh."

For a time everything was gold. My heart beat love, made me calm, and I cocooned myself against my sister.

Then, in a small voice, she said, "How could a weapon have disappeared?"

I pulled back from her. My hand slapped Emma across her cheek, slapped it again. "You ruin everything!" I said. A small fire exploded at the back of my neck and under my arms. I got up from the floor, made it creak, and headed for the backyard, *if she wants all this horror so much, I'll show her.*

I walked outside to the pear arbor and sat under leaves, let the fruit sweep my hair. I reached my hand up and pulled down on a pear, took a bite, let juice drip. Teeth ground teeth and my skin heated. Emma and her constant questions. Why do people care so much about what I did that day and what I saw?

I went to the barn, walked in. Pigeon feathers lay on the ground. I kicked them, made clouds. I climbed the ladder up to the loft and looked out the window onto the house. I hated everything I saw. I rushed over to the little box in the corner of the room, *I'll show her.* I lifted the cover and looked inside. What I expected to see had become invisible. Panic in my heart. I looked again. I rubbed my forehead. From outside I heard my name being called and I climbed down the ladder, decided never to go back into the barn again.

———

After the final prayer, the coffins were taken out of the parlor and into the street, the sequoia cherry wood bright and sunny against dark-green tree leaves. We followed them to the hearse, hemmed in by the crowd that stretched six houses to the left and six houses to the right. Emma crossed her arm over mine and her body tilted, caught off balance by the small waves of sound. I held her tight, walking straighter than I ever had before. It was easy. Some of the neighborhood women reached for us, said, "We are sorry for your loss," and "Is there anything we can do for you?" I smiled at them, *these people who will always love me.* Two children from Sunday school pressed their sweat-sticky hands into the side of my dress and said, "We'll pray for you, Miss Borden. May God protect their souls."

"Thank you, sweet ones. How thoughtful of you." There's a certain love that comes in grief. Tastes sweet in the heart.

I looked up at the house towards the guest room where Mrs. Borden was found. The house caught a handful of sunlight and shone it in my eyes and there in the window I could see her looking down at me, her hair tangled, falling below her round shoulders. The house moved around her. She closed her eyes and as the house began to shut its curtains, shadows poured over her face, her cheeks swelled into mountains, growing past her head and body until they filled the room and made it a cave.

"I don't want to live in the house anymore," I said.

Emma pushed into my ribs. "But it's home."

It was difficult to breathe.

I wanted us to go to Europe then, sit in front of fireplaces and sip champagne. I'd make Emma my student, show her new ways of living, stop her from thinking that we belonged in this ugly house.

"Tell us what you saw, Lizzie!" women said.

"Tell us so we can find them!" men said.

These chalky voices in my ear, *all these questions.* I covered my face with my hand and Emma swept her arm over my back. Uncle helped us into the carriage, giving me a look, and I knew that I would be alright.

We followed Father and Mrs. Borden down Second Street. Their coffins swayed slightly at the back of their carriage, a final waltz, right onto Rock Street where we walked once, all holding hands. The breeze picked up, cooling us, and letting out a sigh, I took Emma's hand and stroked it, tried to put her sad and empty face to the back of my mind. I had seen this face only once before, when I had told her that I didn't love her anymore. After she had made me promise never to say it again, she told me, "It's important that we're together, Lizzie."

The coffins were taken to the undertaker's quarters as our carriage continued down the path, through oak tree soldiers, towards the family plot where Mother and baby Alice were waiting. When Mrs. Borden's family had arrived and after the priest shook hands with the men, Father and Mrs. Borden were brought to us.

"This is it," Emma whispered to me.

There was no need to answer. I watched Father sink low into the ground and settle next to Mother while Mrs. Borden came for both of them in her hard wooden cage. I rubbed my forehead.

The priest blessed the earth and held his cross over the grave, grinding prayers into the ground, his voice pleading with God to take care of this husband and wife in death as much as he had in life, *ah, but here they are butchered and betrayed*, and he prayed for Emma and me, their heaven-sent children.

I could feel Emma's heavy heart pounding her into the dirt inch by inch, past the tree roots, burying her too early. We stood arm in arm on top of the earth that would one day be our own. The ground looked so small. I wondered how I would fit.

The priest stepped away from the graves and a short broad-shouldered man with a shovel took his place and began locking Father into eternity: dirt bounced then thudded onto the coffins and I realised that I would never see Father again. There would be a day, *when, when, when will that be?* that I would forget what he looked like, would forget all the tiny murmurs he ever made. When Father brought us here to see Mother all those years ago, he told us that she wouldn't leave our minds, that she would always be right here when we needed her. But he lied about that. The dead don't come for you.

Dirt continued to fall into graves. Tree branches danced. Everything slowed and the faces surrounding us looked metallic. My hand rushed to my eye, *I am still intact*, and everything slowed and felt like a dream. Shovel lofted dirt and coffins continued to be covered. Emma kept squeezing my hand, twisted my skin like modelling clay, the pain taking me far away from words.

When dirt hits wood with force, there is no echo. Only blunt sounds, like an ax through tree stump, through bone. At least, that's what I heard the police say. Breaking bone is a terrible sound, the way it shrieks through your teeth landing on tongue. I heard myself whisper, "Goodbye," and it seemed strange to know I wouldn't say anything to Father again, that I wouldn't say another word to Mrs. Borden ever again.

Emma began to cry. I wrapped my arm around her shoulder, *I could be an even better sister*, heard a little voice inside my mind begin to say, "I have a secret but you have to promise not to tell like you always do . . ."

My spine hung like a beehive, a honey fizz pushing towards my head, and I felt ready to explode. Everything slowed. Uncle ran a finger over his lips, eyed the spot where Mother lay buried. I was ready to explode. Inside my ear I heard the clock on the mantel tick tick.

"Emma," I wanted to say, "do you want to know my secret? I've remembered something about that day." I could see myself standing at the bottom of the front stairs, staring into the sitting room the morning Father died. I heard the three of them in the dining room at the table, Father, Uncle and Mrs. Borden. They talked about agriculture and I thought some nasty things about you, Emma. "I hope she's having a terrible time," I told the house. I wrapped my hand around the banister as tight as I could until my fingers turned white then blue. The house trembled and I did it again.

I went into the sitting room, opened the door to the dining room. Bridget walked around the table, poured Mrs. Borden more tea, and I saw Uncle smile at Bridget, make her blush.

"Why don't you join us?" Uncle said.

I moved towards them. "What are you all doing today?" I said.

"I'll be leaving shortly. Think I'll spend the day attending to business." Uncle chewed his middle fingernail.

"I'll be at the office." Father, busy not looking at me.

"When will you be back, do you think?"

"This afternoon." He looked up.

"Oh," I said. I watched them eat johnnycakes and old mutton soup. Slurp, slurp, slurp. Something inside me wanted to laugh.

"Why don't you eat with us?" Mrs. Borden swivelled her tongue around, silver like a pig.

"I'm not particularly hungry."

"You should eat, Lizzie," Father said. Slurp, slurp.

"I said I'm not hungry." I saw a bird fly by the dining room window, shadow flight. "I'm going to feed my pigeons," I said and made my way to the side door.

Father called out, "Lizzie, wait."

Emma, I wanted to say. The sun was sugar warm that morning. It dripped onto my fingers and neck and I felt like dancing, felt like everything in life was going to be all for me. Grass prickled my ankles and my skin jumped. I opened the barn door and went inside. A strange smell stung my nose, was sharp against lip and tooth. This smell of rotting flesh. I went to my pigeons.

Emma, I would tell her, I didn't eat breakfast because I knew there was something bad about it. Please don't tell anyone.

Okay, she would say. I won't.

It's just that I was so mad at everyone.

If only I'd been home.

I would tell Emma that I'd considered telling the police how very strange it had been when I found blood on my hands after I touched the banister on the front stairs landing. I put the blood on my tongue but couldn't place the taste, and I had washed and washed my hands outside until blood disappeared, until I began to wonder if it had been there at all.

I would tell Emma that after the clock struck ten that day, I saw Father inching towards the house in his dark-gray suit, his boots dragging behind him. All morning I'd been thinking about him, had been thinking about every feeling I ever had, every thought I ever had. It was there on my tongue. There were parts of me that were angry about the pigeons and I couldn't understand how Father could have been so cold and cruel, *maybe he really hates me.*

Father had knocked on the front door, the boom noise filling the house, and Bridget unlocked the bolt on the front door, let him inside. He came further inside the house, placed his hat on the coat rack then moved like old time into the sitting room. Seeing him like that made me giggle. I came down the front stairs, looked at the guest room door.

I had so many things I needed to tell Father, I thought I might spark and burn away. I worried that he wouldn't listen, the way he hadn't listened to me for so long.

I shook my head and continued down the stairs, listened to Father grunt as he tried to lengthen his body along the sofa. His stomach sounded war; churn-churn fire pit, a small crying devil.

I surprised myself. When I saw Father resting on the sofa, I began mouthing my favorite prayer, "As the Lord liveth, there shall no punishment happen to thee for this thing." Father had taught me the prayer when I was tiny, had wrapped it tight around my brain and heart so that it would never leave me.

Father held his head in his hands. I wanted to be inside him, to see and hear all the thoughts that never came out to speak to me. I wanted him to hear me, to really know me.

Father opened his eyes and looked at me, his body hunching deep into the back of the sofa. "I feel so unwell, Lizzie." There was a buzzing coming through the floor into my feet and legs, travelling all the way to my head.

I smiled at him. "Let me look after you, Father."

He watched me and I smiled again, felt my teeth raw on lips. A few weeks before, I had dreamed about him. Father was a tiny baby sent to me to be looked after. I bathed him and nursed him, both of us happy. He was a small puppet for me to play with, to make him do whatever I wanted. Baby Father was warm in my arms and when he looked at me, I saw myself and kissed his cheeks. The beginning of love.

The clock on the mantel ticked ticked. Father kept watching me and the dream feeling disappeared. When I looked at him on that sofa my arms and hands became heavy. I stepped towards him, hoping that being closer to him would release me, make me happy again, *I want my daddy to love me*, and I could see him stare, stare, stare. I wanted to tell him so many things. I walked closer to him, and I thought I heard him say, "Is it too late for me to be a good father?"

The conversation we could have.

"What do you think a father does?" I would ask sweetly.

His face would pucker like dried fruit. "I'd let you live the life you deserved. Everything for you and Emma."

"Would you marry Mrs. Borden?"

He shook his head, an earthquake. "I wouldn't make that mistake again."

I walked closer and we watched each other. Father blinked. I felt a twist in my heart and my body turned arctic. I considered everything. "I wish it could be different. But it won't," I told him.

Father looked at me, eyes wide, confused. I wondered what Emma was doing. I missed her. "Everything will be better when Emma comes home," I told him. The ceiling popped and ice ran the length of my spine. The clock on the mantel ticked ticked and I began to feel warm, warmer.

How old he looked there on the sofa with his white hair and white beard; I saw how different we were. I wanted to ask him, "Can you tell me one more thing?"

"Yes, Lizzie. Anything."

"Can you tell me something from when there was only me and Emma and Mother and you?"

"Once, there was love. All love."

"Yes. All that love. Once." I smiled. A father returned.

I stepped closer to him, heard birdsong in my ear. This was the beginning of my happiness. I would show him that I could finally love him more.

"Lizzie?" Father's voice was loud.

I nodded. Father's eyes widened and he grunted a little, words becoming stuck to the side of his mouth. He began crying, *I didn't know this was possible*, and for a moment, I felt confused. I stepped closer to Father, said, "All that love, once," and he cried some more. The clock on the mantel ticked ticked. I folded my body all the way down to his, kissed him on the head. He cried. "It's alright," I said, my angel voice.

Birdsong was loud in my ear and happiness was about to begin. Above me, the house opened up, just like I had always wanted it to. I felt the sun come for me, wanted Father to see it.

"Look up!" I said. "Look up."

Father did. I watched his hands, saw the golden circle on his finger. I smiled. The sun burned bright. He shielded his eyes with his hand.

I knew he was waiting, just like I was. Waiting for all my happiness. Together we closed our eyes. I lifted my head towards the sky, *everything is magical! I want to touch the sun!*

I raised my arms above my head.

Fall River timeline

September 13, 1822: Andrew Jackson Borden is born at 12 Ferry Street, Fall River. He is the eldest of five children.

September 19, 1823: Sarah Morse is born. She is the eldest of nine children.

January 21, 1828: Abby Durfee Gray is born.

1833: John Morse is born.

1845: 92 Second Street is built. It is designed to house two families.

December 25, 1845: Andrew marries Sarah. He is a cabinetmaker, she is a seamstress.

March 1, 1851: Emma Lenora Borden is born.

May 3, 1856: Alice Esther Borden is born.

March 10, 1858: Alice dies at home from "hydrocephalus" (commonly known at the time as "dropsy on the brain'').

July 19, 1860: Lizzie Andrew Borden is born at 12 Ferry Street, Fall River.

March 26, 1863: Sarah dies of "uterine congestion" and "disease of spine." She is thirty-nine. Andrew is forty. Emma is twelve. Lizzie is two.

On a certain date: Andrew meets Abby at Central Congregational Church, Fall River.

June 6, 1865: Andrew marries Abby. Abby is thirty-seven years old. Andrew is forty-two. Emma is fourteen. Lizzie is almost five.

1866: Bridget Sullivan is born in County Cork, Ireland.

1875: Lizzie goes to high school.

1877: Lizzie leaves high school in her junior year.

May 24, 1886: Bridget arrives in New York on the SS *Republic*.

1887: Lizzie stops calling Abby "Mother."

October 1, 1887: Andrew sells Emma and Lizzie 12 Ferry Street, Fall River, for $1 as a gift and as an attempt to soothe tension in the household. As owners of the house, the sisters will collect rent and make an income.

November 1889: Bridget is hired as a servant at the Borden household.

June 21–November 1, 1890: Lizzie takes her Grand European tour. She is gone for nineteen weeks.

June 24, 1891: Daylight robbery takes place at 92 Second Street. Lizzie, Emma, and Bridget are at home. Andrew never pursues an investigation. It is believed that he suspected Lizzie committed the crime.

End of June 1891: Both indoor and outdoor doors are kept locked at 92 Second Street at all times.

End of June 1892 and July 10, 1892: Uncle John comes to visit.

July 15, 1892: Because 12 Ferry Street was always in dire need of repair, Lizzie and Emma actually made a loss on the house (that is, they couldn't ask for higher rents from tenants). They sell it back to Andrew for $5000.

July 21, 1892: Emma goes to Fairhaven.

August 3, 1892: Uncle John comes to visit.

August 4, 1892: Andrew and Abby are murdered.

August 6, 1892: Andrew's and Abby's funerals are held; 2500 people gather in the immediate vicinity of 92 Second Street.

August 11, 1892: The bodies of Andrew and Abby are exhumed and autopsies are performed. The heads are removed, retained as evidence. Lizzie is told she is the main suspect of the murders and is taken into custody just before seven pm.

August 12, 1892: Lizzie is taken to the jail located in Taunton, Massachusetts. She is refused bail.

August 17, 1892: The decapitated bodies of Andrew and Abby are buried once again.

June 5, 1893: The trial begins.

June 20, 1893: Lizzie is acquitted. She spent ten months in jail leading up to and while the trial was held.

Twenty days later, 1893: Lizzie and Emma buy 7 French Street, Fall River. Lizzie names the house "Maplecroft."

Early 1905: Emma abruptly leaves Lizzie and Maplecroft. The sisters never speak again. Lizzie begins to call herself Miss Lizbeth A. Borden. Emma takes on an assumed name until her death.

1906: Emma travels abroad. She visits Scotland.

June 1, 1927: Lizzie dies of pneumonia. She is sixty-six years old.
June 10, 1927: Emma dies of chronic nephritis. She is seventy-six years old. The sisters are buried side by side at Oak Grove Cemetery in the family plot alongside Andrew and Abby.
1948: Bridget dies in Montana.

Last will and testament excerpts

Lizzie, January 30, 1926

Section 1. "To the city of Fall River the sum of five hundred dollars, the income therefrom to be used for the perpetual care of my father's lot in Oak Grove Cemetery in said Fall River."

Section 28. "I have not given my sister, Emma L. Borden, anything as she had her share of her father's estate and is supposed to have enough to make her comfortable."

Emma, November 20, 1920

Section 1. "I give and bequeath to the treasurer of the City of Fall River . . . the sum of one thousand dollars ($1,000) . . . IN TRUST, the income thereof to be used and applied for the perpetual care and improvement of the family burial plot, and the monuments and stones thereon . . . which was owned by my father, Andrew J. Borden, at the time of his death."

Section 6. "If my sister, Lizzie A. Borden, shall survive me and I shall own an interest at the time of my death in that tract of land with the dwelling house . . . situated . . . [at] French Street . . . then I give, devise, and bequeath all my right, title and interest . . . to my said sister, Lizzie A. Borden.

"If, however, at the time of my death I shall have disposed of my interest in said tract of land . . . on French Street . . . and my said sister, Lizzie A. Borden, shall survive me, then I give and bequeath to my said sister the sum of one thousand dollars ($1,000)."

Acknowledgments

WRITING IS SOLITARY but you never truly do it alone. Over the years I have had tremendous support in all forms. Without it I would never have finished.

There are many, many people I need to thank but in particular I'd like to give a shout out to: Christine Balint for early supervision, encouragement, and advice. The MA/PhD group from 2006 to 2010: amazing. A big-hearted thank-you to Antoni Jach. Your unwavering support over the years has meant so much.

Very special thanks and big love to: Kylie Boltin, Kalinda Ashton, Kate Ryan, and Alice Melike Ulgezer. Your friendship, advice, long talks, and reading the manuscript at crucial times has meant so much to me.

To MC VI: Jacinta Halloran, Rosalie Ham, Leigh Redhead, Jenny Green, Yvette Harvey, Mick McCoy, Moreno Giovannoni, Lawrence McMahon, and Lyndel Caffrey.

To Lyndel Caffrey in particular: you've no idea how much you've helped me.

The wonderful writing group: Evelyn Tsitas, Erina Reddan, and Caroline Petit. You've been so supportive, wise, and generous. Thank you from the bottom of my heart.

Huge thanks to my work colleagues, especially community engagement: your generosity, support, and laughter means a lot.

To dearest squirrel eyes, Felicity Gilbert: you let me outsource my emotions to you when I needed it most. Thank you for advice, reading, and friendship.

Over the years chunks of this novel were written with the assistance of Varuna, the Writers' House and the Eleanor Dark Foundation. Thank you also to Peter Bishop.

While this is a work of fiction based on true events, I couldn't have written the book without gleaning information from people who dedicate their time to this fascinating case. Their hard work and keen research made the non-fiction aspect of writing easier. I'd particularly like to mention the folks at lizzieandrewborden.com who unlocked the best treasure trove a writer could wish for. A wonderful resource, *Parallel Lives: a Social History of Lizzie A. Borden and her Fall River* was produced exactly at the right moment. I also spent time at the Lizzie Borden Bed and Breakfast Museum and for that I am forever indebted to Lee Ann Wilbur for her generosity, hospitality, and insight. Thank you also to the wonderful staff at that magnificently creepy house on Second Street.

To Vashti Kenway and Susan Johnson, and to all my dear friends in my life: thank you and I love you.

To my parents, Michael and Alana for always encouraging me to make up stories and for accepting the moment I started primary school and told you that I just wanted to be a writer when I grew up. Thank you for your love and support.

My wonderful brother, Josh, and my dearest Andrea Parker. Words cannot express.

Thank you also to my extended family: Ian, Deb, Rhonda, John, Vicki, and Tara. Extra thanks to Emma and Marty for reading the manuscript at various stages. Thank you to John Parker and Honor Parker for Ireland.

Thank you to my wonderful agents Pippa Masson, Dan Lazar, Gordon Wise, and Kate Cooper: you have changed my life. Thanks also to Luke Speed.

Major thanks to everyone at Hachette Australia but especially: my wonderful publisher Robert Watkins, Karen Ward, Ali Lavau, Nathan Grice, Anna Egelstaff, Tom Saras, Daniel Pilkington, Andrew Cattanach, Louise Sherwin-Stark, Justin Ractliffe, and Fiona Hazard. Thank you Josh Durham for the beautiful pigeon.

To Corinna Barsan, Leah Woodburn, and Sarah Savitt and the entire publishing families at Tinder Press and Grove Atlantic. I'd especially like to give massive thanks to: Georgina Moore, Joe Yule, Amy Perkins, and Yeti Lambregts for the beautiful rotting pear at Tinder and to: Morgan Entrekin, Judy Hottensen, Deb Seager, and Zachary Pace at Grove Atlantic.

To Cody and Alice: two kinds of love that held me safe so I could journey to the dark places. You are everything.

And lastly thank you to Lizzie Borden, whoever you are. Thank you for choosing me but it's time to go now.